MARK RADCLIFFE

Mark Radcliffe was born in Bolton and now lives in Cheshire. He is currently a presenter on BBC Radio 2. He is married and has three daughters.

ALSO BY MARK RADCLIFFE

Showbusiness

MARK RADCLIFFE

Northern Sky

HODDER

Copyright © 2005 by Mark Radcliffe

First published in Great Britain in 2005 by Hodder and Stoughton
A division of Hodder Headline

A Hodder paperback

1

A catalogue record for this title is available from the British Library

ISBN 0 340 71569 3
Typeset in Sabon by Hewer Text Ltd, Edinburgh
Printed and bound by Clays Ltd, St Ives plc

Hodder Headline's policy is to use papers that are natural, renewable
and recyclable products and made from wood grown in sustainable forests.
The logging and manufacturing processes are expected to conform to the
environmental regulations of the country of origin.

Hodder and Stoughton Ltd
A division of Hodder Headline
338 Euston Road
London NW1 3BH

For Bella, with love

THANKS TO

Caroline Chignell and Jenny Rhodes at Pbj, Nicola Doherty at Hodder, Charlie, Doc, Donal, Jock and Rusty Mahone. Special thanks to Christy Mahone. Love always to Holly, Mia and Rose.

1

We were all folkies, you know, folk singers, and I don't suppose any of us had ever been able to envisage a life as a threadbare suited clerk waiting in a back alley garret office above the dampened flagstones for the city clock to chime five. Instead we'd clung on to the music.

We'd known each other for years, on and off, but had been drawn back together by the Northern Sky Folk Club, which was, in reality, nothing more than a raggle-taggle band of like-minded artisans who didn't want their music processed by some faceless corporation and defended the right to wear trousers that didn't really fit. We'd no truck with being told how jeans should hang this season, any more than we'd be dictated to by the music industry, style magazines and radio goons about what we should be listening to. The funny thing was that we finished up dictating to them.

Well, that's a bit of an over-statement as there would be no more than a few hundred people who'd ever heard of any of us when it was all over. For a time, though, it did seem possible that some of us, and one in particular, would make our mark. To be honest, I was surprised that anyone was interested at all, although in a way there was something inevitable about it. The sense of disillusionment with manufactured pop was bound to lead people back to more earthy roots music with a bit of history and tradition to it. Not that it was all about old stuff. It's not a dead music, not a museum piece, and yet the best folk tunes do appear to have been exhumed rather than written last week.

There were six of us: Freddie, Mo, Lane, Matt, Jeannie and Ed. That's me. Ed Beckinsale. I'd moved back to town after having been sacked from a campus university in the North Country for refusing to follow departmental guidelines on syllabus. The idea that in this day and age men could come to blows over the number of lectures that should be devoted to Spenser's *Faerie Queene* is little short of incredible, especially in a seat of learning. And yet didn't Christopher Marlowe get killed in a brawl in a boozer? So I can't say I regretted socking Professor Bede Raynsford by the stainless steel shelving that had held clingfilm-smothered, inadequately filled sandwiches since the late nineteen fifties. He had it coming and I was glad to be the delivery boy, although a senior lecturer called Mark Lambert, one of the few members of staff I'd actually call a friend, had separated us after no more than a token exchange of blows.

I didn't bother to attend the hearing before the vice-chancellor. Instead I left a note with the English department secretary, an unfeasibly large matriarch in crushed velvet called Bernice, informing them that I wished my case to be considered in absentia and to send their findings on to my mother's address.

And that was it. No leaving 'do' with limp vol-au-vents containing indeterminate fillings and bottles of Chardonnay served at room temperature. No back slapping from bumbling dons with leather elbow patches, money belts and Cornish pastie shoes, puffing on pipes like minor characters from Kingsley Amis. No presentation of a briefcase, carriage clock or stirrup cup bought with the proceeds of a collection, seventy-five per cent of which was contributed, under the stern tin rattling of Bernice, by fellow staff who had never spoken to me. So at least I was spared those particular indignities, and for the first time in years I was free. Free to do what at that point it wasn't easy to say, but free none the less.

I never made a conscious decision to go home, it just kind of happened. I suppose it was simply that there was nowhere else I could go. I phoned my mum to let her know I was coming back to stay for a while and of course she was thrilled. Since my dad had died, the days had seemed that bit longer to her, the evenings that bit darker, the silences that bit deeper. I knew how she felt. My social life had been generally full of the buzz and whirr of a low-ranking campus university where younger members of staff, wrongly, considered themselves indistinguishable from the students and hung around the union bar seeking to impress pretty female undergraduates with their wealth of experience. It's probably fair to say that I had impressed the odd one but rarely enough to warrant a night-cap back at my rooms, and even more rarely enough to warrant a tussle under the duvet. Most nights ended with a half-hearted strum of the guitar, a contemplative Armagnac and the suspicion that life was drifting by without notable achievements.

It was much harder for Mum, of course. She'd stayed on in the house they'd shared, and in which my brother Jack and I had grown up. Thirty-seven Wordsworth Avenue was an unremarkable semi on an unremarkable estate where the unremarkable streets were named after remarkable men. Across the bottom of Wordsworth Avenue ran Keats Avenue, which in turn led to Coleridge Close and Shelley Drive. Byron, for some reason, was reduced to being a stubby cul-de-sac of charmless dormer-bungalows tagged on almost as an afterthought just round the dog-leg of Coleridge. Far be it from me to try and get inside the dead head of a romantic poet but you would have thought that George Gordon Lord Byron would have felt severely insulted. A cul-de-sac! The indignity of it.

That my old mate Maurice Pepper still lived on Byron Crescent was a certainty. And not only because I'd phoned him before coming home to make sure there'd be at least someone I could go for a pint with whilst I pondered what to do with the rest of my life. That Mo still lived in the same house was a certainty because he was conceivably the most bone idle waster ever to drag himself to the dole office. Since leaving the University of East Anglia with a first class degree in Classics, he'd chosen to reject his adolescent devotion to Homer in favour of a thus far longer standing devotion to idleness. Except for practising the guitar, of course, but then we'd all done that. On reflection, perhaps Mo Pepper wasn't the ideal sounding board for my ponderings on the future, as he had little discernible future of his own. Or so we thought.

When I put my hand on the familiar decay of the once green gate of 37 Wordsworth Avenue and pushed, it was as if I was sixteen again, coming in from school. The gate, dangling even more precariously than I'd remembered from the corroding hinges that my DIY-allergic father somehow never got round to looking at, scraped once more, creating the tell-tale grind that let her know I'd arrived. The dim glow of the hall light spread into the gloaming, revealing the stout, beaming presence of my mum, in all her knitwear glory.

'Edward Beckinsale, look at the state of you! Come here

and give your old Mum a hug and let's get you inside and sorted out.'

That's the great thing about mums and coming home. You need sorting out, otherwise you wouldn't be back. They know you need sorting out or you wouldn't be back. You know they can't sort you out any more and they know you know that, but there's still the illusion that they can. That they will. And whilst you haven't got the heart to tell them they won't, you've got even less heart to admit it to yourself.

'Edward, what are we going to do with you?' she said. 'Your father was so proud of you. Twenty-five years old and a lecherer at a university polytechnical college. And you had to pack it all in.'

'I didn't actually pack it in, Mum. They more or less packed me in, you know.'

'Yes, but only after you'd walloped your boss, that nice Professor Rainsmoor.'

'Raynsford, Mum, Bede Raynsford.'

'That's the chap. A real gent. Lovely soft hands.'

My mum reckoned she could tell a lot about a man from his hands. My dad had spent years cutting and bruising his on a butcher's block, so anyone with soft hands was a cut above in her book. Certainly Bede Raynsford had had a privileged upbringing and knew a thing or two about manners. What was also certain was that he had no greater regard for, or interest in, my mother when they met than he had for the poor soul who had to clean the private lavatory in which he spent hours perusing the *Times Literary Supplement*.

'Bede Raynsford was not a real gent, Mum. Bede Raynsford was a bully and a snob who needed bringing down a peg or two.'

'Oh, and of course the great Edward Beckinsale had to be the one to do it. Your father would be ashamed of you. He was a big man, a strong man and yet he never had a fight. And he never would have dreamed that his precious lad, who'd not only gone to college but got a job there, would have been chucked out for brawling. He hated violence, your dad. He'd feel so let down right now, he'd have taken you out in the yard and given you a good hiding.'

I knew this to be untrue.

'He wouldn't, Mum. He'd have taken me out to the Fox and Barrel and bought me a pint of Black Sheep. He'd have said, "You did right, son. Stand up for what you believe in. Don't let the buggers get to you. I'm proud of you, Eddie boy."'

'Like bollocks, he would,' she said mischievously.

'Mum! Bollocks? That's not a word that mums are allowed to use.'

'Not while your father was around maybe, but it's me who's got to knock some sense into you now. Let me see your hands.'

'Oh, Mum, come on. I'm not a schoolboy any more. You're not going to tell me to wash my hands before tea ever again.'

'I don't want to see if your hands are clean. I just want to see what state they're in generally. Your dad never wanted to see you with rough hands. He wanted you to have hands like Professor Raynsbrook.'

'He never met Bede Rayns-bloody-ford,' I said exasperatedly.

'Language, Edward!'

'You're the one who just said bollocks, Mother. And if Dad had ever had the misfortune to meet the blessed Bede he'd have taken me to one side and said, "Watch out for that wiley old fox, son. He's a bad 'un." '

'Well, let me see your hands anyway. I want to check you've still got college hands and not tradesman's. Come on, let's be having with you.'

I knew resistance was futile. My mother's obsession with the extremities of the arm was too deeply grounded to be shaken now. I placed my open palms at her disposal whilst she ran her starchy fingers over and under like an ageing manicurist, fretting at the discovery of every callus.

'Your hands are in a mess, Eddie Beckinsale. Tomorrow I'll get you a pumice stone. You've been wasting too much time with that bloody guitar as usual.'

Whether the time spent refining my guitar technique was wasted or not was debatable. It's true that I had spent more hours than was probably healthy alone, hunched over my beloved Martin Grand Ole Opry, but I was striving to be as good as I could be. Ever since I'd been an adolescent, and most of my school mates had been into chart music, or prog-rock or most commonly heavy metal, I'd lost my heart to singer-songwriters like Ralph McTell, Bert Jansch, Richard Thompson, John Martyn, Nick Drake especially, and I wanted to be able to do what they did. The way they could hold an audience with just a song and a voice and a finger-picked guitar transfixed me. It was as impressive in its own quiet way as seeing a comedian make people laugh with nothing but a microphone and a few choice observations.

I was under no illusions that I'd ever be in the same league as my heroes, not least because, though I could hold a harmony, I would never be a proper singer, and Mo was already a far better player and songwriter. But surely the hours spent with knitted brow over the fretboard couldn't be said to be wasted, could they? Admittedly I'd earned very little money from music over the years but all musicians hang on to the remote possibility that that could change at any moment. That discovery lurks around the next corner. Taking a pumice stone to my hardened fingers, therefore, didn't seem like a priority.

'Mum, I do not want a pumice stone. And that bloody guitar is a Martin spruce top Grand Ole Opry Limited Edition from 1966. That bloody guitar is worth about three thousand pounds.'

She tutted. 'Well, that bloody guitar cost more than your dad put down on this house, which is bloody stupid. So what did you have in mind to do to earn some money so you won't have to sell that bloody guitar to feed yourself?'

A good question, and one I'd been pondering. I didn't have an answer yet but what was certain was that, without anything else in my life, music was going to have to fill a big part of it, and that meant getting back into Northern Sky at some point.

'Well, I thought I might try and earn at least some of my income by playing that bloody guitar.'

'Well, bloody hell. Now I know you're puddled.'

'Mum, stop swearing,' I said. 'When I used to swear you used to say you were going to wash my mouth out with soap and water. I'll make the same idle threat to you if you're not careful.'

'Aye, you're right, son. It's just that you get me all worked up and since your dad died I don't have to mind my language. He thought a lady should speak like a lady, and seeing as he treated me like a lady it always seemed fair enough. Now there's no one to care about how I speak, so I just enjoy cursing when I want to. Any road, don't mind me. You play your guitar if you want to. Now get the sodding Baileys out and we'll have a little drinky before bed.'

She didn't say sodding really. I made that bit up. But we did have a Baileys. And then we did go to bed. And the following day I did get round to Mo's.

2

Twenty-four Byron Crescent was not in any intrinsic way a more offensive structure than its neighbours; it's just that its occupants had worked hard to make it like that. In contrast to my dad, Mo's father, Arnold Pepper, was a DIY fanatic who'd removed whatever limited dignity that dormer bungalow ever possessed. Tyrolean shutters, giant mutant butterflies clinging to the pallid brickwork, charmless carport of rusting pole and Perspex, wishing well with wrought iron winding apparatus; think of any unpleasant adornment for the family home and Arnold had botched it.

Maybe it was his parents' obsessive dedication to the desecration of a perfectly good dormer bungalow, if that's not a contradiction in itself, that had made Mo turn out the way he had. It was almost as if his utter disregard for the way he looked was a direct rebellion against what his mum and dad called 'home improvements'.

I rang the front doorbell. The theme tune from *Born Free* echoed around the lemon woodchip of the interior hall. Nothing happened for a while but then that was only to be expected. Arnold would be at the exhaust centre, Miriam would have several hundred school dinners ready to microwave, and Mo would be hauling himself out of bed to see who had interrupted *Trisha*.

Eventually his familiar figure appeared behind the frosted glass, moving with no great urgency down the inspirally carpeted hall. However, anyone assuming that

his shambling gait and diminutive stature were tricks of
the light refracted through the distorting glass would have
been disarmed of this notion when he opened the door.

He was a gnomish individual, standing about five feet
four inches in his stocking feet. Which is a peculiar way of
saying he was a short arse with socks on. His hair of
corkscrew curls was shoulder length, although this was
not immediately apparent as it was held in a limp ponytail
with what I believe is called a scrunchy. His clothes were
shapeless and baggy, in the gardening and not high fashion sense, and didn't appear to touch his body anywhere
except the outer reaches of his beer gut. An appendage of
impressive size for a little bloke. His grizzly stubble and
pillow-creased cheeks gave testament to the fact that here
was a man who had not started the day on a treadmill.

He was the same age as me, although at that moment he
could quite easily have passed for fifty. In fact he appeared
strangely middle-aged, even on our first day at grammar
school. Amidst the lanky, athletic, shiny-haired hordes
this slumped, shapeless, baggy figure appeared, somehow,
to be a kindred spirit. If I regarded the tall lads, like Lane
Fox, as being effortlessly cool and myself, unrealistically,
as moderately cool, then here was someone who was
emphatically uncool. Perhaps I was just looking for someone who would be even less likely than me to be picked for
the football team but when, whilst whispering at the back
of assembly, he started enthusing about the new Christy
Moore album, our friendship was sealed.

'All right, Eds? Cup o'tea?' he drawled, expressing not
the slightest surprise at my turning up unannounced for
the first time in nearly eighteen months.

Now I come to think about it, aside from my call the
week before we hadn't had any kind of contact in that

year and a half at all. I'd probably phoned once or twice but hung up during the eternity it took him to get to the phone. We could have written, I suppose, but . . . well, we're blokes.

'Yeah, go on then, if it's not too much trouble, Mo.'

'You know me, Edwardo, nothing too much trouble as long as you're not in a hurry.'

'I'm not in a hurry any more, Mo. Take as long as you like. I'm going nowhere.'

'Join the club,' said Mo, proceeding to the kitchen at a speed normally associated with sullen teenagers or pensioners with zimmer frames.

Inside, the house hadn't changed at all. Ruche blinds hung in every window in ever more fantastical lace and satin cumulus formations. Glass-topped occasional tables with gilded legs competed for floor place with a hostess trolley and white leather three-piece suite with wooden arm rests. Horse brasses hung in elaborate display between batons randomly nailed to the wall and then stained with dark chestnut Cuprinol to supposed Tudor effect. An effect not assisted by the swirling Artex. Miriam Pepper was conceivably the only woman left in the entire world who considered spare toilet rolls less offensive if covered by a crocheted doll. They even had a wall-mounted tea caddy.

Mo filled the kettle and put it on the stove to boil. The celebrated tea caddy was pushed three times to send the PG Tips into the Portmeirion teapot. This impressive bout of potentially exhausting activity over with, we dragged chrome-legged stools up to the breakfast bar and hoisted our behinds on to the black vinyl seats.

'So how come you're back, then, Professor Beckinsale? Your mum told my mum you were doing really well up there.'

I laughed. 'Oh, come on, Mo, everyone's mum tells everyone else's mum that they're doing really well.'

'Mine doesn't.'

'No, well, perhaps that's because you trudge up and down the same streets everyone else's mum lives on, looking like a binman who's given up on himself. You really are the scruffiest creature I've ever met, Mo, and that's after spending two years teaching at a seventies campus university that attracted every scruffy git in the British Isles.'

'I'll take that as a compliment then. So why'd you jack it all in?'

I could have tried to explain but didn't feel like going through the whole sorry affair again.

'Oh, you know, usual thing. Intellectual tensions and mindless violence.'

Mo shook his head.

'You don't change, do you, Ed? Remember that time Freddie had the audacity to suggest that he thought Nick Drake was overrated? What was it he said – "Drake was a middle-class tosser wallowing in self-pity"? You went for him like a bloody panther. If me and Lane hadn't pulled you off I think you'd have done him real damage.'

'I know. I just can't seem to help it and I hate that about myself, you know. Always have done. I hate violence and yet it keeps hiding round corners and jumping out on me.'

'I don't get it really, Ed, because ninety-nine per cent of the time you wouldn't hurt a fly and then . . . wham . . . someone's tipped you over the edge. Next time you feel like that, do me a favour and give me the nod so I can finish my pint and get out of the pub. Or try and imagine how your precious Nick Drake would have reacted to similar provocation.'

'Probably by increasing his medication, moving into a blacked out bedsit in Belsize Park and not coming out for three years. Not really an option, is it? Better just to have a scrap and have done with it.'

But Mo wasn't having any of this.

'Fine as long as you don't mind being barred from every boozer within a five mile radius and every folk club in England. It's only because violence is so rare in folk circles that the rest of them are too shocked or too pissed to give you the kicking you really deserve. You wouldn't try it on if you were on the biker scene. Actually you're that daft when the mood takes you, you probably would. But it's got to stop, Ed. You're my mate and all that but I'm not dealing with the moron you turn into after ten pints of Gravedigger's. You can start a row in an empty room when you're like that, which on the folk circuit gives you plenty of opportunity.'

He was right and I knew it. It depressed the hell out of me that most of the time I was a sensitive soul: widely read, substantially qualified, good on the guitar, part-time beat poet, competent if unremarkable singer, affable drinking buddy, and yet it could all go wrong in the downing of a fateful half. I hated myself for it but had never managed to control it. This time, though, I was determined. I'd have to be. Every time I'd achieved something, gained recognition or acceptance in any small way, I'd blown it by lashing out. Even to my everlasting shame inadvertently slapping Jeannie during that fight over the honour of Nick Drake with Freddie. I hadn't meant to hit her, of course, her very minor injury being a bit of what you might call 'collateral damage', but when you're 'fired' upon it's not much consolation to know that it's 'friendly'. Particularly when it's been unleashed by your boyfriend.

Which naturally enough, immediately after that incident, I wasn't. If my dad had seen me at that moment hitting a woman; drunkenly, unwittingly, but hitting a woman none the less, he'd have been too disgusted even to punch me. There hadn't been a lot of these incidents, perhaps half a dozen or so. I'm not a violent man. It's just that at key moments I've lost control and blown it. Bede Raynsford, Freddie Jameson, Mr Mortimer when he kept me in after physics the night I had a ticket for Fairport Convention and, most lamentably, Jeannie McBride.

'Mo, I'm really not going to let that happen ever again. I was such an idiot. Those were good times at Northern Sky and I'd do anything to have things back the way they were. Singing, drinking and going home to fumble with Jeannie on the couch. Halcyon days, mate. How are things down at the club? You still doing a regular spot?'

'Absolutely.'

'And is Jerry Snow still running it?'

'Well, kind of, but Matt O'Malley's been muscling in there and trying to take over a bit. You know what he's like.'

I certainly did. We'd known Matt for years as he had once lived on Keats Avenue until his dad's stationery business took off, at which point the family moved to a detached house on Riverside Drive. Though loosely a friend of ours, he was the kind of bloke who couldn't resist trying to take charge of whatever situation he found himself in. The magical moment Mo and I became best mates as we discovered our shared love of folk during 'All Things Bright and Beautiful' on the first day of term had been curtailed by the policing of Matt O'Malley, who'd been installed as class prefect, despite the fact that Mo and I had been unaware that there'd been an election. Matt

15

was an annoyingly effortless all-rounder at school. Brilliant at English, he had won the reading prize a record-breaking three consecutive years. The record still stands. He was also irritatingly good at sport and was not only house captain but also skipper of both the first eleven football and cricket teams. As if that wasn't enough, he was moderately good looking, in a clean cut, public schoolboy sort of way, even though we were at state grammar, and was accordingly the first of us to have a proper girlfriend. Even if it was Kimberley Medcalf, who was, as popular opinion had it at the time, frigid.

Naturally, then, Matt was also the first of us to get a guitar and so it came as a welcome surprise to find that he was useless on it. We all worked pretty hard to master the rudiments of chord shapes and finger picking, those who could afford it from teachers, the rest of us from books, and it became apparent at an early stage that Matt O'Malley was rotten. And the best thing was that it annoyed the hell out of him. He'd been so used to being the best that he just couldn't accept that when it came to the guitar he was way behind. He did perform occasionally and once memorably brought three Taylor guitars set to different tunings on which to perform three songs. He stumbled through Tim Hardin's 'Reason to Believe', a passable version of Dylan's 'Don't Think Twice It's All Right', and finished off with one of his own deathly compositions: 'Days of Yesteryear'. Four grand's worth of craftsman-built guitars to sound, at best, competent.

Of course, he continued to succeed in other ways. The local newspaper took him on as a part-time copytaker and cub reporter as a Saturday job which paid him thirty quid a week when the rest of us still had paper rounds. A year or so's wages bought him his first Taylor, a 310, which was by far and away the best guitar any of us had ever seen. It was a peach of an instrument and in the right hands would have sounded stunning. Unfortunately, it was only in the right hands on the rare occasions Matt condescended to let Mo have a go. Deciding that being a musician was not his natural calling, although ironically I think it was the only thing he really wanted to be, Matt breezed through a journalism and creative writing degree course at Warwick. Returning home with the anticipated first, he waited for the inevitable call from a national newspaper to head south and take up his rightful place as a political leader writer with a sideline doing music reviews for the Sunday supplements. Sadly for Matt, though I'm ashamed to say not without a certain satisfaction to his close so-called friends, the call never came and so it was with a sense of slumming it that he returned to the local paper where he'd started out. Eventually he would write something for a national newspaper, though not under the circumstances he'd imagined, but he never lost the belief that he was somehow better than the rest of us. And that must have been why Matt had thrown himself into running the folk club with Jerry. He was certainly never going to be a major player as a performer.

I wasn't sure how he'd react to seeing me again, as he'd managed to work himself into a frenzy over the Nick Drake showdown, but at least Mo was still playing.

'Typical O'Malley. But you're still going down all right when you do a set, are you?'

'Yeah, I do all right. It's a good crack and there's still some of the old crowd down there. Lane stills plays from time to time, you know.'

'Really?' I was intrigued despite myself, as I would have thought the fantastic Mr Fox, the coolest bloke we knew, would have moved on to bigger and better things by now. 'Hollywood hasn't called then?'

'No, he's still strutting around, dipping into the old trust fund, and him and O'Malley seem pretty close these days. He's no competition though. In fact I think I've got a bit better recently and it might be something to do with this. Follow me.'

Putting down our Andrew and Fergie mugs, we left the kitchen and headed for Mo's bedroom, in all its aromatic glory. A hearty push of the bedroom door revealed the anticipated aftermath of a small yet destructive whirlwind. The floor and the single bed he'd slept in since his cot was removed at the age of three were strewn with socks, t-shirts, full ashtrays, Spitfire bottles, a copy of *Guitarist* magazine, a copy of *Razzle* magazine, a rancid bowl of chilli and other objects, or possibly lifeforms, in advanced states of disarray and conceivably decay. If the scene could have been transported to the Tate Modern, Charles Saatchi would have bought it on the spot.

Mo lurched unsteadily onward, pausing to kick a Marlboro packet out of his path, and flung open the cupboard door with as theatrical a flourish as he could be bothered to manage.

'Da-da! Whaddya think, Beckinsale? Look at that and weep!'

I was initially grateful that I hadn't copped either an eyeful of soiled y-fronts or a nostril full of ripeness, but gratitude gave way to wonder and genuine admiration.

'Bloody hell, Mo. You finally got yourself a decent guitar. All those years on your Eko Ranger Six, not that it stopped you showing the rest of us up, but all those years struggling with that plank and now this. She's a beauty. A Fylde, eh? Nice one.'

'Not just any old Fylde, Edwardo. A Fylde Gordon Giltrap Signature spruce top with ebony fingerboard and Florentine cutaway, that's all.'

I couldn't take my eyes off it.

'Gorgeous, Mo. Gorgeous. How much?'

'Two thousand notes,' Mo said proudly.

'Jesus, Mo. Where'd you get two thousand pounds from?'

'Ah, you know. Saved some from gigs, got five hundred when my gran died, put a bit by from jobseeker's allowance.'

'Yes, bit of a misnomer in your case, "jobseeker's allowance", Mo, but what a guitar. So why's it in the wardrobe?'

'Well, I haven't actually admitted to Mum that I've blown the equivalent of one sixth of Dad's annual salary on a guitar.'

'Yeah, but don't they hear you playing it?'

'Of course, but they don't know it's a top of the range model. They wouldn't know the difference between a two thousand quid guitar and a junk shop model that cost a tenner.'

'But won't your mum cotton on when she sees it? Doesn't she go in your wardrobe?'

'Would you, Ed?'

He had a point.

'So go on then, give us a blast.'

'Aye, fair enough. I've been writing some new stuff, as it happens, so you can be the first person to hear it and can tell me it's crap.'

Mo picked up the guitar lovingly, and clearing a bum-sized space on the bed, sat down cradling it across his knee. He began to play, finger picking in a minor key. I hadn't seen him play for a while and so it came as a shock to rediscover how brilliant he was. How stubby little hands like those with fingers like undercooked chipolatas could produce such a delicate, rippling sound was a mystery. Then he started to sing and, if his guitar playing was a mystery, his voice was nothing short of a miracle. Higher pitched than you'd expect from his gruff speaking voice, it was as pure as it was unexpected. Close your eyes and you'd think you were in the same room as an angel. Open them again and you were with a gnarled goblin wearing shapeless jogging pants in a less than fragrant back bedroom.

He sang two songs. One was Ralph McTell's 'Barges', a perennial favourite of ours, and the other was a new song he'd written. It was called 'Summer's End' and was about two people who'd had summer jobs on a seaside fairground going their separate ways at the end of the season. It was astonishingly good. Mo had always written songs and he'd come up with several crackers, but nothing as good as this before. I felt a bit embarrassed being an audience of one, but also honoured to have heard it first. I remember thinking at the time that it would be a tragedy if hundreds, thousands, no, millions of people didn't get to hear it. Of course, in the end thousands did. But for now there was just me.

'Mo, that is . . . I just don't know what to say.'

'Look, if it's rotten just tell me, Eddie. I can handle it. Might not believe you, like. After all, who gives a toss what you think? So go on, hit me.'

'Mo, it's fantastic. It's a work of genius. It's the best thing you've ever done. You have got to get it heard.'

'Yeah? Do you really think so? You're not winding me up, are you?'

'Mo, honestly, it's brilliant. Have you got any more?'

'About a dozen or so. I've been sitting in this sodding bedroom day in day out for nigh on three years now writing songs, and planning the running order for my first album. Which of course I'll probably never make, but inside my head I'm already outselling David Gray.'

'So you haven't played them to a real, live, whites of their eyes crowd yet?' I couldn't believe it.

'No. I was thinking of giving them a run out at the club on Friday night. Fancy it? You could even get up and do a spot yourself.'

I had to admit it sounded tempting, but I knew it would be a bit too soon for that.

'Oh, I don't know about that, Mo. I haven't been playing that much. Fingers have got a bit stiff. Strings on the Martin a bit rusty. You know how it is.'

'Not really. Playing the guitar is about the only constructive thing I've done since leaving UEA. So forget playing and just come down anyway.'

'Oh, I don't know. I'm not sure I'm exactly welcome down there. Major bloody Champion did bar me, remember?'

'Jimmy Champion's not the landlord any more, Ed. It's Sally Fisher. You know, used to have the Dun Cow. Good old girl, she is. No baggage there. And Freddie Jameson isn't going to stick one on you. That night's water under the bridge, mate. And I don't even know if Jeannie's going to be there. She's not as regular as she was before . . . well, you know. In any case, you can't avoid her for ever. So come on, what do you reckon? Friday night. Lane's doing a set. It'll be like it was before you went away. The old crew back together again. Go on, you know you want to really.'

'I don't know, Mo. I'll think about it.'

3

Trudging those familiar lanes with the air dampening as the river drew closer, I attempted to fool myself into believing that I hadn't yet decided whether to go into the folk club or not. As if I could stay away. Without it I was rootless.

We'd first managed to sneak into Northern Sky when we were still a couple of years shy of a legal pint and I remembered that evening so clearly. The expedition had been planned by Matt, because he was in his element when he was planning things, and Lane Fox, who was the only one we were confident would get served at the bar.

Choosing what to wear had been the first challenge to overcome because dressing to blend in with an older crowd is a trick very few adolescent males can pull off, in contrast to their female counterparts, who seem to be able to do it easily. What we didn't know was that the dress code for an evening of traditional song and ale is that anything goes as long as it doesn't look like you've thought about it for more than thirty seconds. Folk clubs are probably the only clubs where 'smart casual' is actively frowned upon. Freddie, Matt and I went for the safest possible option of our scruffiest jumpers and jeans with, despite our protestations to our respective mothers, ironed-in creases. Mo, demonstrating his own sartorial idiosyncrasy even at that age, wore a garish Fair Isle waistcoat and bright red flares with purple patch pockets.

Lane, with his tattered denims, black moleskin jacket and steam-pressed hair, looked like he'd been frequenting nights like this his whole life. How we envied him for that.

Getting into the club proved surprisingly simple as the door policy at Northern Sky in those days was one of benign neglect. Jerry Snow had long since given up sitting at a rickety table at the entrance because this kept him away from the bar for too long. Wandering in, we scuttled to the table furthest from the bar, clinging for comfort to the shadows in the alcove, whilst Lane harnessed all his youthful swagger and poise to get a round in.

Once my underage drinker's nerves had begun to float away on a second pint of mild, I began to take in the scene around me. The smell in particular is one I'll never forget: a mix of spilt beer, heavy shag, damp wool, river mist and slowly rotting timber. It was a smell that would come to be as comforting over the years as the peculiar smell of home or a decent bacon butty.

The singers that night weren't established names, but local amateurs closing their eyes as they lost themselves in the music, taking turns to sing and joining in with each other's choruses. I'd never experienced anything like it. They were all individuals and yet with a strong collective spirit to bind them together. Sitting in loose circles in the half-light of that old boat-house, they were secure and adrift in their own world and we knew we had to be a part of it. And how much I wanted to be part of it again now.

The Rising Sun was a gothic, red brick building with mullioned windows and solid oak doors on the banks of the river, about three miles along the towpath from the bottom of Shelley Drive. Miraculously, though it was located in a 'highly desirable residential area', it had never become a family theme pub. Mercifully, the Sun had remained that rarest of things, a good, solid traditional boozer: one where you could get decent beer, a perfectly acceptable steak and kidney pie, where you take your mum on Mother's Day for lunch and return later the same day for a session with your mates.

That it had survived pretty much intact was principally down to the recently departed former landlord, Major James Champion. We really owed him a huge debt of gratitude because he had not only fought off numerous developers and brewery big cheeses, but had also allowed the Northern Sky Folk Club to run from the boat-house at the end of the beer garden for more than twenty-five years, not of course out of a sense of altruism but because it doubled his bar takings. He ran a tidy boozer, as I imagine he once ran a tidy battalion, and had never really left army life behind, which was why he insisted on being called Major. I'm always suspicious of people who have to be known by a title long after they've left the job that bestowed the title on them in the first place. Matt O'Malley, a man desperate for status, had been made captain of Borrowdale House at school but I don't think even he expected to keep the title for life. In retrospect, I can see that this was not a topic of discussion likely to be warmly embraced by a retired major waiting to close his pub and go to bed. Especially from a be-stubbled college lecturer slurring after his eighth pint of Jennings. In all honesty, I think I'd have barred me as well. Of course, I could still sneak into the folk club direct from the riverbank but I was persona non grata in the snug and lounge bars. However, Major James Champion had not managed to keep control of his arteries which had, demonstrating a dereliction of duty which would have astounded their owner, completely furred up and mutinied. Shortly after he'd pulled his last pint.

His unexpected departure left a power vacuum at the Sun and it had been a nervous time not only for the folk fraternity but also for the regulars, who wondered if this meant the end of their local as they knew it. The appointment of Sally Fisher was therefore greeted with widespread relief. Sally was a woman in her mid-fifties with a fearsome head of peroxide hair welded into a style that was known as a pageboy when she'd first adopted it in the late seventies. She was known to us all as the benevolent landlady of the Dun Cow on Ashburton Street who'd happily served us since we were fifteen. I'm not condoning under-age drinking, you understand. On second thoughts, I probably am, but it was reassuring to have a publican in charge of the Sun who would let the folk club carry on its long and fine tradition and expected to be greeted with no higher title than 'love'.

The boat-house was a long narrow black and white wooden structure with a veranda running down each side. At the far end was a rickety staircase leading down to the waters of the River Arn. For as long as anyone could remember this building had been home to the Northern Sky Folk Club. The exact date was a matter of some discussion. It had certainly been up and running when Major Jim took over the licence in 1978, and there were those who maintained there'd been evenings of traditional song going on there as far back as the sixties. It was widely rumoured that Simon and Garfunkel had appeared there before they even had a record deal and when Paul Simon's hair still covered his head, but there was no official record. Sun elders remember men in jumpers carrying pewter tankards disappearing into the boat-house as far back as 1969, although it can't have been called Northern Sky back then because the Nick Drake song of the same name wasn't released until 1970. But certainly it was one of the established folk clubs on the circuit and had seen the likes of Bert Jansch, Martin Carthy, Lindisfarne, and Donovan pass through down the years.

I took a deep breath, pushed the familiar brass handles of the double doors and re-entered the boat-house for the first time in quite a while. The familiar smell was as immediately nostalgic as an old family photograph and, despite my agitation, it was good to be back.

The room was packed. The tables in shady nooks, even the remote recess we'd twitchily occupied as schoolboys, were all taken, as were most of the woodworm-infested pews and ladder-back chairs that cluttered the main floor area. Evidently the club was going through one of its periodic boom times. These had come and gone in the past and were hard to explain or predict, although they did seem to coincide with pop music hitting a dead end again. The sound of endless remixes and cover versions spewing from tin-pot radio stations certainly seemed to convince people that there had to be more to musical life than this. And generally, if they could be bothered, they found that there was.

There was no sign of Mo which, in truth, was not in the least bit surprising. He was always easily the shortest male in the room, even at the Christmas party for the members' kids. Tonight he'd be extra difficult to find because he was performing and didn't like to chat much before he sang. I don't think it was saving his voice or anything precious like that. He just liked to focus on his set. Perhaps that was part of the reason he was so good. Well, that and the fact that all he'd have had to focus on for the rest of the day was the toilet bowl as he attempted not to dribble on the tufted pedestal mat placed there by his mum.

So I wasn't really expecting to find Mo, but all the same it put me in an even more jumpy mood as I knew he was in my corner. After what had happened last time I wasn't so sure who else would be.

'Well, well. If it isn't the Ricky Hatton of the folk world. Left the boxing gloves at home tonight, have we?'

There was no mistaking a voice like that. Somewhere in the depths beyond bass, it was reassuring and yet at the same time caused such low rumblings in the abdomen that an instant enema seemed a distinct possibility. Jerry Snow was in his late fifties and had been an active member of the club for more than twenty years. A dextrous, though infrequent, concertina player and a huge bear of a man, he had a head like an off-duty Santa Claus and a body to match. He was the owner of truly the most vile collection of shirts I'd ever seen. Where those extra, extra large silk blouses in a range of psychedelic swirls were bought from I have no idea but wherever it was it should have been closed down by environmental health. A genuine folk fanatic, he had an encyclopaedic knowledge of traditional songs and, alarmingly for a brute of his dimensions, dances. His enthusiasm and dogged determination had kept the club going through its darkest days, when attendances of a dozen or so like-minded souls were commonplace and, without the Snowman, it's eminently feasible that Northern Sky would have clouded over completely.

'Hello, Jerry. Yes, I guess I deserve that. Come on then, let's get it all over with. Is my membership still revoked or what?'

'Dear boy, of course not. Everyone makes mistakes, though I must say I've never cuffed my own girlfriend in full view of the old gang. An accidental cuff but a cuff all the same, you young rapscallion. Next time you want to get at the ladyfriend, buy her something from one of my shops. I've got crap in there that even Gerald Ratner would wince at.'

Jerry was the owner of a small chain of jeweller's and was what you might safely call affluent, not that you'd have any indication of this from the state of his appearance.

'So I'm forgiven then?'

'Well, in the words of Nick Lowe: "What's so funny 'bout peace, love and understanding?" Mind you, it's not me who needs to forgive, is it? Now come along and let's have a drink. I do believe it's your round.'

'Yes, Jerry, I do believe it is.'

Whether it was or it wasn't, it seemed churlish to contradict him under the circumstances.

I scanned the pumps to check out the guest beers and, spotting that they had Speckled Hen on, pulled a tenner from my pocket and shouted in the direction of the second barmaid, who was at the till with her back to us.

'Two Speckled Hen over here when you're ready, please, love!'

The effect of my voice brought a more immediate reaction than I could ever have dared hope, but not in quite the way intended. The barmaid froze for a moment before looking up at the ceiling and then slamming the till drawer shut with a startling crash. She spun round and faced me. It was only then that I recognised her. It was Maria McBride, Jeannie's sister. In the words of those most lyrical of punk poets, the Buzzcocks: 'Oh, Shit'!

'Well, look what the cat sicked up. Ed Beckinsale. Flyweight tosspot of the world.'

'Hello, Maria. You're looking good.'

'Do you think for one minute that I care about how I look to you?'

'Probably not but, look, I'm really, really sorry about what happened. I just lost control and it will never happen again. I promise.'

'You're dead right there, Lennox Lewis, because you'll never be on your own with her again. She hardly ever comes in here, thanks to you, and you know how much she used to love this place. God knows, Ed, it's been hard enough for her to live a normal life as it is and this was one of the few places she felt at home. But you screwed all that up for her, didn't you, bully boy?'

There wasn't a thing she'd said that wasn't true and fair and so it was fortuitous that Sally Fisher chose that moment to intervene.

'Maria, dear, there are about a dozen people who want serving so can you have your go at this berk when you're on your break?' Once Maria was out of earshot, she continued,

'And it's nice to see you back, love. Don't worry about her, she's only being protective of her little sister but I know you're not a bad 'un. Bloody hell, if I'd barred everyone who'd ever had a fight in the Dun Cow I'd have had to close the place down. It'll blow over, Ed. Just keep your head down for a night or two.'

It was just that kind of maternal advice you look for in a landlady. I felt a glow of gratitude as Jerry and I meandered across the club and found a couple of feet of spare floor space by the fire exit that had been chained and padlocked since 1987 when Mo set fire to the curtains with his new clay pipe.

On stage were a well respected local trio called Full

House who were about halfway through 'Sir Patrick Spens'. Only about another twenty-three verses to go then. Not one of my particular favourites, the song could test the resolve of all but the most dedicated traditionalist, but the mandolin and fiddle playing was top drawer. Relieved to have got away from Maria, I was gradually beginning to relax. Other club regulars gave me nods that seemed to hold no hint of malice, and Jerry's close attendance seemed to indicate that I had been welcomed back into the fold. Full House moved on to Richard and Linda Thompson's 'I Want to See the Bright Lights To-night' and all was well with the world.

Then I felt a tap on my shoulder.

'Ah, the return of the prodigal.'

I didn't need to turn round to recognise the voice of Matt O'Malley.

'Yes, I'd heard you were back and wondered when you'd show your face,' he went on. 'You're bloody lucky not to have been barred for life, you are.'

'Look, Matt, I've kind of had the talking to off Jerry, so I know where I stand. If it's all the same to you, can we skip the lecture? I just want things to be how they were, all right? I need some friends right now, if it's not too much to ask.'

This was a long shot as Matt and I had never been pals in the true sense. We'd been continually thrown together by circumstances and rubbed along reasonably well at times and yet we'd never bonded. Not really. Not like I had with Mo or Freddie or Jeannie. Especially with Jeannie. Matt was all right in his own slightly smarmy way but he never forgave me for being better on the guitar than him. And I guess I never forgave him for being cleverer than me, better at football than me, better looking than me and having more cash than me. I suppose that made us equal.

'Ed, listen, I've no major beef with you myself, and Mo told us that you were coming home, so it's not as if seeing you is a surprise. It's just that you upset a lot of people that night and they don't all forgive as easily as Mo. But as I'm one of the few people you didn't actually land one on, I'm prepared to let it go and start again.'

And with that he drifted off, acknowledging nods from other members across the club in a slightly more diffident way than was strictly necessary. He always maintained that he was just a conduit for the wishes of the member-ship in how the club was run but, in truth, he was hooked on the power. He had to control everything and I think that what eventually happened upset him even more because ultimately he'd been unable to.

After Full House had finished their set, they left the tiny stage to warm applause. Mo was going to be on next which gave me about ten minutes to get a top up and empty the last one out.

At first I thought there was no one in the gents which, for a man on a night out, is always something of a disappointment. A moment of solitary contemplation is no substitute for exchanging platitudes with the chap at the next stall but one. As it turned out, though, I wasn't alone. From behind the door of a melamine cubicle came the sound of someone pulling up his trousers whilst depositing his loose change on the floor, followed by the flushing of a cistern. At this I permitted myself a smug grin. Admittedly, I'd had a cool reception from Maria and initially Matt, but at least my beer money was in my pocket and not in a rancid pond on a toilet floor. The door to the lavatory was flung open.

'Bloody hell. It's Raging Bull.'

'Hello, Freddie.'

Freddie Jameson looked just the same. Curly shoulder-length chestnut hair, earrings, twinkly green eyes, denim shirt, pint. His parents were both tax inspectors but it was hard to believe there wasn't a splash of gypsy in there somewhere. He wasn't what you'd call devilishly good looking, but he had an easy smile, soporific manner and gently weathered finish from working in the open air at the timber yard that more than made up for it. If I'd been gay, I guess I'd have thought about it. Which doesn't, of course, mean that he'd have said yes.

We'd spent a good deal of time together, Freddie and I, not least because we'd performed as a duo for several years in which my steady guitar playing and harmonies attempted to provide adequate accompaniment for his demon fiddle, occasional finger-picked guitar and soaring lead vocal. It seemed to work because, even though we were both good players, we compensated for each other's deficiencies. He made up for my lack of charm, charisma, singing ability and confidence. I made up for his inability to count the money.

'So how are we then, Fred? You know, after, well . . . you know.'

'After the great battle of Drake, you mean? Look, I know you worship the bloke. I shouldn't have said anything really. I knew it would wind you up. No, it was just the beer talking as usual, so I'm not at all sure it shouldn't be me who's apologising.'

'No, Fred, it's me who socked his mate one. I mean, yes, Nick Drake is beyond criticism as far as I'm concerned but that's no excuse. What was it you said anyway?'

'Just that not everything he ever did was the work of

genius you think it is. In particular, though *Five Leaves Left* is a pretty good album, there's some chaff on there as well.'

'Hummmmm. Like what?'

' "Man in a Shed". '

'Yes, you may have a point there. So why did it end in a fight?'

'Because you're a lightweight who can't take his ale.'

'Fair enough. So we're all right then?'

'Bloody hell, Eds. I'm hardly likely to let a daft argument and a badly executed girl's punch ruin one of my longest friendships.'

'Well, that's a relief because I've not had the warmest of welcomes here tonight.'

'Why, who's been getting to you? Not the Snowman?'

'No, Jerry's fine but Maria was a bit prickly.'

'Ah yes, Maria. Well, you'll probably just have to take that one on the chin, old son. Protective sister and all that.'

'I know, I know. She was always so different to Jeannie though, wasn't she? Much harder, much more obnoxious.'

'Nice arse though.'

Freddie cracked his cheeky grin and winked and I was, for a split second until I regained my equilibrium, in touch with my feminine side.

'God, it's good to see you, Freddie. Have you seen Jeannie?'

'Yeah, I've seen her. She comes in from time to time.'

'And?'

'She's okay. I've seen her looking worse. I don't think she's eating a lot from what Maria says, but she's okay.'

'Do you think she'd see me?' I asked as casually as I could.

'Oh, I expect so. She always does, doesn't she? Just don't go round when Maria's in or you'll really cop for it.'

'Right. They still live at Lanercost then?'

'Of course. Mother McBride says they'll carry her out of there in a box. So Maria tells me anyway.'

'Maria seems to be telling you quite a bit. You're not . . . ?'

'Me and Maria? Naaah. Never. Too stroppy by half. No, she just talked to me a bit after the Jeannie business because she was under the impression that I was your mate. I said you were just some pillock I knew from school but she wouldn't have it. So we just sort of got into the habit of having a couple of drinks at the club and that's it really. I don't fancy her or anything.'

'Except for her arse.'

'Except for her arse.'

'I've missed this. It's so good to see you. Shall we go for a pint and watch Mo?'

'Good idea. I hear he's written some cracking new stuff.'

'Well, he played me one called "Summer's End" and it's brilliant. Like John Martyn at his best, crossed with a bit of Coldplay. It's a shame really – it could be a hit if it wasn't being sung by an ugly gnome.'

'Cruel, Beckinsale, very cruel. By the way, it's your shout.'

'Yes, and I reckon it will be for quite a while.'

We sloped back into the club room and Freddie joined the Snowman, whilst I went back to the bar to discover that Maria had gone on her break. Mercifully, I could now buy beer without getting my head bitten off.

Mo's appearance on stage always caused a stir. Partially because his performances were much anticipated, in a

low-key local kind of way, and also because if you hadn't
seen him for a while you forgot what a peculiar-looking
creature he was. That night he'd chosen to wear shapeless
tweed trousers, and a scrubby brown vest, tie-dyed with
orange penumbras and torn around the navel, offering a
glimpse of his hirsute underbelly. As he mounted the dais,
the animated conversation gave way to a nervous sussura-
tion as the audience began to wonder if they hadn't
unwittingly become involved in a care in the community
project.

Mo never bothered to say anything before he began his
set. He knew that the best way to wipe out the quizzical
looks was just to get on with it and let that voice soar. He
strapped on the Fylde and eased himself into the traditional standard, 'Claudy Banks'; and within a verse you
could see the mouths drop open, the doubt drift away.
Anyone with ears knew that this was the kind of voice you
don't hear often. High and pure but with a slight rasp
spilling over from his speaking voice around the edges. I'd
compare it to someone else if I could find the right person,
but to be honest, there was no one like him. There were
perhaps traces of Neil Young and Michael Stipe, sometimes a reverberation of Peter Gabriel or Brian Kennedy,
but faint echoes were all they were. Mo's voice was
unmistakably his own.

He finished the song to a reception that already began
to border on the reverential, and then began to work his
peculiar elfin charm on the audience.

'Evening, everyone. Thanks for that. I imagine that
there were a few of you who wondered if I'd got up here
to sing or sweep the stage but I hope you'll hear me out for
a while. Not all singers can be golden gods like Robert
Plant, y'know. Look at Joe Cocker – great voice but a man

who always looks as though he'd be more at home fixing a sink. Anyway, this is a new song about drinking whilst walking from St Bees in the Lake District to Robin Hood's Bay in North Yorkshire on the Wainwright trail and this is called "Coast to Coast".'

Once again his chubby digits effortlessly skated across the rosewood fretboard, producing delicate clouds of notes through which his voice shone like a milky sun.

Bloody hell, I thought to myself, good job you didn't say that out loud or they'd think you were a right nonny Fotherington-Thomas.

'Jesus.' Having mentally re-phrased, I ventured to go public. 'He's a bloody genius, the little gimp.' Better.

'To be sure, to be sure, lad,' offered Jerry Snow, 'as good a songwriter as has passed through here in all the years I've been booking.'

Freddie readily agreed. 'Yep, he certainly is the most talented Capuchin monkey I know.'

'Coast to Coast' was received with the appreciation it quite obviously richly deserved and was followed by two other new Pepper songs: 'Misty Morning' and 'Long Shore Drift'. Both were sickeningly good.

'I don't know how he does it,' said Jerry. 'Where does he find the time?'

'Well, that's the least mysterious part of it, Jerry,' said Freddie. 'Where the inspiration for stuff this good comes from I've no idea 'cos as far as I can see he spends his days scratching his knackers whilst waiting for his mum to bring him pizza and oven chips so he doesn't miss any of *Bargain Hunt*. How a slob like Mo can turn out such beautiful songs really is a mystery, but where he finds the time is easy. He spends all of every day doing nothing at all.'

It was true as well. We'd all written songs and most of us, Matt O'Malley excepted, had composed stuff that went down well enough with the punters. But none of us would ever quite match Mo, who by this time was charming the pants off the crowd with 'Summer's End'.

'If he's not careful he'll be in dire danger of copping off with a woman,' said Freddie, 'and that'll ruin his image as a sad little chump who's only got his hand for company.'

The Snowman leapt to Mo's defence. 'Frederick, please. No discussions on that subject, unless you're prepared to be candid about your own recent reliance on, how shall I put it, the hand-pump. Which reminds me, whose round is it for the old hand-pulled?'

Silence fell over the table as Freddie drained the dregs of his pint and Jerry feigned interest in a bluebottle circling the ceiling fan. Bastards!

4

Several Speckled Hens later, it had turned out to be an expensive evening, but an enjoyable one nonetheless. In particular, it had been great to see Mo on such good form. The club was even busier now and a particularly animated crowd had gathered round him. I caught his eye and signalled the time honoured gesture to enquire if he needed a top up. I needn't have bothered. Despite having a drink in each hand, no doubt paid for by a new acolyte or two, he nodded cheerfully. He was never a man to turn down a free drink. Even when he'd once famously vomited over ten pints of Old Hooky into the Arn from the balcony, he still managed to gleefully accept a large Baileys to 'settle his stomach' from a wide-hipped woman in plaits and a skirt that appeared to have been woven out of raffia.

I raised my eyebrows in mock indignation at him and continued on my way which, as I wasn't looking where I was going, I found immediately blocked as I collided with the chest of a substantially taller individual heading the other way. Carrying a tray of drinks. But not for long. It's at times like this you wish you were a fan of heavy metal. The sound of four pints and two chasers hitting a hard floor can be all but obliterated in a club pumping out Metallica. Even if you receive a smack in the mouth for your trouble, you're still spared the indignity of everyone looking round to see who's at the centre of the maelstrom.

In a folk club the noise of shattering glasses is cacophonous enough to stop everyone in their tracks. Not that stopping many of the regulars in their tracks was hard, as after three or four pints they moved like arthritic sloths in pullovers. I was also conscious that there were those who, seeing me in the centre of the room with dampened corduroys, surrounded by shards of pint pot, would assume that another incident was in full swing. I hurried to make amends.

'Look, mate, I'm really sorry. All my fault, wasn't looking where I was going.'

I scrabbled about on the floor, trying to pick up the larger pieces of glass and put them on to the tray, whilst coming to terms with the realisation that my already pricey round was about to get positively ruinous. Ah, well.

'Edwardo Beckinsale. Stand up, you recalcitrant urchin, and let me see if you've got any uglier.'

Lane! I hauled myself on to my knees and used the long, denim-clad thighs in front of me to claw my way fully upright, passing a taut torso swathed in lumberjack cheesecloth on the way. Not that a lumberjack would wear cheesecloth, I thought. Not that that was really the issue at hand.

Lane Fox was another bloke I'd known since school and, being the oldest of the group by a good six months, he'd always had an air of insouciant superiority. I suppose being rich and handsome helped too. He'd even managed to age so gracefully that he'd ended up looking younger than the rest of us. Admittedly it wasn't hard to look younger than Mo, who was one of those people who appear to have been born middle-aged, but Lane Fox was sickeningly attractive. Tall, whip thin with velveteen curtains of hair that made Laurence Llewelyn-Bowen look like one of the Levellers, he had proved irresistible to countless women and I daresay a few men, as he made no distinction and flirted with either. It was as if, realising he had the raw materials, his parents had sent him to irresistible lessons, which for a chap of his background was by no means an impossibility.

His father, though christened Arthur, was a former flower child of the sixties who'd actually been at Woodstock where he spent his twenty-third birthday whacked out on brown acid, flinging his hair to Santana. The following lunchtime he had woken to find his throbbing head perilously close to an effervescing latrine but apparently safely in the lap of a flaxen haired willow from Hoboken called Marielle. They'd been together ever since and it was due to his American mother that the heir to the Fox fortune had found himself christened Lane; last names doing pretty big business in the States in lieu of first ones.

That Lane was able to carry it off only added to his unshakeable cool. He also had the ability to dress in the perfect clothes to suit the occasion, a knack which admittedly benefited from a seemingly unlimited trust fund with unregulated access that enabled him to blow a fortune, looking as if he'd stumbled across just the right gear in a charity shop. You know, the kind of worn-in gems you always think you're going to find but never do. The money came from his parents who, naturally being anti-capitalist drop-outs from the summer of love, had made a considerable fortune being the first people in the area to recognise the potential of home and office computers, and had secured an early import deal with the fledgling Microsoft. It was even rumoured that Arthur Fox had actually met Bill Gates. Local legend also had it that Marielle Fox had slept with him, utilising the Woodstockian free love manifesto to seal a lucrative franchise. It was probably apocryphal but with the Foxes anything seemed possible. They just seemed to exude a bohemian glamour without really trying. Which I suppose is the trick really.

'So, Edward, keeping a low profile, I see. Wise move, wise move.'

'Look, Lane, it's not like it was intentional. Do you want another drink or what?'

He didn't look too bothered about the drinks, but I got the feeling that he was going to enjoy making me queue at the bar again.

'Yes, sure, if you want, Ed,' he said vaguely. 'Off to the bar then, there's a good lad.'

God, he could wind you up like no one else, could Lane. Over the years we'd had times when we'd become quite close and, knowing that everyone wanted to be seen hanging out with him, I was always grateful for the occasions he chose me to accompany him to a gig some-where. Disappointment would surely follow though as he, quite reasonably, plucked someone else from the pack the next time. I suppose I wanted to be more important to him than I would ever be and, whilst this made it difficult for me to like him as much as I wanted to, it made it impossible for me to ignore him.

I returned to the bar for what was going to have to be the last time tonight. In fact, with finances as they were, it was going to have to be the last time for about a week, unless someone would take pity on me, which didn't seem likely. My band of merry men had been generally pleased to have me back but they were obviously happy to let me foot the bar bill for a while. I suppose I'd have done the same.

Back at the table, Lane had joined Freddie and Jerry, and Matt O'Malley was advancing with his arm round the shoulder of a perspiration-soaked wood sprite which on closer inspection turned out to be the bard of Byron Crescent, Mo Pepper.

'Brilliant set, Mo,' I enthused, handing him a pint before remembering that he was just about the only person in the club who I hadn't actually bought a drink for in that round, meaning I was going to have to go back to the sodding bar again.

'The new songs are fantastic, mate, just fantastic.'

'He's right, Maurice, and that's not something you hear said often,' threw in the Snowman. 'You really are too good for this place. Someone should take you to a higher plane, dear boy.'

'Yeah, I've been thinking about that,' said Matt.

'Oh, here we go, the Richard Branson of the folk scene is about to outline his plans for world domination. Parked your ballon outside, have you, Sir Matthew?'

'You're such a smart-arse, aren't you, Beckinsale? I really wonder what Jeannie ever saw in you. But listen, a mate of mine who works on the G2 section of the *Guardian* is putting together a big feature on the increasing popularity of folk with all this so-called new acoustic movement thing, and the surge of interest in traditional songs and instruments. Apparently there's loads of music fans out there who just don't feel part of anything that gets played on the radio. Y'know, not everyone wants to mosh to skateboard punk or lurch about to banging techno at four in the morning. Believe it or not, there's a whole bunch of people who'd be happy just to hear the odd decent song.'

O'Malley looked around to check we were following, and continued.

'So look, the *Guardian* are interested in doing a piece about folk at grass roots level, and by that I mean a feature on a folk club and the cretinous singer-songwriters like you lot who hang out in it. Now, the bloke doing the main piece is an old buddy of mine from Warwick and I think I can persuade him that Northern Sky is just what he's looking for. You know how much *Guardian* readers lap up any reference to Nick Drake.'

'That's a great idea, Matt,' said Jerry. 'I'm sure we'd all be thrilled to be immortalised in print.'

'Yeah, but I'm wondering if there might not be even more to it than that. This same mate reckons that the record companies are all desperate to sign some new acoustic acts because, even though they're not entirely sure there's a boat there at all, if there turns out to be, they don't want to have missed it. So this publicity could really lead to some life-changing opportunities. Even for you, Beckinsale, if you behave yourself. Now, what I propose is to sell them the feature, then focus on our two biggest assets.'

'Which are?'

'Well, apart from your gut, Jerry . . .'

'And Maria's arse.'

'Yes, thanks for that, Freddie, most useful. So apart from Jerry's belly and Maria's backside our biggest assets are the blatant star quality of Lane and the songwriting talents of the goblin here, so it makes sense to stick those in the shop window, as it were. Of course, you'll all get a look in. We'll have the odd quote from the Snowman, the old retainer, and we could even have a footnote about the dreaded Jameson-Beckinsale duo, if you can get your act together. What we need to do is put on a special night where all the Rising Sun regulars perform, and use that as the backdrop to the piece. What do you reckon then?'

'Sounds all right, Matt,' chirped Mo, 'but what's in it for you?'

'Publicity for the club and a possible in with a broadsheet, but also I thought that if any record deals came as a result of it, I could handle the business side of things for you in return for a percentage.'

'Jesus, you've got this all worked out, haven't you?'

'In contrast to you, Ed, some of us do indeed have things worked out and don't go through life screwing everything up by lashing out whilst snot-flying drunk. What's wrong with that anyway? Why shouldn't I manage you, if I've set it all up? Let's face it, there's not one of you going to get anywhere if it's left to you. I can't see the combination of Beckinsale and Pepper being a galvanising force in the world of public relations.'

It was a good point, well made. It being Matt's idea it was inevitable that there was that sense of deja-vu: here he was trying to take over again. On the other hand, he was the only one of us who would ever get something like this together, so resistance was pretty futile. There was a general mumble of tentative agreement as Sally rang the bell for last orders.

'Well, don't look at me, lads. I'm stony,' I said before anyone could start.

'Yes, well, even I can see you've put your hand in your pocket enough for one night,' admitted Matt graciously. 'I'll get these. But one last thought. What we've got is a bunch of lads. Some more photogenic than others, but all lads. We need a female presence and you all know what that means.'

'Jeannie.'

'Exactly.'

O'Malley turned and headed for the bar, leaving Jerry in the chair.

'So who's going to talk to her then? Lane?'

'I don't think so, Jerry,' said Lane. 'Jeannie hasn't been down here to sing in weeks. She slips in at the back occasionally but why would she leave Lanercost and subject herself to the press right now? Who's honestly going to be able to convince her to do that?'

Mo put down his pint.

'You're right, Lane, it's a tricky one. Someone'll have to have a go at talking to her though.'

He turned to face me just as I became aware that Jerry and Lane's eyes were fixed on me as well.

'Oh, come on, guys, you can't be serious. I'm the last one she'd talk to. And even if she would, I'd never get past the twin dogs at the gates of Hades: Maria and Mother McBride.'

'Actually, Eds, Maria did happen to mention that she and the old battleaxe are on an all-day shopping trip tomorrow, followed by tapas and *The Marriage of Figaro*. You're probably in the clear.'

'Right, thanks for circumnavigating that excuse for me, Fred. What about her dad though?'

'Patrick McBride's a pushover, as well you know. He'll open the door to you with a stern expression that he'll be able to keep up for about five minutes before he's offering you sherry. And once you're back in with him, Jeannie's bound to at least talk to you. You know how close she is to her dad and if he's prepared to forget about what happened, she'll let it go too. Maybe.'

'So all I do is nip round and confront that little Electra complex scenario, swig a schooner of amontillado and bring Jeannie back down to the club to have her picture taken for a national newspaper.'

'Excellent,' said Jerry, pushing his chair back. 'That's settled then.'

'No, it bloody well isn't.'

'Well, look at it this way, Ed. You're going to have to face her some time. If you do it down here on one of her rare visits you're going to have to do it in front of everyone. Not least Maria. And if you run into her by chance, you won't be prepared for it and you'll make a fool of yourself by stammering out the wrong thing.'

'You don't know that for sure, Freddie.'

'This is you we're talking about, Eds.'

'Carry on.'

'And if you call round on the off chance, there's a very strong possibility the door will be answered by Jeannie's mum who might conceivably throw her arms around you and open a tin of salmon, or might more conceivably beat you savagely around the head with a dustbuster.'

'And so?'

'And so the best thing you can do is to go round whilst the coast is as clear as it's going to be and get it over with. It's the only logical course of action.'

'Apart from going for a pint and pretending it never happened.'

'Good idea, except for the fact that you can't afford to go for a pint.'

'Right then, the words corner and backed into spring to mind, and not necessarily in that order. I don't have much choice, do I?'

'Excellent,' said Jerry again. 'As I said, that's settled then.'

'What's settled?' Matt had returned from the bar with yet more Speckled Hen. He was going to need it.

'We've decided who's going round to talk to Jeannie.'

'And who's that?'

'Ed.'

A spray of foam like that from a beachbound breaker erupted into the air as O'Malley spluttered into the head of his pint.

'You are joking.'

5

'Edward. Breakfast's on the table.'

True to form, Mum had responded to my return to 37 Wordsworth Avenue in the only way she knew, by acting as if I was thirteen. It was seven fifty exactly, the time I'd always had to get up if I was going to catch the bus to the grammar school on the more upmarket side of town. Not that living on Wordsworth Avenue was the front line exactly. The pitched street battles that ran for the summer months of 1981 never directly affected life on Coleridge Close. There was once an incident involving the unemployed man from number 45 with what my mother described as 'disreputable sideburns' and a bottle of Scrumpy Jack that required the appearance of a panda car, but it hardly qualified as looting on a grand scale.

'Edward. Did you hear me?'

I began to contemplate emerging from the duvet, which in itself had been the subject of a frank exchange of views ten years earlier. Mum prided herself on the pristine condition of her linen, stiffened with liberal lashings of Robin starch, even if the prominent sensation of waking up in one of her freshly laundered beds was that of having been committed to a psychiatric institution during the night. She had viewed the duvet with the deep-rooted suspicion normally reserved for single mothers, Chinese food and women who drank beer from glasses with handles. All women who drank beer in this way were 'loose' according to my mother, a theory I was able to disprove after exhaustive field research in the union bar as a fresher. And indeed in the second and third years. She eventually gave way on what she called the 'continental quilt', the word 'continental' carrying implicit distrust, on the assurance that it would mean she would never again have to make my bed. Dad was then officially sanctioned to make the purchase from British Home Stores, despite Mum's mystifying misgiving that 'the Scandinavians are taking over the world'. Although anyone who's queued to get into Ikea on a Sunday may well be inclined to agree.

'Edward, it's nearly eight o'clock.'

I was aware of this from the luminous display on my radio alarm clock, a device which had evidently been designed to prevent tuning into stations with any degree of precision. This inevitably resulted in being woken to pulsating swathes of static and white noise with occasional wisps of travel news floating like apparitions in the FM ether. Getting out of bed was work in progress. I wasn't being totally indolent. I knew that this was Mum's house and if she wanted breakfast to be a depleted family occasion at eight in the morning then that was up to her. I had left behind the blissful vegetative larva state but had yet to be transformed into the full-on butterfly when reality bit. I had promised to go and see Jeannie.

Across the suburban rooftops the city clock chimed eight.

'Edward, I don't want to have to come up there.'

She was right there. The previous night's Speckled Hen had had certain nocturnal consequences which were proving distinctly unpleasant, even to the source.

'Yes, Mum, I'll be right down.'

I hauled myself up on to one elbow and opened one

rheumy eye. The room that slowly materialised had changed little since it had been my permanent home. The wardrobe, desk and chest of drawers were still the same ones that had been passed on to me when Uncle Frank had died. That was when I was about five or six and, try as I might, I don't remember what I had before that. Perhaps it was nothing. Maybe I slept in a room devoid of furniture, waiting for a relative to die. Certainly it seemed as though our house was equipped with stuff that had already done a tour of duty somewhere else in the family. My elder brother Jack had to endure taking mates up to his room which was dominated by Grandma Beckinsale's old dressing table. He always insisted to his smirking pals that it was a desk but they weren't having it. How many desks do you know with octagonal mirrors? At least the rosewood monstrosities stuck in my room were distinctly masculine in their ugliness. And the bed was emphatically my own, bought from the Co-op and delivered wrapped in cellophane. No one else had ever slept in it but me which was more than you could say about Mum's bed. Obviously Dad had shared it for a good few years but before that it had belonged to Great Aunt Mary. Mary was an idle spinster who had managed to spend a whole life doing absolutely nothing. In fact my dad often speculated that she'd avoided getting married because she'd have had to get off her backside and cook the occasional meat and potato pie or wash the odd sock. When my mum had left the room he also confided in his teenage lads that another reason she'd never got hitched was because she didn't want to have to exert herself in 'the old carnal relations'. We were thrilled to be taken into his confidence in this way, and would sit quietly nodding at him in front of the fire. Even though we had no idea what carnal relations were, but dearly hoped they weren't going to snuff it and leave us with more bad furniture.

I still missed those chats. I still missed him like crazy. Especially here. I missed his baritone burr, the smell of his shaving soap, his raincoat hanging on the peg in the hallway. It was just so weird to think that I would never have him there again. It's a funny thing losing your dad. If you're unlucky enough for it to happen when you're a kid I suppose you're left with no option but to grow up that bit faster. If it happens to you when you're a bit older, as it did for me, it's a shock to find that it leaves you realising that you hadn't grown up quite as much as you thought you had. One minute you're secure in the independent life you're leading, then something happens to throw you off kilter and you're back to being a boy who wants his dad again. And you can't have him.

'Edward, the kettle's boiled.'

Oh well, better get a shake on then. Heaven forbid that we should have to go to the trouble of switching it on to boil again.

'Yes, Mum, I heard you.'

I pulled myself up into the sitting position and managed to prise open the second eye. This brought into focus the full hideousness of the swirling turquoise and beige wallpaper that had obviously been designed by some acid casualty after a particularly bad trip. In my youth I had put up posters to try and dilute the effect. I put up pictures of sports cars, though I had no interest in or experience of them, pictures of fighter planes, though I had no interest in or experience of them, and pictures of full-breasted girls in bikinis, though I had no experience of them. All of these had been removed when I left home to go to university. When I asked why this had happened with what seemed to me unseemly haste, I was told that it was because it was becoming 'the guest room'. That no guest had ever slept in it from that day to this did nothing to change matters. Devoid of guests it had forever been, the guest room it steadfastly remained. Evidently, like a serving hatch, hostess trolley or Miriam Pepper's wall-mounted tea caddy, it was just one of those things that you had to have.

'Edward, I haven't got all day, you know.'

I leaned over the side of the bed and reached for my guitar and began to strum Nick Drake's 'Pink Moon', the title track of his minimalistic last album. Had he, perhaps, once similarly lain in bed at his parents' house in Tan-worth-in-Arden, tinkering with the guitar, wondering where his life was going, whilst his mother berated him from the kitchen?

I'd been obsessed with Nick Drake since the very first time I'd heard him. A mate of our Jack's had come round with the debut album *Five Leaves Left*, and as I lay on my bed I could hear it clearly floating across the landing. It was simple, beautiful, intimate and more engaging than anything I'd ever heard, and this was before I knew anything about him. I quickly bought a copy of the record for myself, as well as its follow-ups *Bryter Later* and *Pink Moon*, and began to sit in my bedroom with a cheap Spanish guitar endlessly trying to unpick the mysteries of those extraordinary songs. Other instruments would appear on some tracks, often there were gorgeous, sympathetic string arrangements by his college friend Robert Kirby, but at the centre there was always Nick, hunched over his guitar, singing in his soft, breathy tones as if he was in the room with you.

Naturally I was inquisitive about who this new found hero was and so I read up on him in the public library. It came as quite a shock to realise that he was already dead, but the manner of his passing only fuelled the enigma. He was born to upper middle-class parents in Burma in 1948 and had passed through Fitzwilliam College, Cambridge, before drifting to London, where he became a shadowy presence on the folk scene. Other people knocking around at the same time included Bert Jansch, John Renbourn and, in particular, Fairport Convention, whose bass player Ashley Hutchings had first recommended Nick to legendary producer Joe Boyd. It was Fairport, too, who gave Nick the chance to play at the Royal Festival Hall, an experience that so traumatised him, he gradually withdrew from public life completely. He withdrew from life altogether in November 1974 when he was found dead in his bedroom at the family home in Tanworth. The coroner's verdict was suicide, but there are those who maintain he'd mistakenly taken too many prescription drugs. Whichever, a great talent and unique artist had been lost at the age of twenty-six, and this added even further potency and poignancy to the tracks he left behind. That it had all been so transitory made it, if possible, even more special.

'Edward.'

There she blows. Final warning. No reminders of the time or the heat attained by kitchen appliances. Just the name.

'I'm up, Mum. Won't be a minute.'

A half-hearted hunt through the tangled garments on the floor eventually turned up a grotty towelling bath robe that had, in a previous life, been navy blue. Shrugging it on over last night's t-shirt and boxer shorts, I scratched several straws of limp hair from my forehead and made my way down to the kitchen.

Mum was sitting at the table in her winceyette dressing gown reading the *Daily Express*. She was sipping strong tea from a china cup with the first of the day's Lambert & Butler's propped in the ashtray she'd bought on holiday in Kilkenny, which explained the presence of the ceramic leprechaun who gleefully guarded the collected dog ends. Symbiotically Terry Wogan was on the radio.

'Morning, Mum.'

'Morning, son. Not dressed yet?'

'Well, in a manner of speaking, as I appear to be wearing most of what I was wearing last night, yes. But in the way you mean, no.'

'Your father wouldn't have dreamed of coming down at this time without being properly dressed and shaven.'

'Yes, well, that was because he had to go to work and even I can see that serving pig's trotters and chitterlings in a mouldy bath robe and stinking of last night's ale wouldn't be good for business. But whilst we're on the subject, you're hardly pristine yourself, Ma.'

'Well, what's the point of getting dressed in a hurry? We've nothing special on today, have we? We can take our time.'

'If that's the case, then why have you been bawling up the stairs at me for the last half hour?'

'Because you won't get your lazy arse out of bed.'

'But I don't need to get my lazy arse out of bed at ten to eight if we've nothing to do today.'

'Well, how am I to know if you've got anything to do today?'

'Because if I've got things to do today, Mum, then I'm more than capable of getting myself up at the right time to do them.'

'No, you're not. You were snoring away when I got up.'

'What time was that then?'

'Half six.'

'Half six! Why shouldn't I be sleeping at half six? It's been a while since I had a paper round, Mum.'

'Aye, but the way your life's going it won't be long before you need another one.'

'Well, thanks for that vote of confidence. Any tea in the pot?'

I sloshed an inch of Long Life milk into the bottom of a mug, on the side of which was fired a poorly drawn sketch map of the Yorkshire Dales, and filled it up with stewed Typhoo.

'So what are you doing today?'

'Actually I'm going to see Jeannie.'

'There you are then. Good job I got you up.'

'Yes, but you didn't know that. And I wasn't planning to go round at eight in the morning.'

'No, you'll leave it till you think the coast's a bit clearer. I imagine you'll leave it till her mum's gone out.'

'Yes, and you're not supposed to know that either.'

'I am your mother, you know. I know you think I'm a gibbering idiot but I do have some common sense.'

'I know, Mum, I know.'

'Look, son, it was an accident. Wasn't it?'

'Of course it was an accident. You don't honestly think that you and Dad brought me up to be the kind of bloke who would hit a woman, do you?'

'Well, I would have hoped we'd brought you up not to be the kind of bloke who would hit a university professor but, no, I know you wouldn't lay a hand on a woman. Least of all Jeannie.'

'Exactly. But try telling her mum that.'

'Ed, you and I know that Penelope McBride is an ocean-going snob. The thought of her precious Jeanette being caught up in some pub brawl was always going to hit her where it hurts. At the golf club. Talk of the clubhouse it was, and you can imagine how cut up Lady McBride would be with that. She likes to forget that when she was Penny Battersby of Shelley Avenue she had it away with a coalman in the car park of the Dun Cow.'

'Mum!'

'Well, it's true. Daughter of Percy Battersby who worked on the bins, she was, and to hear her speak now you'd think she was a baronet.'

'Baronetess.'

'Eh?'

'Baronets are men.'

'Really?'

'Yes, Mum. Barons and baronets are men. Baronesses and baronetesses are the female titles.'

'And which is more toffee-nosed?'

'Baronesses are further up the social ladder than baronetesses, I think.'

'Right, well, you'd think she was one of them then. But she's not.'

'Well, I'm glad we've cleared up what she isn't.'

'Look, Edward, at the end of the day it's going to be down to what Jeannie thinks. Her mum'll have to come round to whatever Jeannie wants, and after a while Maria will get over it as well. You know what they're like, that family. Maria sides with her mother and Patrick always falls in with Jeannie. Now there's a fine man. Patrick McBride. Started with next to nothing and became a master joiner, owner of that timber yard and maker of craftsman-built furniture. I'm told he even built a desk for String.'

'Eh?'

'Yes, built a desk for the pop star String.'

'You don't mean Sting, do you, Mum?'

'No, it's definitely String.'

'Right. So he made a desk for String. What's that got to do with anything?'

'Nothing.'

'I see.'

'But he is a very nice man and if Jeannie wants to see you then you can be sure Patrick won't stand in your way.'

'Maybe.'

'Definitely. Have you been in touch with her?'

'Not recently. I did write to her though, on more than one occasion.'

'Did you say you were sorry?'

'Only about a thousand times.'

'Did she forgive you?'

'You know Jeannie, she'd forgive anyone anything. She did say she thought it might be better if we didn't see each other for a while though.'

'Well, perhaps it's been while enough.'

'Perhaps it has. Right. What's for breakfast?'

'Cereals in the cupboard, bread in the bread bin.'

'But forty-five minutes ago you shouted up that breakfast was on the table.'

Her hand stretched out and stubbed the smouldering remains of the Lambert & Butler into the leprechaun's charred groin.

'Mine is, son, mine is.'

I sloped round to the cereal cupboard and filled a bowl with Crunchy Nut Cornflakes.

'D'you think she'll see me, Mum?'

'I don't know, son, but you'll not be happy until you know. You either sit round here wondering whether she will, or go and find out and run the risk of her shutting the door in your face. You're in a Catch 23 situation.'

Which was one worse than I'd been anticipating.

6

Standing on the corner of Marsh Lane and Riverside Drive, Lanercost took its name from a priory in North Yorkshire and was itself possessed of a faintly ecclesiastical grandeur. Protected from prying eyes by convent-like walls of grey render to the rear, at the front it enjoyed uninterrupted views across the meadows on the far side of the River Arn. Many idyllic days had drifted by for us there in summers past, lounging on the lawns drinking cans of Scrumpy Jack, watching cabin cruisers chug their weary way up stream, wondering what it would be like when we were all famous. Jeannie had that special way of looking at me that really made me think that, just possibly, it was all going to happen. Even Maria seemed lost in the lazy calm of those hazy afternoons as she sniggered at Freddie slipping down the banks into the muddy shallows in search of the bottle of Thunderbird he was cooling, hidden from the watchful glare of Penelope. As dusk descended over the marshlands, the belief that we would all one day have our names in the music press evaporated as the combination of cider, cheap wine and sunshine resulted in a series of skull-numbing headaches. But for those golden hours, anything seemed possible.

Deprived of strong sunlight, or perhaps because I was aware of a sense of steadily rising dread at the task in hand, Lanercost now began to brood like a latter day Wuthering Heights with neater gardens.

It was eleven fifteen. I'd managed to waste a bit more time by walking the three miles or so from Wordsworth Avenue rather than catching the bus. I felt certain that Maria and her mother must by now be safely in the communal changing room of some designer clothes emporium, steadily wasting the McBride family fortune.

I paced one last time around that bend in the road where Marsh Lane turned into Riverside Drive. That bend I knew so well from the adolescent hours I'd wasted hanging around there with Freddie and Mo, just hoping that Jeannie would come out so I could ignore her. You know, playing it cool. Cool that had already been unwittingly shattered as the McBride sisters observed us from behind the net curtains of the guest suite, giggling uncontrollably as we failed to light Consulate menthol cigarettes in a gentle breeze.

Reasoning that I couldn't sensibly walk the bend another time without alerting Neighbourhood Watch, I pushed the tall oak gate and headed between the lawns up the familiar path that led up to the front door. I swallowed heavily, mentally straightened an imaginary tie, and sent a sharp crack echoing across the quarry tiled floor of the entrance hall with the brass knocker, buffed to the level only ever attained by professional cleaners.

Except for the distant barking of the dog, a lovably boisterous chocolate brown labrador called Whitley, there was a brief period of inactivity. For a moment or two I started to feel hopeful that there was nobody in. Perhaps I'd be able to go back to the Rising Sun and tell them, hand on heart, that I'd tried to see her but she hadn't been at home. But then I'd only have to build myself up to it again and anyway, getting her to agree to come back down to the club was only part of the reason for being there. And not even the main reason at that. I wanted her back. And if that wasn't possible, I wanted at least to be able to talk to her again, to see her from time to time. Would it be too much of a cliché to ask her if we could be friends? Was it beyond the realms of fantasy to think we could enjoy a platonic relationship? And could occasional sex be deemed to be part of it?

I raised my hand to knock again, but as I did so the door opened and the disconcertingly sterner than I'd remembered crinkled face of Jeannie's dad manifested itself, with the slavering visage of Whitley somewhere down below.

'Mr McBride. Nice to see you again.'

A disconcertingly bushier than I'd remembered eyebrow raised itself, Roger Moore-like, above the left eye. Whitley growled that superficially threatening growl that meant he just wanted to play. Or bite me savagely in the throat. One or the other.

'Mr Beckinsale. Nice to see you again too. Or is it? Let me think about that.'

So there we stood, facing each other on the doorstep in silence, save for the slobbering of the dog that brushed past me on his way into the garden. A period of time elapsed. It may have been a minute, it may only have been fifty-five seconds. Either way it seemed like an eternity to me. Or a minute and a half at least.

'On reflection, Mr Beckinsale, I think it is quite nice to see you because I've been wanting a word with you for some considerable time. Won't you come in?'

In the literal sense this was a question with two possible answers. In reality it was clear that 'no' wasn't really an option.

'Right, yes, thanks, Mr McBride, love to, yes, thanks, right, good.'

I followed him across the hallway and into the less formal sitting room on the right. It was a large room dominated by an inglenook fireplace with bench seats under small leaded windows to either side of the hearth. The last time I'd been here I'd been sitting in one of these recesses, gently merry on punch, clasped if not to the bosom then certainly to the cleavage of the family, as Pat and Penny celebrated their fortieth wedding anniversary. It seemed unlikely that relations would be similarly cordial today.

'Sit down, Edward.'

He'd dropped the mock formality of surnames. Was that a good sign?

'Not in the inglenook, son. On a proper chair where I can see you.'

I perched gingerly on the edge of a studded chesterfield and initiated what I thought would be an ingenious decoy manoeuvre.

'This is a fine piece of furniture, Patrick. Is it one of your own?'

'Don't give me any of that bollocks, Ed.'

That was that cunning plan foiled then.

'I think we'd just better get something straight and out in the open.'

'Yes.'

'You hit my daughter.'

'I did.'

'And as I understand it, it was an accident.'

'It was, it really was.'

'The kind of accident that could befall anyone . . .'

'That's right . . .'

'I hadn't finished. The kind of accident that could befall anyone who can convince himself he's the Incredible Hulk after ten pints of Bombadier.'

'Actually it was Gravedigger's.'

Actually it really was Gravedigger's. I was trying to be honest as part of my meek act of penitence but the subtle reddening of his jowls and the discernible bristling of his grey sideburns suggested that correcting him on minor details was not perhaps the wisest policy.

'Edward, do not mess me about because I have something to say to you that you are going to hear, so shut up now. Do I make myself clear?'

He did. Crystal. But was I supposed to shut up before or after I confirmed this? I nodded vigorously. Good move.

'Right. Now I'll be honest with you, Ed . . .'

Shortened version of name. Must be good news, right?

'. . . when I heard what had happened my initial plan was to come and find you with an off-cut of dowling and beat you around the head with it.'

Wrong.

'The only reason I didn't is that Pen said there was no way I was leaving the house to go brawling in the streets. Not in my new Pringle sweater at any rate. Then, when Jeannie told me how it all happened, my anger wore off and I decided to let it lie. Especially as she said she wasn't going to see you again. Now I'm telling you this, Ed, because I liked you. Jeannie said you hadn't meant to hit her and that we shouldn't think badly of you. Of course, that hasn't stopped Pen and Maria holding you in about the same regard as Michael Barrymore.'

Oh, come on. Surely my reputation hadn't sunk that low.

'I, on the other hand, could see that Jeannie still cared about you and, even though she didn't want to go out with you any more, didn't want to see you crucified. Fair enough. So what I want to say to you is this. I will go and ask Jeannie if she wants to come down and see you. If she does, I won't stop her. If she doesn't then you leave quietly and don't come back.'

'Okay.'

'But what's more, if you do see her and possibly go out with her again, if I hear of one finger laid upon her under any circumstances, or even a harsh word said to her, I will personally take my orbital sander to your testicles. Do we understand each other?'

I had no idea what an orbital sander was but I got the idea.

'We do.'

'Look, Ed. If Pen and Maria find out you've been here they'll throw a right wobbler, but you know I only want what Jeannie wants, and if she wants you then it's all right by me. But don't be an idiot all your life, son. Stop drinking when you can still control yourself and keep your fists to yourself. Have five pints of Bombadier instead of ten.'

Gravedigger's. But this time the correction remained unspoken.

'I will, Pat. Honestly I will. I'm really, really sorry. It won't happen again.'

'All right, son. I'll go and talk to her.'

He rose from his wing-backed chair and padded out of the room in his sheepskin slippers. As he disappeared through the doorway he was passed by Whitley coming the other way. His cocked face bore a quizzical look of recognition. For a minute I thought he was going to come over to be stroked, but then he seemed to change his mind and slumped down in front of the fireplace to attend to the necessary tongue-twisting ablutions. It was as if he was waiting to see if I'd been accepted back into the fold before we could restart petting.

That made two of us then.

7

Several minutes elapsed, leaving me sweating in the
overheated sitting room, the house silent except for
the rumblings of the central heating and the considerably
closer lappings of labrador tongue. I paced the floor,
trying to absorb myself in the family photographs in
filigree frames that lay in meticulous arrangements on
highly polished occasional tables. One was of Maria's
graduation. The beaming graduate was flanked by her
ecstatic parents, basking both in the July sun of the
Manchester quadrangle and the success of their elder
daughter who'd been awarded the cherished 2:1. To the
left, at a slight remove, was Jeannie. That was so her.
This was Maria's moment and she wouldn't have wanted
to compete for centre stage. And yet she was centre
stage. Your eyes couldn't help but be drawn to the
willowy figure at the edge of the shot: slender, with
curtains of tawny hair draped across her gamine features. Despite the sense of someone having their picture
taken under duress, there was an unmistakable glimmer
in her sea-green eyes, a mischievous lopsidedness to the
suggestion of a smile. And even though she was doing
her best to bow out of the direct glare, the light had
caught her perfectly. At this moment it struck me that
although William Wordsworth would have found few
echoes of his work in the anonymity of the eponymous
avenue where I had grown up, Jeannie McBride could

have brought to mind his lines from 'She was a phantom of delight':

> She was a phantom of delight
> When first she gleamed upon my sight;
> A lovely apparition, sent
> To be a moment's ornament.

That's how she seemed to me anyway. In the photo at least.

As I turned away from the table, she was there in the room about six feet away. The fact that I hadn't heard her enter just added to the otherworldly quality she seemed to exude without even trying.

'Jeannie. You look wonderful.'

This was quite patently a lie and she knew it. She had always been thin but had battled with the periodic compulsion to starve herself since she was fourteen. Who knows what triggers these things off? Some perceived slight in the school changing rooms about an inch of puppy fat, some emaciated catwalk freak portrayed as the ideal woman, some stray drunken punch in a seedy scrap in a pub back alley. What was certain was that at times of emotional turmoil Jeannie took solace in the empty groaning of her rumbling belly and each angular protuberance of bone through ever tightening skin. I'd seen her look a lot worse, but the glow she had in the photograph was notable by its absence.

'Don't lie to me, Edward. I'm here, aren't I? You can at least be straight with me. You owe me that at least.'

'You're right and a good deal more besides. I am sorry, you know.'

'I know you are. Really I don't hold it against you. Yes,

you were paralytic and I could deal with that. It's just the transformation into a wild animal I found difficult.'

As if on cue, Whitley, apparently satisfied that his undercarriage was suitably pristine, picked himself up, crossed the room and rubbed against Jeannie's right leg, begging for attention. She braced herself against the six stone of solid canine muscle that seemed, momentarily, to be sure to push her over.

'Everyone thinks that I was upset that you hit me but, believe me, I never went around saying that. I wasn't exactly thrilled to find my boyfriend's knuckles smashing into my temple but I knew you didn't do it on purpose. You're not a woman-beater, Ed, I know that. It was just that I'd tried so hard to live a normal life and Northern Sky was where I felt most at home in the whole world. I felt safer there than anywhere, even here. At the club I didn't have to worry about Mum checking up on me every five minutes to see that I didn't have my fingers down my throat. And you took that away from me. Music, mates and a couple of drinks, that was my recipe for a quiet night out. Not twenty drinks and a brawl with those mates about the music. Jesus Christ, Ed, not everyone thinks that Nick Drake marked the second coming.'

'I know, I know. But it can be like that again. I've been back down the boat-house and made my peace with everyone. Even Freddie.'

'Maria?'

'Well, all right, not exactly with Maria. But the Snowman and Mo are cool.'

'Oh, come on, Ed, the Snowman and Mo would have a cheery pint with Jeffrey Archer as long as he was buying. What about Matt?'

'You know Matt. It didn't even directly involve him but

he managed to act like the most injured party of all. It was
Freddie who copped for it, and Mo and Lane who waded
in, but the way O'Malley went on you'd think he'd been
right in the eye of the hurricane.'

'Hurricane? You and Freddie Jameson? Don't flatter
yourself. Light breeze'd be more like it. Don't be too hard
on Matt though. It is his club.'

'It bloody is not, he just likes to think it is. Jerry Snow
was booking acts into there, and dealing with Jimmy
Champion's grumbles, when Matt was still trying to
master B flat major seventh in his bedroom at Keats
Avenue. And he never did get on top of it.'

'Yes, well, I can see you're quite the peace envoy these
days, Ed. What a transformation. Quite the tranquil soul,
eh?'

'Oh, I'm sorry. It's just O'Malley gets to me, you know.
He's so bloody superior. We're not on the school football
field now. Things have moved on.'

'Have they? I sometimes wonder if things have moved
on at all. We all seem to be living at home for one thing,
not exactly indicative of having travelled great distances in
our little lives, is it?'

'I moved away. I was away quite a while.'

'Yes and then you thumped someone and moved back
in with your mum! Very grown up. How is your mum, by
the way?'

'Oh, you know, just the same. Still treats me like I'm
thirteen.'

'My point exactly.'

'Hmmmm. I see what you mean.'

There was a break in the conversation. I'd been dread-
ing that. In full flow there was almost the illusion that
things were as they had been. From somewhere deep in the

bowels of the house came the sound of a power tool starting up. Was that the orbital sander? My scrotum tightened at the possibility.

'So what do you want, Edward? If you want me to forgive you face-to-face then fine, I forgive you. You can go for a pint with a free conscience. I daresay you've got Maurice Pepper waiting to hold your hand in a snug bar within walking distance.'

As a matter of fact Mo had mentioned something about meeting Fred for a lunchtime pint in the tap room of the Chetwode Arms approximately ten minutes' stroll away but this was purely coincidental.

'Come off it, Jeannie, Mo'll be in bed for at least another two hours yet. No, it's not just about making sure you don't hate me. I just wanted to be sure you didn't hate yourself.'

She dropped her face slightly, and for a fleeting moment a shaft of sunlight flashed across her unbrushed hair, making the girl from the photograph appear in the room before disappearing just as quickly. It was enough though. Enough to know that the 'lovely apparition' was still in there somewhere.

'I've been better, I've been worse. I eat at least once a day. I go out for walks with Whitley and Maria. Occasionally with Lane.'

'Lane? What do you want to hang around with him for?'

'Because he's a good listener, and funny, and kind and he's not likely to get into a fight all that often.'

'Yeah, and he wastes no time moving in on other people's girlfriends.'

'Meaning me? Well, for a start I don't think Lane Fox has much problem in attracting women of his own, and anyway I had stopped being your girlfriend, in case that had slipped your mind. According to Lane, we were a bad combination all along.'

Cheers, Lane. With friends like that . . .

'You being too good for me, I suppose? And how often do these character assassination nights out take place then?'

'Oh, don't be childish, Edward. In any case I don't go out at night much. I'm not really ready for all that, although I have been down the boat-house a couple of times. They had a band on there doing medieval stuff a while back called the Time Bandits. They were good. And sometimes I'll just nip in to hear Mo or Lane sing. Have you heard Mo's new songs?'

'I have, yes.'

'And are they any good?'

'They're fantastic. One in particular is just brilliant. "Summer's End" it's called. He's got talent coming out of his pointed ears, that lad.'

'I know. It's not fair really, is it? He's a bit of a genius on the quiet and yet all the women still hang around Lane. Mind you, he is thoroughly gorgeous. I don't mind being seen out with him myself.'

She said this with a wry smile, and a flash of green eyes that told me she knew I was jealous. A good sign. A glimpse of the old Jeannie.

'I'm not jealous if that's what you think.'

'You bloody well are, Edward Beckinsale.'

'I bloody well am not. Why should I be jealous of Lane Fox? I mean, what's he got that I haven't?'

'You don't really intend me to respond to that as if it was a serious question, do you?'

'No, but money, looks and charisma aren't everything, you know.'

71

'No, but they're a pretty good start. And he's an amazingly attentive lover.'

'All right, all right. I'm not rising to that. I know you haven't slept with him.'

'How do you know? You haven't seen me up till now.'

'No, but I have seen dreamboat Fox and if he'd slept with you he'd have wasted no time letting me know.'

'True. He may be close to perfection but there is still one flaw in his make-up, a chink in his armour.'

'What's that then?'

'He's still a bloke and blokes can't wait to tell their mates when they've "had" someone. Especially someone else's old girlfriend. You're all the bloody same. You're basically nothing but a bunch of immature little school-boys comparing seedy little notes.'

'See, I told you I was as good as him. If we're all the same I must be.'

She screwed up her nose and shoved me playfully in the chest.

'Do you want a drink or something, Ed?'

A drink! Result.

'Yeah, that'd be great.'

'What do you want?'

'I'll have whatever you're having.'

'Right, two Complans it is then.'

It was going better than I could ever have hoped for, but could I get her to be a part of the club scene again? Could I get her to sing in public again? Could I get her to share a bed with me again so I could brag about it to Lane Fox? She was right. We were all the same. I was disgusted at my own shallowness. One civil conversation and already my mind had leapt on to thoughts of cosy double rooms in remote farmhouse bed-and-breakfasts. We'd spent the weekend in one in the Lake District once. We'd taken moonlit walks round Tarn Hows, after which we'd tumbled into a king-size bed and lain under the skylight staring up at the stars, eventually falling asleep until breakfast: two fried eggs, four rashers of back bacon, black pudding, beans, mushrooms and, of course, Cumberland sausage. I think Jeannie had the muesli. I tried to persuade her to order the full English and scrape it all on to my already overfilled plate, but she wouldn't have it.

'They'll know it's not for me,' she whispered when the landlady had disappeared into the kitchen.

'It doesn't matter,' I hissed back, 'because we've paid for it if we want it.'

'I don't care. It's just you being greedy. I don't look like a full English sort of guest so I'm not ordering it. If you want a double breakfast then you order it, you great hog, but wait till I'm out of the room before you embarrass me.'

The practically spherical farmer's wife, whose face was adorned with the kind of round, rosy cheeks you only see in children's books, walked back in with what she considered a reasonable helping of toast for two, about eight slices. Should do for starters, I thought.

'Are you sure that's all you want, love?' she said, looking at Jeannie as one might at a stray kitten. 'A little bowl of sawdust isn't going to keep you going up the Old Man.'

This was not, for those unfamiliar with Lakeland, a frank reference to any bedroom activity going on under her slate roof, but a reference to the Old Man of Coniston, a notable peak we'd planned to scale that day.

'No, I'm fine with this, thanks. I leave the eating to Guts here. He scoffs enough for both of us.'

'Aye, well, I like a boy with a healthy appetite. Do you

want hers as well, lad? You might as well, you've paid for it.'

I turned to Jeannie with what I now see to be a look of sickening triumphalism.

'See? Thank you very much, Mrs Milnthwaite. D'you know, I think I will.'

We then spent another quarter of an hour with Jeannie contemplating with bemused disgust the cholestorol overload taking place on the other side of the dark oak dropleaf table.

'No better way to start the day,' I said, wiping the last of the egg yolk with another slice of toasted farmhouse loaf. White naturally. 'That's set me up for the day.'

What it actually did was set me up for acute indigestion which meant that we had to park up near the centre of Hawkshead so I could writhe in the passenger seat clutching my distended belly whilst making periodic dashes to the public conveniences. Jeannie, returning from an amble around the village, had looked at me with an unmistakable 'told-you-so' expression on her face, but to her credit it stopped some way short of sickening triumphalism.

Oh, for another day of blissful gut-rot in the company of Jeannie McBride. Ten minutes talking to her again and I wanted her back so much it hurt. Even more than having a stomach bunged up with four eggs, a white cottage loaf and three colossal Cumberland sausages.

She drifted back into the room and handed me a glass of what looked disconcertingly like quick set cement.

'Cheers. What's this then?'

'Complan. You did say you'd have what I was having.'

'Yes, very funny. Do you seriously expect me to drink this stuff?'

'It'll line your stomach.'

'Looks like it would line the foundations of a medium-sized block of flats.'

I took a swig. Timmy Taylor's Landlord it wasn't.

'So are you going to start coming back down the club then?'

'I've told you, I do go when I feel like it.'

'Yeah, but why don't you think about coming back and really being a part of it? They all really miss you down there, you know.'

'What, you mean sing again?'

'You could try it. Have you been singing?'

'Yes.'

'Have you been writing new songs?'

'A few, but mostly I've been trying to remember songs I used to sing. You know, Joni Mitchell, Suzanne Vega, Vashti Bunyan, Cowboy Junkies, all that stuff. And some of my own.'

This was great news because Jeannie's presence as a live performer was something we all knew should not go to waste. Technically she was flawless, her finger picking as accurate as it was delicate. Her singing too was perfectly pitched and phrased, despite being as low in volume as it was possible to be and still be considered a public performance. Soft, breathy, without vibrato, it hovered briefly in the air as if it would be swept away by the slightest breeze. Visually too there was the sense that you were gazing on something so fragile, so ephemeral, it might melt away before your eyes. Dressed simply in jeans and a shapeless linen top, she would stare down at her Taylor nylon-strung guitar so that lengths of hair cast shadows across her face. Occasionally she would swap to a Lowden Avalon Dreadnought that her dad had given her in an effort to reawaken her enthusiasm for music, for anything. The Avalon dwarfed her and only added to the illusion that you were watching some tiny creature from a parallel universe. Or perhaps it was just me. Perhaps everybody else saw a skinny girl with a big guitar, but there was definitely something beguiling about her introspection. You only had to witness the hush that fell across the boat-house when she started to sing to know that she had some unfathomable quality that drew people in.

'So do you think you could get back in front of an audience again?'

'I don't know. Sometimes I feel like I should try and then other times I feel like running away, you know, doing a Vashti.'

'Doing a Vashti' was something Jeannie often talked about. It stemmed from her fascination with Vashti Bunyan, a little known singer of the late sixties who released a solitary album called *Just Another Diamond Day*. The songs are so bare and simple that you feel like you are eavesdropping on someone vocalising their innermost thoughts, unaware that anyone is listening. The accompaniment comes from well respected sources: Dave Swarbrick and Simon Nicol from Fairport Convention, Robin Williamson of the Incredible String Band, though it's the singing and strumming of Vashti herself that make the record unforgettable.

But what appealed to Jeannie most was the story of how Vashti came to write the songs. Discovered in London in 1964 by legendary producer and Rolling Stones impresario Andrew Loog Oldham, she had actually been given a Jagger–Richards song to record as a single for Decca. However, in 1968 she decided to leave the capital behind and head for the hills. So far so *Good Life*, and 'getting it together in the country' was hardly a unique concept in hippiedom. Never one to do things by half, though, Vashti not only made for a destination that was about as far as you could get, the Outer Hebrides, she undertook it in an old green wagon pulled by a horse called Bess. A bloke called Robert and a dog named Blue also figured, as I recall. She wrote the songs over the course of two summers and a winter's travelling, and eventually recorded them in 1970 under the watchful eye of producer Joe Boyd, the man who had so lovingly tended Nick Drake.

Vashti Bunyan's story had made a deep impression on Jeannie. The thought of running away from everyone and everything you'd ever known, writing songs that you didn't know if anyone would ever hear, singing them under the stars to no one but yourself was just such a romantic notion that 'doing a Vashti' became something she often talked about. Especially as Vashti herself 'did a Vashti', vanishing into complete obscurity before re-appearing for a solitary concert at the Royal Festival Hall as part of one of the Meltdown festivals early in 2003.

'Well, if you want me to hold the reins while you strum the old Lowden, just let me know,' I said hopefully.

'Yeah, but it'll never happen, will it? If I had it in me to go I'd have gone by now.'

'Oh, I don't know. Perhaps you never found your Bess. Or Blue. Or . . .'

'Or Robert?'

'I was going to say cart.'

'Right, yeah, never found the right cart.'

This wasn't what I'd wanted to hear and I felt a little deflated. Putting my own feelings to one side, though, I still had to try and persuade her to come back to Northern Sky.

'But how do you feel about coming back down the club and maybe singing a couple of songs? Everyone'd love to see you up there again. What do you think?'

'I have been wondering about that myself.'

'Come on, it'd be great. I'll buy you a bottle of Spitfire.'

'You smooth-talking rake. You've not lost your touch, have you?'

'And a bag of crisps.'

'What flavour?'

'Thai Sweet Chilli.'

'Exotic. Now you're just showing off. And how do you think our Maria's going to react to this cosy date?'

'Oh, it's a date you want now, is it, you pushy cow? Honestly, a bag of Walker's Sensations and you presume I'm after your body.'

'Incorrect. I shouldn't think anyone is after this ravaged body.'

Damn. I'd said the wrong thing and we'd been jibing each other like we used to. She didn't seem unduly crestfallen though. A beat of silence left us looking at each other wondering where exactly we were. Were we going to try again? Were we just going to be the dreaded 'friends' in the tortured sense that former lovers who could never quite commit or let go were 'friends'? Would she change her mind and 'do a Vashti' after all?

'So what do you think then?'

'I suppose I could give it a go. The question I've got to ask myself is have I given up singing for good. Am I really never going to do it again?'

'No.'

'Yes.'

'Yes, you are never going to do it again?'

'No.'

'You said yes.'

'Only in response to your no.'

'So no was right?'

'Yes.'

'So you're not going to sing again?'

'No, you plonker. Am I really never going to sing again?'

'Aaaah. You're not never going to sing again, so the answer is no.'

'Yes.'

8

'Right, shall we make a start?' said O'Malley in his best milk monitor voice.

He'd arranged for Mo, Fred, me and Lane to meet at the Rising Sun to talk about his masterplan and whether we were all happy to go along with it. There wasn't much doubt about that. We had no alternative plan and therefore very little to lose, presuming, as we did, that we'd all benefit equally.

'Oughtn't we to wait for the Snowman, Matt?' asked Mo.

'Well, as the next Northern Sky night isn't until Thursday we'll have quite a while to hang about doing bugger all, won't we? About seventy-two hours by my reckoning.'

'You mean he's not coming?'

'You'd have to get up pretty early in the morning to put one over on you, Edward. Well done that man. Correct. He's not coming.'

'Funny,' mused Freddie, 'it's not like Jerry to miss a folk club meeting.'

'Yes, well, strictly speaking this isn't a folk club meeting.'

'You mean he hasn't been invited then, Matt?'

'Right again, Ed. You're not as thick as I thought you were. Now can we get on, please?'

'But why hasn't Jerry been invited?' piped Mo. 'He'd want to be a part of this, wouldn't he? I presume we're talking about the *Guardian* article and if it's going to be about a night at Northern Sky then it's got to involve the Snowman.'

'Yes, your concern for the local gut-bucket is all very heart-warming, I'm sure,' said Lane, 'but if Matt undertakes to inform the eminent corpulesence in question at a later date I wouldn't mind getting on with this.'

Freddie was troubled. 'That's all very well but it doesn't change the fact that Jerry should be here if we're talking about the club.'

'Oh, come on,' snapped Lane. 'The rest of you might not be able to see further than the ends of your noses, but there's a whole world out there. If you're that bothered, Freddie, why don't you toddle off and sort out the club raffle with the great Snowman or something? That's about the level you're comfortable with, isn't it?'

Freddie looked at Lane with disgust but it was me who spoke out.

'Lane, don't patronise the rest of us when all we're doing is making sure things are done in the right way. Jerry should be here and that's a given.'

'Right, m'learned friend here says that's a given,' retorted Lane, 'so we all bow to his supreme knowledge and accept that it's a given. What's also a given is that he's not here and is not coming, so can we get on?'

The fact that Jerry Snow was not only not going to be there but hadn't even been told about the meeting should, in retrospect, have set some alarm bells ringing. He wasn't what you'd call an ideas man. He'd never had much to offer in terms of taking the club forward, branching out into other areas or using some PR savvy to advance his own or anyone else's career, but he was a thoroughly decent man and a comforting presence. You just felt instinctively that no one would be stitched up if Jerry knew about it.

Head prefect O'Malley brought the meeting to order.

'Now listen. I've had a chat with Dom Casey, my mate at the *Guardian*, and he's up for it. All this new acoustic movement as antidote to knucklehead pop and cyber metal gubbins is going down a treat with your average broadsheet-scanning music fan who likes to think they're above being force fed GM-enhanced songs. So to tie in with a special issue of *G2* they want to do this piece on a grass roots folk club with a bit of a tradition behind it and Northern Sky will suit them fine. So we just need to decide when, who we want him to talk to, and what the running order for the night in question is going to be.'

'Well, Matty . . .' Matty? Why did I say that? 'My view is that he should talk to me and Mo and the Snowman, and that Fred and I should go on last because we're great and the rest of these chancers are a bunch of gimps.'

'Yes, well, that's about as helpful as I expected you to be, Eds. Let me outline some of my thoughts on this. The main interviewees should be me and Lane.'

'Really, Matt? You do surprise me. I imagined you'd be keeping a low profile in this. Not like you to take centre stage.'

'Sarcasm really doesn't suit you, Mo.'

'Well, it suits him a lot better than that Bavarian pig castrator's overall he's wearing,' said Lane.

Though it pained me to admit it, he may have had a point there. Arriving for the meeting fashionably late thanks to having arrived unfashionably early and ridden the bus to the next stop, necessitating a ten minute walk back, I'd bumped into Mo at the bar. Knowing full well the rest of them would be at the large table round the corner by the dartboard, he was in the process of buying himself a pint before ambling apparently aimlessly in that direction to react to their presence with faux surprise. That way he avoided having to buy a round. It therefore irked him that I'd arrived at the very moment he was handing over his crumpled fiver to Sally, the landlady.

'Bloody hell. Talk about timing, Beckinsale. I suppose you'll be wanting a pint then?'

'How very generously offered, Maurice. How could I refuse when it's put like that.'

As he went about ordering my drink I had the chance to fully appreciate another unique Pepper outfit. He was wearing a pair of drainpipe trousers, evidently cut from deckchair fabric, and the sort of lace-up leather jerkin that might have been issued to those Merry Men assigned by Robin to tree-felling duties. He looked ridiculous but that still didn't stop my hackles rising when Lane Fox pointed it out.

'Well, you're just showing yourself up there, Fox,' I said. 'Didn't you know that the medieval wood-cutter look is set to be very big this season?'

Matt was getting impatient.

'Right, now fascinating though this discussion on Mo's wardrobe is, would there be any chance of getting down to business? I want to get a few things straightened out before Danny gets here.'

Danny? Danny who? I wasn't aware of knowing any Danny.

'Errmm, hang on a minute, Matt.'

'What is it now, Edward?'

'Who's Danny exactly?'

'Danny Goulding.'

'Who is?'

'Danny Goulding of Goulding, Goulding and Latimer.'

'Who are the new Peter, Paul and Mary?'

'Don't be a pillock all your life, Beckinsale.'

'Well, how the hell should I know? Emerson, Lake and Palmer for the new millennium then?'

Matt tried once again to make some headway.

'Right, look, this is all most diverting and I'm sure if Dorothy Parker was here now she'd be dissolving the Algonquin circle to throw her lot in with the Rising Sun wits but I would at some point like to get on.'

'Fine, Matt, then tell us who Danny Goulding is.'

'Danny Goulding is a lawyer, Ed, a solicitor.'

'Thank you. So what do we want with one of those then?'

'Well, I thought we should just make everything legal and above board. Now are there any more questions?'

Freddie was evidently as bemused as Mo and me. 'Errmm . . . Matt?'

'Yes, Freddie.'

'What are you talking about, "make everything legal and above board"? Are we planning to adopt some Romanian orphans here or have I missed something?'

Matt glanced at Lane and they exchanged a look in the self-satisfied way that hi-fi salesmen do when confronted with a customer who doesn't know a woofer from a tweeter.

'Contracts, Frederick. If we are going to get national press and start actually going out and playing to people around the country, who knows, even put out some records, then we are going to need contracts. It's for your benefit really. If it's all in an official document then you'll know where you stand and Danny is a partner in one of the top practices in town. He's also, as it happens, big on his music.'

'Is he also big on his stationery?'

'You what, Ed?'

'Well, is he, by any coincidence, involved in any legal work to do with your dad's stationery business?'

'Not really, though his father, Murray Goulding, is. I don't see that that's got anything to do with it though. What's your point?'

'Well, firstly that you're asking us to get involved with friends of your family. Secondly that you're throwing legal documents at us out of the blue. And thirdly that even if we wanted to sign a contract for whatever reason, you want us to sign with a bloke we've never even met.'

'Yes, but you wouldn't be signing with someone you've never met because you'd be signing with me.'

'No, you've really lost me now.'

Matt put on his most patronising face.

'Edward, listen. Danny Goulding is a first class lawyer, not unknown to the music business through his work with Lightwater Concerts.'

'The promoters.'

'Correct. Now he let me know that he was interested in exploring other business avenues, particularly of a musical nature, and so last week he and I formed a new company called Northern Sky Artists to manage and represent a stable of burgeoning musical talents.'

'And does the Snowman know about this?'

'No. Should he?'

'Well, if you're using the name Northern Sky it does rather suggest an affiliation with the club of the same name with which Jerry's been centrally involved for most of his adult life.'

'That's true, Ed, but the name Northern Sky no more belongs to Jerry than to you or me or even, come to that, the sainted Nick Drake, who happened to write a song of that title in 1970 and stick it on his *Five Leaves Left* album.'

'*Bryter Later*.'

'What?'

'"Northern Sky" is on *Bryter Later* not *Five Leaves Left* but carry on.'

'Thank you. My point is that no one owns the title and this is just something Danny and I want to have a go at. I don't have anything against Jerry, I just don't want to get into bed with him on this one.'

There was a pause while we all contemplated the horrors of sharing a divan with a fully bearded eighteen-stone beer monster. Perhaps there were actively homosexual, sea-shanty-loving members of CAMRA somewhere for whom this prospect would induce a ready erection. Not round this table though.

'So if we could just agree that we're all on board before Danny arrives, then we'll be getting somewhere. Lane's already on board.'

Mo, Freddie and I looked at each other quizzically. The others made no attempt to speak, however, so it was left to me again.

'Well, why am I unsurprised by that? So you two have had a pre-meeting before the meeting unbeknown to the rest of us, have you? Well, fancy that. So what do you think, guys?'

Before either Mo or Freddie could speak Lane Fox butted in.

'What do they think? What is there to think about? Matt and his stinking rich partner are offering to invest some time, money and effort in trying to get your fledgling musical careers kick-started, though with some of you it's debatable whether that's possible, and you want to think about it? What have you got to lose? Unless you're expecting a call from Simon Fuller, the celebrated S Club Svengali, who's identified a gap in the market that could be filled by a little vagrant in antique slaughterman's attire.'

'Does he mean me?'

'By process of elimination, Mo, I would say yes.'

'Perhaps I should explain,' said O'Malley. 'Last night Lane Fox agreed to be the first artist to sign to Northern Sky Artists and as a result the demos of his latest recordings are already on their way, registered post, to Johnny Leonard at Mulberry Records at his personal request.'

This was, I had to admit, impressive. Not only because we had no idea that Lane had recorded anything, but also because we knew nothing of any connection with Johnny Leonard, who for several decades had run the biggest and most successful independent label for roots music in Europe. That Lane might be on the brink of a record deal was slightly galling, though ultimately thrilling. The idea that one of us might actually get an album out made everything seem so much more real. We weren't going to just sit around talking about it as we'd done since school, we were actually going to do it. Well, one of us was anyway, and once Fox's record was released it would make it a whole lot easier for the rest of us to follow suit, wouldn't it?

'So do you actually know Johnny Leonard then, Matt?' I asked speculatively.

'Well, I wouldn't say I know him as such, Eds, but I have met him. He does a lot of work with Lightwater who do a lot of work with Goulding, Goulding and Latimer and, well, you know how the old boys network works.'

'Come off it, Matt,' sniggered Mo. 'Do we look like we know how the old boys network works?'

'A good point, Maurice. Look, suffice to say that though not the best of buddies or anything, Johnny Leonard and Murray Goulding were at Cambridge together and helped run a college folk club. In fact Murray told me that Johnny once booked Nick Drake.'

A direct connection to Saint Nick! This was more than impressive. It was incredible. The thought that I could sign to a management company where one of the director's dad's mates had once put on Nick Drake in the back room of a boozer. How well connected would that make me? Christ, I'd be practically folk royalty. I took a sip of Pedigree and looked at Freddie and Mo.

'Well, what do you think, boys? Shall we sign our lives away with big shot O'Malley and his legal pal or . . . ?'

'Or what, Ed?'

'Or shall we not bother.'

'What, and just miss out on what might be our big chance and waste the rest of our lives?'

'Bloody hell, Mo, you've happily wasted your whole life so far, why change now?'

'For that very reason. The only thing I'm interested in doing is playing the guitar and singing my songs to people who'll listen and this is about the best chance I'm going to get to do it. And can I just say that I resent you saying that I've wasted my whole life. There was the time I helped my dad build a summer house in the back garden, and you're also forgetting my lifesaving badge.'

This gentle good-natured verbal arm wrestling was all getting too much for Lane, who often liked to imply, in the time honoured manner of the idle rich, that he had pressing engagements elsewhere.

'Gentlemen, at the risk of stating the bleeding obvious, we all know you'll have to sign because none of you is ever going to get anywhere at all under your own steam, and if you don't hitch yourself to Matt's train you're going to be left in the sidings for ever. Personally I think you're bloody lucky to be given the chance at all, so if I were you, and thank God I'm not, I would snatch Matt's hand off and put Mont Blanc to quarto.'

'Yes, we got you the first time, Lane. We know where you're coming from. What do you reckon, Freddie?'

'Oh, come off it, Eddie. We don't have anything to lose because we're starting with sod all, never the strongest position to negotiate from, and if we finish up with sod all then we've lost precisely . . .'

'Sod all?'

'Correct, Maurice. So, Eds, much as I enjoy watching you stall things to rile Lane and Matt, and I look forward to lots more of that in the future, right now we may as well just sign our lives away and get on with sorting out the big night.'

O'Malley managed to look both taken aback and smug at the same time. He plonked his glass on the heavily ringed table.

'Well, well! A welcome, if rare, outbreak of common sense from Frederick Jameson. It looks like you're the only one with doubts about this scheme, Ed, and whilst that is of course entirely your prerogative, I have to tell you that I'll be proceeding with or without you. I'd be glad to have you on board, but I think we can probably crew the ship without you.'

'Crew and ship! Where's all this nautical crap coming

from, Matt? Why can't you talk in plain English like the rest of us?'

'Ahem. Au contraire.'

'Sorry, Lane. Not you obviously.'

O'Malley, sensing that his prey was mortally weakened, came in for the kill by putting on that concerned elder brother voice that's always so annoying when coming from someone slightly younger.

'Listen, Eds. You're right to question things like this. The music business is full of cowboys but we've known each other since the fourth form, surely you can trust me here, can't you? It seems as if Freddie and Mo are pre-pared to give it a go and so it would be neat if you could see your way to signing up too. Especially as you and Freddie are supposed to be a duo.'

Silence fell on the assembled company. I wanted to be swept along like the rest of them. There was a tingle of excitement pulsing through my body at the prospect of becoming a real, proper, actual, performing musician who got paid and everything, someone whose playing and song-writing would be discussed in reviews in the real, proper, actual newspapers. But I really did have some concerns. I wanted to be a part of it all as much as anyone, and I certainly didn't want to be left out of something involving Mo and Fred, but what were we getting into? Even though we had little we could lose, did we really want to entrust our lives to a bloke we'd never really trusted, even at school? Could he be relied upon to treat us all as equals? Could he guarantee there would be no favouritism? Would we all get signed by Johnny Leonard? Was Danny Goulding the kind of bloke we wanted to be involved with? These were questions that would have to be confronted at some point. At that moment, though, O'Malley played his trump card.

'Look, Beckinsale, you awkward sod. Danny'll be here any moment and if I can tell him you've all agreed to our proposal, then I'm sure I can get him to write off tonight as a company expense, as we're entertaining our client roster, and we can all get rat-arsed and go for a curry on Northern Sky Artists.'

Game, set and match to O'Malley then! How could I take away the prospect of a night's free ale from Mo and Freddie, who were already looking at me with the expectant eyes of Whitley begging for scraps of Sunday roast at Lanercost?

'Go on then, Colonel Parker.' I shoved my empty pint glass towards him. 'And I'll have a chaser.'

9

As I struggled to prise myself out of sleep the following morning, my thick head confirmed hazy recollections of the night before. In fact, the last time I remembered feeling as bad after a night at the Rising Sun was while we were still at school. And on that occasion it wasn't just the drink that caused my aches and pains.

Initially, it had been a good natured evening, one of the occasions on which a dozen or so folkies had sat in a circle near the dart-board, passing round the guitars and taking turns to sing. Major Jim refused to open up the boat-house on these nights as he always said the heating bill would be more than the bar takings. This seemed unlikely as no one had any recollection of the radiators down there being anything other than stone cold. He was, however, happy to let us play in the corner as it gave him live music without having to pay for it, and doubled the number of pints he sold on a quiet mid-week night.

It was around ten o'clock when I got up from my stool, grabbed what was left of the beer kitty from the table, and made my way towards the bar. I'd played a couple of Nick tunes, 'Which Will' and 'Saturday Sun', I think, and had passed the guitar on to Mo. He'd performed a song called 'Cringle Fields', the name of a local park, which was a lovely number and must have been his first composition, as far as I can remember. By process of elimination that meant it had to be O'Malley or Lane's turn next, and so it seemed as good a time as any to get the beer in.

It didn't take long to get served but as I turned away with a tray laden with pints of Pedigree I found my way blocked by a bunch of handy looking lads with big hair.

'Well, well, if it isn't one of our little fairy folkie friends.'

Baz Buckley was in the year above us at school and, whilst not in the normal scheme of things a nasty character, was quite prepared to give a thoroughly convincing impression of one if he'd had a couple of drinks. He was also a committed heavy rock fan, and had come to the conclusion that admirers of the folk idiom were not to be trusted.

'Having a gay little sing-song tonight, are we, Beckinsale?'

His gang of leather-jacketed be-denimed hairies guffawed on cue.

'Look, Baz, just get out of my way, please. We're not hurting anybody, are we? We're just enjoying the music we like.'

'And we're just taking the piss. We're not hurting anyone either.'

Not for the time being maybe.

'I don't know what your problem is, Baz. That's the great thing about music. We all like what we like, we're all different, and yet no one can tell anyone else that they're wrong.'

'Well, you're wrong for a start because you like a load of poncey music that's for girls. If you were a real man you'd be into Sabbath and Purple and Zep like we are. Like proper blokes.'

'Actually I do like quite a bit of Led Zeppelin, especially the acoustic stuff like "Going to California". Quite folky, that, wouldn't you say? Didn't they used to play a bit of an acoustic set during their concerts with John Paul Jones on the mandolin? And didn't Robert Plant's lyrics involve the odd elf or fairy?'

These were all perfectly valid arguments, although not ones, in retrospect, that would improve the chances of my coming out of that evening unscathed.

I managed to sidle my way through, beer slopping on to the tray as I was buffeted by a well aimed elbow, and got the round back to the circle where Matt O'Malley was mauling John Martyn's 'May You Never'.

'You took your time,' said Mo.

'I know. I ran into a bit of a problem over there. Look.'

Baz and his heavy metal hangers-on had followed me back from the bar and were packed into the doorway, making it impossible to pass through without bodily contact.

'Come on, you big girl's blouse,' shouted Fowler. 'Stop pissing about and do "Smoke on the Water".'

As it was Matt singing, this didn't seem to be altogether a bad idea, but it did little to improve the atmosphere.

'Look, stout brethren of the metal fraternity,' said Lane. 'You are welcome to sit, listen and even join in, if any of you have taken enough time off from drinking Strongbow to actually learn how to play the guitar. If not then perhaps you could go away and compare dandruff and leave us alone.'

Baz snarled, 'You'd just better watch your step, soft lad. I've got my eye on you. One look in the wrong direction and I'll have you.'

Lane raised his eyes to the ceiling, shrugged and proceeded to play a note perfect version of David Bowie's 'An Occasional Dream' as if he hadn't a care in the world.

The stand-off continued until closing time: them standing in the doorway making derisory snorts, us trying our best to ignore them and play our songs. They left shortly after last orders, leaving us to pack away our guitars, say our goodbyes, and even have the odd hug without fear of persecution. However, as we made our way into the car park, and as the door slammed behind us and was securely bolted from the other side by Major Jim, it became apparent that we'd fallen for the oldest trick in the book. From the shadows by the bins came an empty cider bottle which shattered at our feet. Following it came the marauding horde of hard rock Picts, with their Braveheart, Baz Buckley, leading the line.

'Bloody hell, lads, we're for it now,' I muttered.

'Yeah, but at least there's five of us,' said Mo.

'Errm, I think a recount may be in order,' said Freddie, a noticeable tremble in his voice.

Turning, shortly before the first of a dozen blows connected with my head, I noticed the lights of Arthur Fox's Porsche leaving the scene at high speed, presumably with Lane and Matt. We were not five, we were three. And a pretty weedy looking three at that. Looking back, this may actually have helped our cause, as I don't think Buckley and his mates saw us as worthy foe. They liked to go into battle looking for opponents who would give them a good fight, and that certainly wasn't going to be us. Not that Matt and Lane knew that when they deserted us. Admittedly they did contact my dad, who duly came in a taxi to scrape us off the tarmac, and, as they later explained, we couldn't have all fitted into that car anyway. But couldn't they have at least waited? Couldn't Arthur Fox have given one of those 'Dad speeches' and persuaded our assailants to leave us alone? As it was we were left as cannon fodder for the Buckley gang as the city clock chimed the longest twelve of my life.

On the way home my dad sat with an arm around my shoulder.

'Don't worry, son, your mum's got some ointments, bandages and a nice mug of Horlicks ready at home.'

'Thanks, Dad.'

'And we've all had a few fights in our time, lad. You're hurting now, but the bruises will soon go away. It's all character-building stuff.'

'Thanks, Dad.'

'Mind you, you do bring it on yourselves in a way, playing all that girlie music. Why don't you do a bit of that there heavy rock like real men?'

'Bloody hell, Dad, not you as well.'

Happily, the current hangover was entirely self-inflicted, thanks to the largesse of Danny Goulding, who had turned out to be a surprise in more ways than one.

The fact that he was some kind of hot-shot lawyer and a mate of O'Malley's led us to expect a shiny suited, brilliantined slimeball who was not to be trusted. It's one of life's strange rules that people who turn out in clothes a scarecrow might turn his nose up at, topped off with haircuts by the council, feel free to be suspicious of those who dress well, without ever suspecting the opposite process might also be true. We were the scruffy ones so we were the good guys, right? So when Danny turned up, we had to overcome the palpable disappointment of putting our preconceptions to one side. For a start, he was about two and a half hours late, which endeared him to us immediately as it had engendered a state of great agitation in O'Malley – not least because the absence of his new business partner had left him with the unenviable task of getting the ale in. We were also impressed that Goulding had had the foresight and decency to turn up to meet his new charges heroically sloshed. The guy could barely stand up. He was also reassuringly plump; the kind of man who looked unfamiliar with the Atkins Diet, or at least, if he was having meals that were low in carbohydrate he was having them on toast with a side portion of mash. His brown chalk stripe suit may well have been bespoke, but as it was following the contours of a body that was anything but designer built it appeared crumpled, shapeless and not in the least intimidating; perhaps because it had what looked like the remains of a spaghetti carbonara smeared along one of the sleeves. In much the same way his thinning yellow hair was smeared across his glistening dome. Not with gel, but perspiration.

'Shit, Christ, O'Malley, you great knob, get 'em in, you wazzock.'

Things were looking up.

At that moment Sally Fisher rang the dreaded brass bell.

'Last orders, gentlemen, please.'

Things were looking down.

'Where the hell have you been, Danny? You were supposed to be here at half past eight.'

'Aye, well, got a bit waylaid in town. Went for a swifty after work with the guys from the office and, you know, one bottle led to another. Sorry to have held you all up. I can see you've been waiting for me before getting stuck into the beer, you bunch of dossers. White cider all round, was it? My God, son, what sort of a jacket do you call that? What time's the execution?'

That he had homed in so fast on Mo's clothes only recommended him still further. Matt, predictably, wasn't so easily placated.

'Yes, well, I think we'd have put on a more professional front for the first meeting of Northern Sky Artists if the directors of the company had both been here to put up a united front.'

'For God's sake, O'Malley, get that broom handle from up your arse and loosen up. I work with tossers who are "putting on a professional front" all frigging day, every frigging day! I thought we were going to have a bit of a laugh, a load of ale and try and sell the odd dodgy folk album. And judging by the looks of this bunch of rag, tag and bob-tails, I would think that's about right. If it's professionalism you want you'd better find another bank-roller, and some well honed cabaret artistes with matching sodding waistcoats. Now who's for a curry?'

Danny then proceeded to conjure up a cab, complete with a reckless Jenson Button drive-alike called Salim Chowdry, who got us to the Shere Khan in ten minutes flat, charging through the back streets at seventy miles an hour while he and Danny had an animated chat about the relative merits of Nusrat Fateh Ali Khan and Leonard Cohen. At the restaurant, having been greeted effusively by the waiters and squeezed himself on to a velveteen banquette, Danny ordered Kingfishers all round, and began to hold court.

'Right, gentlemen, eat as much as you can, safe in the knowledge that O'Malley and I will stump up for the lot.'

Matt had been one of those sickeningly fit and well looking blokes since school but his customary rosy glow was growing paler by the minute as his new business partner's entertainment expenditure continued apace. Beer, cabs and now a curry and we hadn't coughed up a penny. Result. You could tell he didn't mind under-writing Lane, he was always trying to impress Lane, and I don't think he particularly minded funding Freddie's evening. But putting his hand in his pocket for Mo and me, that really hurt. Which only added to the pleasurable nature of the outing.

We ordered, as is customary when dining late at night on Indian cuisine, about three times as much food as we needed; most of the dishes including king prawns, which we didn't like particularly, it was just that they were the most expensive things on the menu. As the waiters ferried ever more dishes to the table, Danny outlined his vision for Northern Sky.

'So look, this is how I see it. I've got more money than sense and O'Malley here is an ideal associate for me because he's got more sense than money. The legal business is going from strength to strength but I really want to try and have some fun otherwise what's the point in having the cash?'

'Flash cars, holidays in the Maldives?'

'A fair point, Freddie, but if you drive a flash car you can't have a drink, and they don't serve Jennings Sneck Lifter in the Maldives.'

'Good answer. For a legal bod you're in grave danger of talking sense.'

'I'll take that as a compliment, Mo. But I really am into music, and particularly folk music. My dad Murray was big into it at college and made a lot of mates booking the top folk turns into his college bar. Mates who would then come and kip in the spare room when they were passing through. Many's the time I've come down to breakfast on a school day to find Roy Harper slumped in the armchair by the Rayburn, or Bert Jansch with yolk running down his chin as he rips into a fried egg sandwich. So folk music is in my blood, I've grown up on the stuff. It was either phone social services and risk getting taken into care or get into it myself. Plus, through the business we are very well in with not only Johnny Leonard but also Julian Bellerby and Bill Foster at Lightwater Concerts, so it makes perfect sense to have a crack at it. That being said, what do we need?'

'Your heads testing?'

'In all likelihood, Ed, but in order to have a punt here we need some artists, turns, singers and this is of course where you all come in. Matthew has lavishly sung your praises . . .'

This seemed doubtful to me. Lane and Mo yes, Jeannie maybe, but me and Freddie? Never.

'. . . at least he says that Lane is a star in waiting and that Maurice is a gifted writer and . . .'

Yes?

'. . . that we can't leave Freddie and Ed out because you're all mates, right?'

Right. So we were in. Not on merit but we had too little pride left to worry about that.

'Oh, and he also says that there's someone else who's destined for great things.'

Jeannie.

Goulding shovelled in another JCB scoop of chana masala, thumped himself in the upper ribcage, emitted a belch audible to everyone in the restaurant and resumed.

'So basically we'd like you all to sign up to Northern Sky for no money because you haven't earned any, and perhaps never will. However, we can get Johnny Leonard to listen to your stuff, and he's already agreed to put something out by Lane, and we can get some sort of package tour on the back of the *Guardian* piece through our chums at Lightwater. From what I hear from Matt about Mo and Ms McBride there should be no problem drumming up some interest there. With you two, well, what have you got to lose?'

Freddie and I looked at each other like the last two kids against the wall waiting to be picked for the football teams, which is not the best feeling in the entire world, but, being realistic, it's not exactly the worst. All right, you haven't been picked first but at least you know you're going to get picked, right? We nodded our agreement. He was right. What had we got to lose?

'So we're all agreed then. We'll give it a go. And to cement the deal I'd like to invite you all on board my canal boat for a celebratory cruise and piss up on Sunday. Judging you all on appearances, with the possible exception of Fox here, I'd say you were the kind of people with windows in their social calendars, so we'll get under way at shall we say eleven a.m.? All libations provided by Northern Sky, of course.'

O'Malley could stand it no longer.

'For God's sake, Danny, we'll be going bust before we've even begun. Let 'em buy their own ale and we'll provide the pork pies.'

'Oh, do lighten up, O'Malley, you bloody stiff. All right, you provide the pies and Goulding, Goulding and Latimer will foot the booze bill. I trust you'll all be availing yourselves of our services when you're involved in transcontinental lawsuits? Good. Everybody happy?'

'Just one thing, Danny. Is Jerry Snow invited on this booze cruise?'

'Who, Ed?'

O'Malley hadn't mentioned him. I knew it.

'The Snowman. Perhaps he's slipped Matt's mind, as walruses in lurid blouses do, but he is actually the longest serving committee member at the folk club. So is he invited?'

In contrast to his hawkish partner, Goulding's bonhomie knew no bounds.

'Of course he's invited. The more the merrier. O'Malley, you'd better bring more pies. And big ones if he's a lard-arse like me. So see you all Sunday then at Windrush Marina. Oh, and Edward, bring what's her name with you.'

'Jeannie.'

'Jeannie, of course. Bring her, won't you?'

The bill arrived on a stainless steel platter on which were also placed several sliced oranges. Danny quickly despatched the bill to O'Malley, who took it, studied it and swiftly began to resemble a man who'd been punched, while Danny proceeded to hand round the citrus segments.

'Anyone for fruit?' boomed Danny amiably. 'Come on, dig in or I'll have to eat the lot myself and I don't want to do that. On account of it being good for you, I'm trying to give it up.'

What a man!

10

By choosing the time of my call carefully I'd managed to avoid any contact with the combative Maria McBride and her harridan of a mother, Penelope. Jeannie didn't answer the phone of course but Patrick had said he'd pass on the message. That he would wasn't in doubt, though whether Jeannie would respond was less certain. I needed to see her on neutral ground, not at Fortress Lanercost where I would always have one ear listening out for the crunch of gravel as Penny's Vel Satis rolled into the drive, to be followed by the threatening clip-clop of the dreaded court shoes making their inexorable progress across the parqueted hall. She really was the mother you didn't want the girl of your dreams to have. Over-primped, over-inflated and overpowering, she was one of those women who had the ability to knock the self-confidence out of anyone she met. Rather like being in the company of a thick-set detective constable, when being addressed by Penelope McBride you began to feel as though you'd done something wrong even if you hadn't. Which I kind of had, but you get my drift. And of course the worst thing about girlfriends' mothers from hell is that they know you can't talk back to them because if you want to have any chance of a long-term relationship with their daughter, you have to be unerringly polite to the parents. At least I could tell Maria to piss off. I hadn't plucked up the courage to do it so far, but it was at least a possibility, and Jeannie would give me only a mild rebuke and perhaps withdraw any moist opportunities for the rest of the evening. Not that evenings of moistness were on the agenda right now. But one piss off to the McBride matriarch and the big freeze would be permanent.

I'd told Patrick to ask Jeannie to meet me in town at one of Jerry Snow's shabby trinket emporiums on Crossway. I suppose that this might seem a strange point of rendezvous, as we weren't a pair of impoverished sweethearts looking to waste a fortnight's minimum wage on matching sovereign rings, but I knew Jeannie would be late if she came at all, and would on no account walk into a pub or café on her own. Even if I was there waiting. So hanging about at Jerry's was one of those things I'd spent a lot of time doing over the years, and it was a real tribute to the dreadfulness of his stock that in all that time I'd never felt the remotest impulse to buy anything. In my experience blokes with a keen interest in jewellery are, like Manchester United supporters living outside Manchester and keen golfers living anywhere, not to be trusted. What rogue brain wave makes a bloke wake up in the morning and think about buying an identity bracelet? Who really needs what amounts to an inexpertly engraved hospital identity tag outside of a bling-bling hospice for senile rappers?

I passed the time by talking to Jerry, who was wedged behind the counter in a shirt that contained enough fabric to run up a pair of living room curtains in a pattern Laura Ashley may have dismissed as too floral. His presence was the cause of some irritation to his staff as he quite patently had no intention of actually serving. This was of course his prerogative as it was his shop, but negotiating your way around him in order to reach the christening mugs was proving a patience tester for the manageress, Denise, and her recently acquired assistant, Patrick.

'So O'Malley and this lawyer friend of his want you all to sign up to Northern Sky Artists and in return they'll guarantee you what?'

'Um, a party on a boat.'

'Well, it's something, I suppose. More than anyone else has ever offered you anyway. And am I invited?'

'Of course you are, Jerry. We couldn't have a Northern Sky event without you.'

'Except for the one you already had at the Shere Khan.'

'Yeah, except for that one. So will you come on this trip or not on Sunday?'

'I would imagine so if the invitation was genuine. Do you think Matthew really wants me there?'

'Jerry, what O'Malley wants is neither here nor there. If it's Northern Sky business, you should be involved.'

'I fear that what O'Malley wants may be more important than you might imagine if you're preparing to sign a contract with this new company of his. Was it actually his idea to have me come along on Sunday?'

'Well, not exactly but he didn't object when the idea came up.'

'Well, he wouldn't, would he, dear boy? He's not likely to be that blatant about shutting me out. And to be perfectly fair,' which the Snowman always was, 'there's no reason why I should be involved. I don't own any of you. I just run a backstreet folk club because I like the music and enjoy a pint or twelve with anyone who's prepared to be seen in public with an oversized hillbilly in a bad shirt. I'm sure Matthew would have got around to telling me in his own good time.'

'That's your problem, Jerry, you always give everyone the benefit of the doubt.'

'Present company included, I presume.'

The shop bell sounded as an impossibly young couple entered and shuffled up to the counter.

'Can I help you, sir, madam?' said the resplendently bald Patrick with maximum obsequiousness, adding to their tangible discomfort by addressing them formally for the first time in their lives.

'Errr, yeah. Engagement ring,' said the underfed and over-fake-tanned female of the pair, patting her stomach to indicate the imminent advent of motherhood. 'We want to get engaged.'

'That, sir, madam, is often the ideal occasion on which to purchase a ring of the engagement variety.'

I was beginning to warm to Patrick.

'So what did sir, madam have in mind?'

By the mortified and vacant expression on the pizza face of the father-to-be the only reasonable answer to this question was 'nothing'. Whether the question was about rings or not. His loquacious intended came to the rescue.

'Er, gold.'

'Gold!' said Patrick, as if she'd just suggested lead. 'I'm not sure if we have any gold rings in stock. Let me just check with the manageress. Mrs Baverstock, do we have any gold engagement rings in the vaults that I might display to sir and madam?'

Denise Baverstock suppressed a smirk and raised her eyes to the strip light before muttering, 'Just get on with it, Mr Gallagher.'

Making the customers as uncomfortable and confused as possible, not that discomfort and confusion can have been new experiences to the reluctant shoppers on this occasion, was evidently a familiar way of filling the time at Snow's the Jewellers these days. And why not? How enraptured is it possible to be when demonstrating a carriage clock for the thirty-seventh time in a five and a half day working week?

'Well, do you know what,' said Patrick, wringing his hands unctuously, 'I think you might be in luck. Our colleagues at Tiffany have this very morning despatched to us some of the very rings in question by armoured motorcade. How much were sir, madam thinking of spending?'

Sir stopped chewing his Airwaves and finally found his voice.

''Bout fifty!'

Patrick closed his eyes and nodded sagely.

'How very wise to set a budget before making a purchase, sir. One doesn't want to get carried away, does one? Right, if sir, madam would be so kind as to tarry in situ, one's salesperson will endeavour to return with a velveteen display card forthwith.'

And with that he turned on his immaculate brogues and headed off to retrieve the tray marked '9 carat engagement rings £49.99' from the window, squeezing himself as suggestively as possible against Snow the Jeweller's backside as he passed through.

'Seems like a nice boy.'

'Aah yes, Patrick. Rather fond of dear Paddy. He's certainly livened Denise up. She's a fine woman but she was becoming a bit, shall we say, lacking in motivation.'

'Jerry, she's worked here for fifteen years. How motivated is it possible to be after that length of time selling rolled gold crap to people who think the Koh-i-noor is a curry house on Market Street?'

'The Koh-i-noor is a curry house on Market Street, Edward, as well you know. As I recall the last time you were in there you found yourself in a state of some financial embarrassment and someone else had to foot the bill for your lamb jalfrezi. A debt you promised to repay within twenty-four hours.'

'Ah yes. Fair point, Jerry. Will you take a cheque?'

The Snowman glanced across to the glass-topped counter where, having wrapped up another sale on his way to becoming employee of the month, Patrick had taken a fountain pen from his top pocket and was busy amusing himself by floridly concocting an unnecessarily detailed receipt.

'With trade as brisk as this in the old top of the range ring market, I think I can stand an old friend the odd curry. As can Northern Sky Artists, I believe. So where's the money coming from? Matthew hasn't got any and, if he had, whilst I could see him spending it on Lane, I can't see him wanting to wine and dine you, Freddie and Mo.'

'You're not wrong there, Jerry. No, the cash seems to be coming from this solicitor mate of his called Danny Goulding.'

The Snowman nodded.

'Oh, yes, Danny Goulding. Murray Goulding's lad.'

'You know him then?'

'I know Murray vaguely. Very well connected in music circles is Murray Goulding. Lightwater Concerts and all that crowd. I have had the odd chat with him to get hold of certain artists for the club. In fact his name came up in conversation just the other week when I was talking to Max Dauber. Do you remember Max?'

'The landlord of the Saracen's Head?'

'Exactly, and an excellent cask of Old Salopian he keeps

too. Well, for a time he's been after a small country hotel to run and he was desperate to get his hands on the Pines out Cummerton way. Bit of a wreck these days apparently but bags of potential, as they say. Anyway he went to the auction but was outbid by Goulding, Goulding and Latimer.'

'Really? I didn't know they were in the hotel trade as well.'

'They're not, which is what got Max's goat. What they plan to do with it no one seems to know.'

The bell sounded again as the emaciated future divorcees shuffled out of the shop, already feeling for the packs of Regal in their tracksuit bottoms. Coming past them the other way was an equally slight figure whose wasted frame was lent some bulk by a fading grey duffle coat and chunky multi-coloured striped scarf. Jeannie.

Before I could intervene the irrepressible Patrick leapt into action.

'And how may I be of assistance to madam this fine day?'

'Sorry?'

'What particular avenue of semi-precious pleasure would madam like to investigate?'

The Snowman intervened.

'All right, down, boy. Madam will not be making a purchase, unless there's going to be a break with tradition stretching back at least a decade. This is Jeannie, who's a friend of ours. Jeannie, this is Patrick, who's a sarcastic sod who makes the most of his dull existence as a shop assistant by being monstrously over-polite to the customers so that they feel even more uneasy than usual.'

Jeannie's wan smile flickered across her thin, slightly chapped lips. I could see that the court jester had amused her. Good job he's gay, I thought. He had to be. All men who choose to work with jewellery are gay. Aren't they?

'Jeannie. It's good to see you. I wasn't sure you'd come.'

'No, well, it was touch and go fitting you into my hectic social calendar, Ed. You know there are so many other things I could be doing: Lowdens to be re-strung, toe-nails to be cut, middle-class maternal prejudices to be heard. How are you, Jerry?'

'Never better, my dear, never better. I trust we'll be seeing you down at the club before too long?'

'I guess so. I'm feeling a lot better now and I think I might even be getting to the point where I could sing a song or two again.'

She was smiling, but Jerry's next remark changed her expression completely.

'Just as well, seeing as you're all off on a world tour courtesy of Matthew's burgeoning music empire.'

'Pardon?'

'Bloody hell, Jerry!'

'What is it, Edward? I haven't let the cougar out of the mail sack, have I? You were going to outline the details of O'Malley and Goulding's plan to our favourite wood nymph, weren't you?'

'Of course I was, Jerry. I was just going to pick my moment.'

'Well, it looks like I've picked it for you. Run along now, the pair of you, and sort it out. Jeannie, I expect to see you at the Sun very soon. And Beckinsale, treat her like porcelain.'

I took her by the hand. It struck me that this was the first physical contact we'd had since the incident and though it hardly marked the full resumption of our relationship, it still felt good to touch her. We drifted aimlessly along the rimy flagged pavements of Crossway, passing the glowing tobacconists and squealing heel bars; taking our time, feeling our way as the swarms of worker ants and shopaholic drones buzzed around us. It was a moment I would look back on wistfully. A moment when nothing was for certain, but nothing seemed impossible, and though you were just two ordinary people walking amongst other normal people on a normal street on a normal grubby afternoon, the simple act of holding hands made you feel like you were so different. So different that you couldn't understand why people weren't stopping to look at you, such was the aura you felt you exuded.

And the city clock chimed four.

'So where do you want to go? The usual?'

'I'm not sure we still have a usual, Eds. It's been too long.'

'Okay, fair point. Well, we could go to the milk bar on Coppergate.'

'Naah. Too depressing. Full of old grannies in raincoats and trainers with nowhere to go, eating soggy toast.'

'Okay, well, we could go to the Dun Cow.'

'No. Too smoky. Full of bulbheads in football shirts.'

'Hmmm, well, we could just go for a walk on the city walls.'

'Too strenuous. Full of middle-agers in purple and turquoise fleeces.'

'Right then, clever trousers, let's hear your ideas.'

'The usual?'

'The usual.'

We took a left down a cobbled alley by Sharpe's the bakers, where a woman in an overall to which was pinned a badge proclaiming 'Joanna – Manageress' was already removing the last of the vanilla slices from the window and washing down the plastic trays. At the bottom of the hill we crossed the City Avenue and strolled on towards the meadows heading for the Old Boat-house Tea Rooms situated on the far bank of the Arn opposite the pumping station. The usual.

I hadn't been to the Old Boat-house since I got back. It never felt right without her. Any time I tried to sit and read the *Guardian* over tea and Eccles cakes her ghost had lingered at every turn, which for someone who wasn't dead was a pretty amazing trick. Now, sitting at the same table by the same window with her again, the pieces of the jigsaw slotted in once more.

Like the boat-house that housed Northern Sky, the tea room was little more than an oversized shed with leaded windows and a old gas fire at one end. Permanently flickering away on miser rate, it must have contravened health and safety regulations on several counts, but it lent the place an unmistakable cosy glow.

We sat by the window at one of the tables on which the heavy varnish had been indelibly ringed by a thousand leaky teapots and idly perused the menu. I don't know why. We'd never deviated from the same order in all the years we'd been coming here.

'The usual?'

She smiled. 'The usual.'

Managing to effect a short hiatus in the day's gossip, one of the home-knit cardigan-clad old ladies made her stately way across the floorboards towards us from be-hind the counter laden with doorstep slices of musty fruitcake on doily-lined dumb-waiters.

'What can I get you, dearies?'

'Tea for two and two toasted teacakes, please.'

We knew how to live. Not that she ever finished her teacake. I had polished it off for her every single time.

'So what's all this about Matt and this friend of his then? Gouldman, was it?'

'Goulding. Danny Goulding. He's a lawyer, a big wig in Goulding, Goulding and Latimer.'

'Oh, them.'

'Christ, not you as well. Seems like everyone in this town has heard of them except me.'

'Well, why would you know them? You don't make it your business to keep abreast of goings on in the legal quarter, do you? You're an English literature lecturer. Or at least used to be. Why would firms of solicitors be any concern of yours?'

'Well, I could ask you the same question.'

'Well, you could, but then I would just tell you that Murray Goulding has been for dinner several times at Lanercost on account of the fact that he is my dad's legal advisor to his businesses. So it's not particularly surprising that I know the Gouldings and you don't.'

'God, Jeannie, you sound like your mother. I know your family are better connected in local society than mine will ever be but it's not like you to drone on about it.'

'You patronising git. You brought all this up and I'm just telling you I know the Gouldings. And anyway, your dad was very well thought of round these parts, and quite right too. Lovely bloke, he was. Do anything for anybody, and always gave me a big hug when I came round to Wordsworth Avenue, even if he was just back from work and covered in blood.'

She was right there. Again I got a sudden pang of missing him when she mentioned the condition he came home from work in. That his being 'covered in blood' from the butcher's made him an even more fond memory in her mind just reminded me what a lovely man he was.

'I know. He looked like an extra from *The Texas Chainsaw Massacre* on a bad day, didn't he?'

'Yeah. He did a bit.'

She stretched her hand across the table and gave me a reassuring pat.

'So tell me about this big plan then.'

'Well. Matt and Danny Goulding are forming this company called Northern Sky Artists and they want to sign us all up.'

'But why? There's nothing to sign, is there? Admittedly Mo's got some good songs and Lane is extraordinarily good looking, but it's hardly an empire, is it?'

'No, but they've got this college buddy of O'Malley's who writes for the *Guardian* doing a piece on a night at the club and they've got some direct line of access to Johnny Leonard at Mulberry, plus they know the blokes who run Lightwater Concerts and they think it's all worth a punt. To be honest, I think Danny has got money to burn and wants a plaything, and O'Malley just enjoys a feeling of power. Especially over me.'

'Right, and he still wants to sign you and Fred, does he?'

'Apparently, although I think O'Malley thinks of us like the coffee ones in a family bag of Revels, nobody likes them but they come as part of the package.'

'Well, I don't see why. You're not exactly blood brothers with Lane Fox, are you? And anyway it's not true to say no one likes you. You and Freddie used to go down really well at the club. All right, you might not have been the peanuts or chocolate ones in this allegorical bag of Revels, but you're putting yourself down by saying you're the coffee ones. You were orange at least.'

'Cheers. That makes me feel so much better. But to be honest, it's not just me they're after.'

'No?'

'No.'

A beat.

'Me?'

'You.'

Jeannie cocked her head on one side and glanced out of the window, where a sickeningly well toned crew of beefcake undergraduates swept by in a blur of well practised strokes as the ruddy sun disappeared behind the diminutive baseball cap of the barking cox.

'What do you think?'

'Well, I'm flattered to be included.'

'I don't see why. You were one of the club's main attractions. You were breathtaking some nights, Jean. Going back to the Revels, you were right up there with the Maltesers.'

'Wow, praise indeed. Although if a family bag of Revels is full of duff flavours like vile coffee ones and sickly orange ones and everyone's just hoping for a Malteser, why don't they just fill the bag with Maltesers and have done with it?'

'They do. They're called Maltesers. But where's the danger in that? Where's the dark thrill of expectation when delving into the depths in the hush of a darkened cinema?'

'You really do like to live life on the edge, don't you? But I'm not sure. I think I'm up for singing again, but newspapers and records and tours. It's all a bit much.'

'Oh, come on, Jeannie. What have you got to lose?'

'My appetite? My sanity?'

'Look, it's not like we're going to be propelled into superstardom, is it? There's never going to be more than a couple of hundred people in any given town who are daft enough to part with good cash to see a few dodgy folk singers. It'll probably all come to nothing, but why not give it a go? It'll be a laugh, and, well . . . I'll look after you.'

She laughed. Not a giggle or a snigger, but that full-throated dirty laugh I'd missed for so long.

'My guardian angel. My rock. My oasis of tranquillity.'

'Okay, you've made your point. But what about it?'

'Maybe.'

'Look, this Goulding chappie, who's a thoroughly decent bloke for a friend of O'Malley's actually, he's having a bit of a bash on his canal boat on Sunday which he keeps at Windrush Marina and he wants me to bring you. At least come down to that and meet him and then make up your mind.'

'No harm in that, I suppose. A day on the water sounds like a good idea. And it's about time I started to live a bit.'

'Nice one. I'll pay then, shall I?'

'Charmer.'

I signalled to the creaking waitress, who had spent the last quarter of an hour buttoning herself into an antique tweed overcoat before enthusiastically wiping down the glass display cabinet recently emptied of fondant fancies. The combination of her exertions, the indomitable heaving of the aged gas fire and the thermal qualities of the Harris weave had left her with a toffee apple where her face used to be.

I looked down at Jeannie's plate and for a minute I was taken aback.

'You've finished your teacake!'

'I was peckish.'

'But you never finish your teacake. I always order two teacakes in the knowledge that I'm going to get one and a half. But you've eaten your teacake.'

'I told you I was going to start living a bit.'

11

Windrush Marina was throbbing with activity and the hammer of boat engines as dedicated canal fanatics went through their quasi-religious Sunday morning rituals. Some were absorbed in touching up the elaborate displays of floral paintwork that seemed to be badges of honour, like the dense tattoos on the forearms of thrash metal bands. Contented looking men with white hair the texture of candyfloss poking out from under denim skipper's hats puffed pipes as their elongated craft shuddered and nudged their way out on to the main waterway.

Mo, Jeannie and I strolled languidly along the towpath, waiting for Whitley to exhaust the aromatic possibilities of weathered fence-posts further dampened by decades of territorial canine sprayings. It was a fine day, bright with a gentle wind sending ripples and shimmers across the surface of the navigation. And perhaps it was the chill in the air or the reflections from the clouds and the water, but the light that seemed to radiate around Jeannie in that photograph of Maria's graduation on the occasional table at Lanercost had somehow been switched on again. Even Whitley's coat seemed especially shiny.

Which was not an adjective you'd ever have applied to the briar tangle that sat on top of the head of Mo Pepper. However, if his hair was in need not so much of a comb as a combine harvester, he'd made a real effort with his cruising outfit. A striped boating blazer gave way to what looked suspiciously like fake leopardskin tights and emerald green sparking clogs. There are probably one or two unfeasibly tall and emaciated male models somewhere in the world who could just about get away with this ensemble on the catwalks of Milan without reducing Anna Wintour to hysterical laughter. On a stunted hobbit from Byron Crescent the overall effect was beyond surreal. You began to wonder if the back of Mo's wardrobe didn't contain a secret doorway into some private Narnia where centaurs and unicorns chased each other through enchanted forests wearing tie-dyed leggings and heavily embroidered Afghan waistcoats. And yet because it was Mo, he somehow got away with it. Mainly because we all knew he wasn't doing it for effect. He really did dress as badly as that without ever thinking he stood out. As far as he was concerned he was just one of the crowd, despite the fact that gleeful children were following him, eager for the clown show to start.

The booming voice of Danny Goulding shattered the peace of the canal basin.

'Ahoy there, me hearties! Permission to come aboard.'

He was waving vigorously from the tiller position of what was inevitably the most desirable boat in the marina. It was called *Pendragon* and was sixty-five feet long with a steel Stoke-on-Trent shell and BMC engines. At a glance, I deduced its draught to be about one foot ten inches and its beam six foot ten. I didn't really. Goulding told me all this later in the day and for some reason it's stayed with me, despite not knowing what draught and beam are even now. I suppose that in the light of what happened on that boat it's not surprising that I should remember the statistics.

Goulding, in a lumberjack shirt that would actually

have fitted a real lumberjack and designer shapeless 'Dad jeans', was in high spirits. Indeed his bulk and feverish geniality brought to mind no one so much as Toad from *Wind in the Willows* embarking on his next adventure.

'Edward, Maurice, dear fellow voyagers, how the devil are we this fine wind-freshened morn? And you must be Jeannie. Enchanted, I'm sure. Bloody hell, Ed, what does a little honey like this see in a bruiser like you?'

'Very little, I would imagine. Jeannie, this is Cap'n Goulding.'

Jeannie smiled that familiar smile that was simultaneously shy and yet wise. I could see straight away that her bewitching presence was not lost on Danny.

'Pleased to meet you, Danny. I've heard very little about you. Oh, by the way, I've brought my dog along, if that's okay.'

'A narrowboat without a dog is like a lawyer without a paunch, they do exist but there's always that feeling that there's something missing. What's the beast's name?'

'Whitley.'

Goulding put two stubby fingers in his cavernous mouth and whistled at a volume that matched his bulk.

'Whitley,' he boomed, 'here boy, good dog, bound aboard, you daft hound!'

Whitley nonchalantly hosed down a sapling before trotting haphazardly along the towpath towards the *Pendragon*. It became apparent at this point that Danny was not alone on the boat as a series of sharp bangs emanated from the interior saloon, followed by the smashing of glass.

'Bugger, shit, crap and turds!'

The boat swayed as a person of considerable bulk stomped the length of the lower deck before the shaggy

Spacehopper head of the Snowman appeared in the doorway with a red lump the size of a cricket ball rising on his forehead. Despite having sustained mild concussion, Jerry was his usual cheery self when he realised we'd arrived.

'Aah, boys and fragrant princess of the Lowden. Bloody tight squeeze down there, Goulding, me hearty.'

'Yes, Jerry, but you are, to put it politely, rather broad in the beam.'

'Fair point but I was expecting a bit more width on this bloody thing.'

'Hmmm, and it didn't occur to you at any point that there might be a clue as to the width of a vessel generally known as a narrowboat?'

'All right, smart arse. Where do you want me to stash the rest of this booze? The bottles of Spitfire are stacked in the compact galley, the Sancerre in the toddler's shower and the champagne in the sink designed for elves.'

'Look, you great rancid polar bear, these on-board features are used exclusively for the cooling of the drink, and there's not a craft on the navigable waterways with a shower that would accommodate you.'

Jerry laughed so hard you could see his great white underbelly wobble underneath his Hawaiian kaftan. Good news. I'd been worried that there might be some mutual resentment between Jerry and Danny but they couldn't have been easier with each other. Perhaps their sheer proportions made them kindred spirits.

We stepped on board and wandered below to find O'Malley fussing with what looked like a bit of a gourmet buffet. Judging by the elaborate feast and the look of mild panic on Matt's face it looked like Danny had done the ordering and left the paying to his increasingly bewildered partner. Lane Fox was lounging, in the way only rich people can, on a double sofa bed with a range of scatter cushions propped up against the oak panelling.

'Good morrow, fellow voyagers. I trust we're all brimming with excitement at the prospect of our epic voyage. Maurice, my dear, what an absolutely delicious outfit. Dolce and Gabbana, is it?' He gestured grandly towards the food, taking on the role of host in order to avoid doing anything useful. 'Have you eaten already or could I perhaps interest you in a petit mille-feuille?'

'No thanks,' I said. 'I'm trying to cure my mille-feuille addiction, and anyway I've already had a bacon barm from the caravan outside B&Q.'

'Aaah, the sensory life of the committed Epicurean! Jeannie, great to see you. Come and sit with me and let's get comfortable on this peculiar day bed thing. That way we can watch the view sliding by from this port-hole while the rest of them do all the work.'

'Hello, Lane. Still possessed of the old egalitarian spirit then? I'll come and sit by you a bit later on maybe. In the meantime you could actually get off your lazy, if appealingly scrawny backside, and actually do something useful.'

'Do something useful? Me?' said Lane. 'Come on, Jeannie, I'm the talent.'

He was joking, of course. In his own way. Not even he would come out with a statement like that in all seriousness. And yet you couldn't help thinking that deep down this was what he believed. That he was somehow on a more important journey than the rest of us. And why was the scrawniness of his backside so appealing anyway?

The conversation was interrupted by a sudden thud and sway as further passengers came aboard. Through the hull we could hear the animated tones of Freddie Jameson

interspersed with the twin bass baritones of Danny and
Jerry, and a female voice. Evidently Freddie had brought
someone along for the ride.

'Who's that with Fred then?' I asked.

'Dunno,' replied the clown. 'He's not got anyone on the
go at the moment, has he?'

'I don't think so. If he had you'd have thought he'd have
told us.'

'Yeah. We are his mates after all.'

'God, you're like fourth-formers, you two,' scoffed
Lane. ' "Ooh, Freddie's got a girlfriend and he didn't tell
us about it." Just 'cos you two haven't got girlfriends
there's no reason the rest of us should live like monks.'

This last comment he delivered looking directly at
Jeannie, as if to imply some secret they shared. I knew
he hadn't touched her in that way, scrawny arse or not,
but it didn't stop him irritating me.

'Shut your mouth, Lane,' I barked. 'There's no way
Jeannie would be daft enough to go with you. I know you
think you're so bloody special but she sees through all
that. Don't you, Jeannie?'

'Leave me out of your little boy squabbles, thanks. If
you want to spend what could be a lovely day taking turns
to wind each other up then go right ahead, but don't drag
me into it.'

Typically, Lane appeared to assume that this rebuke
was directed at everyone except him. Raising a superior
eyebrow, he shifted his weight on to his elbow like a
reclining Roman emperor in order to witness the arrival of
the new recruits down the wooden staircase. Freddie's
cherry Doc Martens appeared first, closely followed by a
pair of expensive cowboy boots meticulously scuffed
around the toecaps.

'Morning, all.'

Freddie beamed as he entered the cabin, looking twinkly. In all the time I'd known him I don't think I'd ever seen him look anything less than twinkly. It was sickening. Appearing attractive to women late at night when everybody was drunk was one thing but managing it the next morning as well, which was a trick he'd effortlessly mastered, was infuriating. In many ways it was a betrayal of male solidarity. If men like Freddie Jameson were going to wake up next to women they'd met the night before with clear eyes, a cheeky vagabond smile and tousled curls falling over their brows, where did that leave bloodshot morning-after warthogs like Mo and me?

No one spoke as we waited to get our first glimpse of the latest Jameson conquest until Jeannie whispered into my left ear.

'Listen, Eds, I was going to mention this.'

'Mention what?'

Bloody hell. Mention that! As the cowboy boots lowered themselves fully into view, bringing with them a pair of slender denim-clad legs and drummer-boy jacket-encased trunk, the appearance of the head made it clear that introductions were not going to be necessary. Maria McBride. And damn it if she hadn't had the audacity to look amazing.

'You all know Maria, I think.'

'Of course we all know Maria, Freddie, but we didn't know you knew her this well. How long's this been going on?'

'Oh, and you have a right to know first about everybody's private life do you, Edward? After all, you're in such tight control of your own that I should have realised we have to get your written permission before getting together with anyone.'

'And good morning to you too, Maria. I'm not saying I disapprove . . .'

'Well, that's a weight off my mind, I can tell you. Freddie and I have lost a lot of sleep over what you think. Your approval is so important to me, Ed. I can breathe easily once more. Hello, clouds, hello, sky.'

'Well, this is delightful,' I said. 'As if the day wasn't going to be enjoyable enough, we now have Maria lending her particular brand of sunshine to proceedings. How lucky is that?'

'The pleasure's all mine, Ed.'

'Is it really, Maria? Well, if I feel the need of some later on I'll remember to ask first. But seriously, there's no better feeling than seeing two close friends coming together, but until Freddie cops off with Sally Fisher we'll have to make do with you.'

'All right, you two,' said Jeannie. 'I think that will probably do. We're here at Danny's kind invitation and I for one am determined to have a bloody good day, and anyway it looks like there's someone who's pleased to see my sister.'

Whitley had latched himself on to one of Maria's thighs, much to Mo's delight.

'Hey, Freddie, I'll bet . . .'

But Maria was too quick for him.

'Don't even think about it, Maurice Pepper. Now will somebody please prise this heaving brute off me.'

'Hey, Freddie . . .'

'I won't tell you again, Mo.'

From somewhere in the bowels of the boat came the splutter of engines, and from somewhere above, the sound of Jerry calling to Goulding as he pushed us off from the mooring. As the reassuring chug hit a steady rhythm there was a sudden lurch to one side as the Snowman sprang aboard. Not that springing gives an accurate description of the airborne jeweller. I was down below with the others but from the impact of the size thirteen Gore-Tex fell boot on the hull it would be safe to assume that there was very little gazelle-like elegance involved. We fell silent as Danny steered us through the marina, past waving children and immobile parents sitting proudly in folding chairs by their narrowboats, as if ownership was somehow an end in itself without the need to actually take to the water. Lane stretched over to the drainer of the Lilliputian sink and grabbed a bottle of champagne which he opened expertly, sending the cork crashing into a the row of miniature Toby jugs proudly rubbing their distended bellies in a dwarf display cabinet. The shattering of ceramic tri-corn hats alerted the tillerman.

'Oi, watch my Toby jugs, you tosspots. Those are my pride and joy, and that collection is worth a small fortune.'

'Really, Daniel?'

'Of course not, Fox, you great fop. Do you really think I would waste my time and money with little beer-gutted bastards in frock coats? No offence, Mo! Bloody hell, smash the lot if you want to. They just came with the boat and I haven't found the time to sling them overboard. Right, shipmates, we will shortly be reaching our top cruising speed of three miles an hour and I'll be pointing out points of interest along the way, such as to your left, a field, and a little later on to your right, a field, and then further upstream on your left, a field with a bull in it. So given that there's bugger all worth looking at, at least until we get to the Five Locks, I would heartily recommend you get stuck in to the booze.'

'You are a most convivial host, Mr Attorney,' said Lane, swigging champagne from the bottle. 'It's all come at the right time for you, hasn't it, Eds?'

'What has?'

'Well, finding someone who's daft enough to foot the bill for your boozing, seeing as you've not got a job or any cash at the moment.'

'Yes, Lane, bless you for pointing out my current state of financial embarrassment.'

'Current? Life-long state of financial embarrassment would be more like it!'

'I've had jobs and money, Lane. It's true I'm going through a bit of a lean patch right now but unfortunately my dad's lifetime earnings at the butcher's didn't run to a trust fund. Not like some.'

'It's a fair point, Lane,' said Jeannie, smiling, 'although there's been more than one lean patch, hasn't there, Eds? In fact I can't remember ever going anywhere with you without having to pay my way.'

'Errm, not fair actually, Jeannie 'my-dad's-going-to-leave-me-a-timber-yard-and-bespoke-furniture-business' McBride. I distinctly remember paying for you to go and see the Richard Thompson Band.'

'Yes, and I distinctly remember having to pay for chips afterwards and then walk home because you'd spent up.'

'You really do know how to treat a woman, don't you, Beckinsale?' sneered Lane. 'Next time Thompson comes around I'll be happy to pay for your ticket and arrange transport home, Jeannie.'

'Yes, he'll probably get his dad to give you a lift, leaving his so-called mates to get a good kicking in the car park,' I muttered, attempting, not entirely successfully, to conceal the venom behind light-heartedness. Lane looked like he was ready to come back at me but before he could say anything O'Malley clapped his hands.

'Right, if I can have everyone's attention for a moment.'

'What's this, Matt, a safety demonstration? Are you going to point out the emergency exits?'

'Hilarious I'm sure, Freddie. No, seriously . . .'

Groans.

'. . . Seriously, I know we're all here to enjoy ourselves but I do want to get a few things straight.'

'Christ, O'Malley, we're supposed to be your friends. Why do you insist on talking to us like a council care worker taking coffin dodgers to an outlet village?'

'All right, Mo, I'm sorry, but can we just have a quick chat about what Danny and I have got mapped out for the next few weeks and then we can all just relax and get stuck in to all this posh nosh that'll be wasted on the likes of you.'

'Hey, just because Lane's here and he's as common as muck, don't assume that the rest of us don't know what a falafel is.'

'What is a falafel, Edward?'

'Good question, Maurice. I'm not sure but I think it's some kind of fish paste served on a crouton to chinless wonders with more money than sense.'

'And what, pray, is a crouton, Edward?'

'Oh really, Maurice, it's a Japanese camp bed, as any fool know.'

'I think you'll find that's a goujon, Edward.'

O'Malley was not amused and in truth I couldn't say I blamed him as the whole point was to interrupt and annoy him. Unfortunately it was annoying everyone else as well.

Not even the normally supportive Jameson could muster a childish snigger. Possibly because he was conscious of the demeanour of Maria, who looked as though she had booked for Center Parcs and ended up at Butlins.

'Right, well, if that's all from Flanagan and Allen here . . .'

'Nice contemporary reference, Matt. I'd have preferred Reeves and Mortimer but there you go.'

'Eds, for heaven's sake shut up and then we can get on with just having a nice time, although that's beginning to look a remote possibility.'

'Sorry, Jeannie.'

That was that then. If the saintly Jeannie was hacked off then it really was time to shut up.

'Thank you, Jeannie. Right, so this is where we're at. Dom Casey phoned me last night and he needs to deliver this piece in about three weeks. Leaving him the best part of a week to write it up, that means getting him down to not the next club night, but the one after that. Now I know Lane's got his act together, so no problem there. He'll top the bill and play the songs he's going to be recording for his album. Mo, I presume you'll have no trouble putting a set together?'

'No bother, matey boy.'

'Good. Which leaves us with the trickier matters of our other troubadours.'

He looked accusingly at Fred and me.

'Oh, sorry, Matt, I didn't know you meant us. When you said troubadours I was looking around for someone in the garb of a twelfth-century French peasant who would sing in Provençal!'

Lane, riled, flopped down on his day bed.

'Right, and who is it who's swallowed a dictionary today? Is that your new career then, trainee pedant?'

I gently placed my bottle of Spitfire down and took two steps to bound across the cabin and hurl myself on top of him, spilling his champagne over the velvet cushions. I think it was all in fun. At least I had no sense of wanting to actually hurt him, just puncture his superciliousness. Before he had a chance to react I placed a knee either side of his torso, pinning down his arms. Then, pausing only briefly to push my sleeves back over my elbows, I ruffled his mane for a second or two before calmly releasing him, pulling my cuffs back down to my wrists, and picking up my beer.

'Sorry, Matt, where were we?'

12

There was silence around the cabin, fractured only by Fox's splutterings as he tried to regain his customary poise. Not easy with a windswept haystack sitting on top of your head and stray dribbles of bubbly making their way across your lantern jaw.

'You really are a moron at least three-quarters of the time, aren't you, Beckinsale?'

'Well, I think half would be closer to the mark, O'Malley, but if you think I'm going to stand here and be called pedantic by the Lord High Pedant himself, you're very much mistaken.'

'And if you think that Northern Sky Artists are going to get involved with people who can't control themselves then you're very much mistaken.'

The tension stepped up a notch but frankly I didn't see the need for there to be any tension at all. I'd only been having a laugh and trying to bring Lane down a peg or three.

'For Christ's sake, O'Malley, I've ruffled his hair a bit. I haven't disembowelled him. I haven't drowned him in the bloody canal. Any normal person would consider it having a bit of a lark.'

Maria decided to stick her oar in. 'Well, I don't.'

'No, but to be fair, Maria, I did specify a normal person.'

The cavalry arrived in the shape of Mo.

'Yes he did, Maria. I distinctly heard him say "normal" so that pretty much rules you out.'

'And you're a reputable judge of what does and what does not constitute normality, are you, Maurice? By the way, what exactly have you come as today?'

Freddie was in a difficult position now. I knew his natural inclination would be to fall in with Mo and me in enjoying Lane's state of disarray and O'Malley's pre-disposition to take himself far too seriously. On the other hand, he had some duty to back Maria up if he wanted repeat performances of whatever favours had been granted last night. He wisely chose the diplomatic route.

'Look, I think we were about to discuss the role Eds and I will be taking in all this and if someone can find Lane a comb and Maria a large glass of red wine, I wouldn't mind sorting that out. Come on, Lane, let it go. It's not like he's broken your legs or anything. He's only mucking around. We are supposed to be mates when all's said and done.'

Lane looked unconvinced.

'You're a bloody lunatic, Beckinsale. If it was down to me you wouldn't be part of this at all. You'll only go and do something stupid and spoil it for the rest of us. And I'd like to see you try to break my legs. I am bigger than you, in case you hadn't noticed.'

'Oh, don't get all macho on me,' I said. 'I don't want to get into a proper fight. I was just messing about. Look, I'm sorry, all right?'

O'Malley took the floor once more, with a huff of disdain meant to imply that this was my last chance. Last chance for what, though? It wasn't like he was offering us a headline slot at the Cambridge Folk Festival or anything. He was playing the big shot without having anything to back it up and it was really beginning to annoy me.

'Right, Freddie, well, this is what I had in mind. I thought that you and your impeccably behaved mate here could cobble together a few songs to start the evening off. You know the kind of thing; a couple of Simon and Garfunkel numbers, something a bit more recent and, if you must, one of your own. This will ensure there's a bit of atmosphere when I bring Dom and the others into the club.'

'What others?'

'Ah yes, well, Danny's arranged for Johnny Leonard to come down as well and hopefully he's bringing Bill Foster and Jules Bellerby from Lightwater Concerts.'

'Right, and so while you schmooze the VIPs we're just providing a bit of background music to which nobody will be paying any attention then?'

'Look for the negative if you must, Freddie.'

'Well, perhaps you could point out the positive then.'

O'Malley was in grave danger of losing his newly assumed executive cool.

'Look, you two, I don't give a toss if you play or not. Quite frankly it's neither here nor there to me whether you do a couple of songs or collect the bloody glasses, but Danny thinks that everyone should get a spot and, seeing as he's putting the money in, I've no choice but to go along with it.'

This was all I needed.

'Well, thanks for being so gracious about it, Matt. We've known you since school and Danny Goulding for less than a week, and already he's sticking up for us more than you are.'

'Don't be so childish, Ed. This isn't a playground scuffle we're having here. This is business.'

'Oh yes, sorry, I forgot. Richard Branson must be

crapping himself. Get real, O'Malley, you're a bloke who part-runs a two-bit folk club and is starting a two-bit agency which will, in all likelihood, never amount to anything. After this *Guardian* piece your mate's writing for you, there's probably not one of us who'll ever get mentioned in the papers again.'

'Look, Eds, your opinion of what we're trying to do is of so little importance I won't even let it hold things up any longer. Sing or don't sing, it's all the same to me.'

He turned his gaze on Jeannie with an insufferable simpering look of fake concern.

'But what I do want to know, and this is something that does matter to me, Jeannie, is will you sing? I'll put Mo on after these two clowns and I just thought that if you could manage even two or three songs before Lane does his thing, well, that would be the icing on the cake.'

Jeannie sighed and looked out of the port-hole at the rushes sliding by. She was calm on the outside these days but it was tricky to work out what was going on beneath the surface.

Maria, ever protective, over-protective, leapt in.

'Matt, just back off. She doesn't want to do it and doesn't want to hurt your feelings by telling you. Why can't you just be a little more sensitive to how she is? If you'd got any brains in that pompous head of yours then you'd never have embarrassed her by asking the question in front of the rest of us in the first place.'

It went against the grain but I had to agree with her.

'You're not wrong there, Maria. You really have no idea, do you, O'Malley? Can't you see that it'll take a long time before Jeannie will want to get up in front of an audience again? Just leave her to do it in her own time. When she's ready she'll let you know.'

Alliances were shifting, and the re-preened Lane Fox unexpectedly joined us.

'Well, I couldn't possibly go so far as to say that Beckinsale is right, Matthew, but I do think you should let Jeannie decide when the time is right without trying to badger her into it.'

'Actually . . .'

Jeannie turned away from the window and looked directly at O'Malley.

'Actually, I think I would like to do it, Matt. Thank you.'

This was unbelievable and tremendous news. The idea of Jeannie having recovered sufficient confidence to put herself through what she loved doing the best and yet what frightened her most was something I thought was several months away. No one said too much as we knew that she wouldn't want a fuss, but there was an unmistakable lightening of the general mood. I'd returned to a fragmented group but Jeannie's decision gave me hope that everything could be as it had once been. I wasn't sleeping with her again yet but I did thread a surreptitious arm around her waist to give her a reassuring squeeze in the soft areas where love handles would never appear. She made no attempt to shrug it away.

This moment was brought to the end by a yelling Snowman.

'Oi, you lot, if you'd care to tear yourselves away from the booze and grub, we're about to enter the Five Locks.'

We reluctantly left the cabin and crowded on to the decks fore and aft to witness at close quarters the thrill of the lock experience. To be honest, I don't think any of us were truly interested but we didn't want to hurt the feelings of either Danny or Jerry, both of whom were hopping about excitedly which, for men of their build, was quite an achievement in itself.

Goulding steered *Pendragon* into the first of the locks, at which point the Snowman leapt with the agility of an aged dik-dik on to the towpath and began to push one of the lock gates closed behind the boat.

'Well, come on, one of you bone idle whelps,' he boomed. 'I can't do everything myself, you know.'

Obligingly Freddie jumped on to the bank and began to undertake duties on the opposing gate. This left just Danny, O'Malley and me at the tiller station with the McBride sisters, Whitley, Mo and Lane at the prow. An intrigued pair of dog-walkers stopped on the towpath to observe proceedings as Jerry and Fred strolled on to the next set of gates to open the sluices that would flood the chamber.

'Enjoying the day, Edward?' Danny clapped me on the shoulder.

'Excellent, Danny, excellent. It's really good of you to take us all out like this.'

'Good man, good man. So no deep rooted suspicions about the motives of a slimy lawyer then?'

'No, mate. I'm prepared to trust you with my career on account of there not being much of a career to speak of and no one else to trust it to in any case.'

'A perfectly sound way of thinking, Eds. Don't worry, you've no need to be wary of me. I've got no secrets, you know. Anything you want to know . . . just ask.'

'Hmmmm, well, there was one thing I was wondering.'

'Fire away, dear boy.'

'Is it right that you've bought the Pines at Cummerton?'

'Ah, you as well. I've already been talking to Jerry about that.'

'So it is true then?'

'It is.'

'And what do you plan to do with it?'

'Well, as a matter of fact we haven't quite decided. It's not really viable as a hotel at the moment. It's been let go in a big way and I wouldn't have the heart to charge people to stay in those draughty rooms full of damp patches and stained sinks. So the options are either to do it up and turn it back into a classy joint, or maybe convert it into flats. We just thought it was a nice building to add to our portfolio. However, in the short term there is another option and I've been meaning to talk about this to you, Matt.'

With the fretful countenance of someone getting used to having surprise schemes sprung upon him, O'Malley took his eyes from the torrents of water gushing around the hull.

'Yes, Danny, talk to me about what?'

'Well, I've got this rusting hulk of a hotel sitting in a state of decay in overgrown gardens. You, or should I say we, have a band of free spirited balladeers we're going to try and promote and yet their free spiritedness is not best reflected by their domestic arrangements.'

'They all live with their parents, despite being well advanced into adulthood. Present company excepted.'

'I live with my mum,' I said, indignantly.

'Yes, but you're not well advanced into adulthood,' replied Matt.

Danny laughed and continued.

'So you see, they all live with their parents, which doesn't create a good image for the artistic type, does it? Where's the romance, where's the danger, where's the mystery? Would Nick Drake have composed "Time Has

Told Me" whilst waiting for his tea to be put on the table at the dormer-bungalow he shared with his mum and dad? I think not. So, why don't we move the whole sorry lot of them into the Pines? It suits me to have someone living there security-wise, and I'm not really looking to make money out of rents if we can just cover the basic costs. And we get the whole of the Northern Sky crew living under one leaky roof.'

'Like some sort of artists' colony or hippy commune?'

'Well, let's not get carried away, Matthew, but broadly I suppose, yes.'

'Or like some new Seventh Day Adventist Waco compound with the prophet O'Malley here the new Koresh.'

'I knew I could rely on you to capture the spirit of the idea, Edward. Remind me to give you the attic with the broken sash window and no access to the fire escape.'

A sturdy two-finger-in-the-mouth whistle from Freddie signalled that we were ready to proceed into the second lock. *Pendragon* chugged into position and Jerry and Freddie heaved the gates shut behind us. It would have been a relatively relaxed and contemplative scene if it hadn't been for the increasingly frenzied barking exchanges between the agitated Whitley and the yapping cocker spaniel straining at the leash on the canal bank. Jeannie and Maria tried in vain to calm him down.

'Whitley, down, boy, stop it, there's a good dog,' coaxed Jeannie in a calming whisper.

Predictably Maria tried a different approach, whacking the frenzied hound on the nose as she yelled, 'You stupid dog. Shut up before you find yourself booted into the canal for a swim you weren't expecting.'

Nothing, however, would dissuade Whitley from the impression that the rather feeble spaniel with its distinctly unthreatening floppy ears was a worthy and serious opponent. He was a reasonably smart animal and common sense should have told him that here was a beast who presented no real danger, and yet it was clear that, rather like Chris Eubank fighting a punchbag of an opponent, some gladiatorial instinct had been unleashed.

Jerry and Fred, high above us on the lock gates, each connected a windlass to the ratchets and began to wind the antique cranks to unleash fearsome thrusts of water through the sluices. In the shadows at the bottom of the dank canal chamber we gazed up at the darkening sky, the yelping of the dogs just about audible over the swirling currents. At that moment a dual scream sounded above the thunderous noise of the water. Jeannie and Maria, powerless to control his rabid excesses, had had to watch in horror as their beloved Whitley made an ill-advised and impossible leap upwards towards the other dog. Scrabbling and scratching with his paws at the sides of the lock, he was still some six feet short of the towpath when he fell back in a twisting, howling stretch, crashing his skull on the side of the boat as he passed into the vicious whirlpools of the lock. Jeannie's calm whisper had been replaced with hysterical keening.

'Whitley, Whitley, where are you, Whitley? For Christ's sake, someone, do something.'

Strangely, perhaps sensing the futility of the situation, Maria had gone deathly quiet.

We knew that there was nothing we could do. To venture into the water at that moment was little short of suicide. I would have done almost anything to save that dog for her, but sometimes 'almost' is not enough. Just once we caught sight of the dog struggling to paddle his way to safety, a look of deep panic in his eyes. Then he sank back out of sight and we heard the sickening thumps as his helpless body touched the hull of the boat on its journey to the stern. Gradually Jameson and the Snowman regained control of the sluices and calm returned to the lock. Weeping, shaking, Jeannie and Maria made their way through the guts of the barge to where O'Malley, Goulding and I stood, mortified, by the tiller. As the final eddies died away and the water settled, there by the spluttering belch of the exhaust outlet, the carcass of Whitley lay motionless but for the gentle bobbing of the water. I threaded another surreptitious arm around Jeannie's slender waist to give her what I hoped would be an even more reassuring squeeze. She shrugged it away.

Across the marshlands, the city clock struck four.

13

How long are you supposed to mourn a dead dog for?

The Victorians had strict guidelines on periods of mourning. If a wife lost her husband, polite society expected her to wear black and look pale for two to three years. A recently bereaved widower, on the other hand, only had to look vaguely crestfallen for three months. By my calculations this means that Victorian England considered the death of a married man to be up to twelve times more traumatic than that of a hitched woman. This, in a nutshell, probably tells us everything about the Victorians that we need to know. Oh, and just for the record a grandparent got six months, aunts and uncles three, great aunts and uncles six weeks, and a parent one year.

This left me with mixed feelings. At first I felt pretty good about myself having given my dad six months over the odds at least. Then I remembered that after being told of the death of Great Aunt Mary I'd said, 'Oh well, she had a good innings', and had gone off to the youth club to play Subbuteo with Mo, and attempt to get Siobhan and Sinead Doherty from Mount Carmel to let us feel under their jumpers in return for swigs of cider. So I owed Mary six weeks. Was mourning, I began to wonder, something you had to do at the time or could I do my six weeks now, over a decade later? Or could I knock the six weeks off the extra months I'd given my dad, which would still leave me four and a half months in credit? If the mourning account worked like this I'd have enough in the bank to cover an uncle or aunt and still have a month and a half left over. Was that enough for a dog? Especially if it wasn't even yours? According to the Victorian rules you can do a first cousin in four to six weeks, so your ex-girlfriend's dog must fall into a lower category than that, mustn't it?

When my father died I'd retreated into my bedroom for several weeks, spending my time listening to records by Nick, of course, and Tom Waits and Joni Mitchell. Sometimes I'd strum along distractedly, other times I'd just stare out of the window. I didn't cry much, which seemed to worry Mum at the time.

'Let it all out, son,' she'd say. 'That way you can start to grieve.'

But I didn't want to 'start to grieve'. That implied that I would one day have to stop. Of course I knew what she meant. No matter who dies, life has to go on. In the deepest pit of her life Mum realised that, and tried to help me through it. But I never did come through it. Not completely. And the reason that I never got over it was that I didn't want to. Somehow, 'getting over it' seemed like a betrayal.

With this in mind, I must confess I felt comparatively unmoved by Whitley's passing. Don't get me wrong, I held nothing against him, even though he had once held his genitalia against my left leg when I was summoned to Lanercost for afternoon tea. Afternoon tea, I ask you. What sort of an invitation is that? The sort of invitation you only get from social climbers like Penelope McBride who don't want you there for an actual meal but still want the opportunity to make you feel uncomfortable by forcing you to sit through some overly formal nonsense with doilies and serviettes. Sitting through a full dinner at your new girlfriend's family home is indeed one of the most excruciating experiences the adolescent male has to negotiate but at least you get roast beef and Yorkshire pudding followed by treacle sponge and custard. With afternoon tea you get all the discomfort but only a flapjack to show for it. That half the flapjack had been tossed to Whitley, much to Mother McBride's indignation, should have cemented a stronger bond between us, I suppose, but I really couldn't get worked up about it. He'd had a Mary-like good innings, hadn't he? He'd had love and affection poured on him by two of the most desirable girls in the neighbourhood. Indeed, many of the lads in our class, O'Malley and Fred included, had often expressed the desire to change places with Whitley for twenty-four hours, and I can't think it was because they felt the irresistible urge to rub up and down the leg of my Wranglers, although with pubescent boys you can never be sure. Of anything. If they'd asked, I'm not sure I'd have turned them down. It was as close to real life sex as I was going to get in those days.

So Whitley had led a bit of a charmed life as far as we were concerned and, as last days go, being fed gourmet titbits and having a good old bark at a cocker spaniel before banging your head on the underside of a narrowboat didn't seem such a bad deal.

I'd phoned her a few times, of course, and it wasn't as if she was refusing to take my calls. It wasn't even as if the security fence around her was impenetrable. If I was unlucky enough to encounter Penny on the other end of the line I just put on my best concerned voice, as if the drowning of their dog had cast a shadow over my whole life. If Maria answered it was a bit easier. After all, she had previously blamed me for many things but not even the tortuous female McBride logic could lay the responsibility of the hound's death at my feet. If Patrick answered the phone, well then, that was okay because he was a bloke and at the end of the day it was only a bloody dog. Not that he wasn't upset, and not that he wasn't having to dredge new depths of solemnity himself, particularly at meal times.

Jeannie didn't seem to have taken it as badly as I thought she might but, as usual when any slight setback befell her, she retreated behind the walls of Lanercost. I persisted in ringing her because I wanted to make sure she was all right. Well, okay, perhaps there's a degree of disingenuity there. I persisted in ringing her because I wanted her to think I was a caring and sensitive soul so that I didn't lose the advances on getting her back I'd so painstakingly made since coming home. She knew this, of course. She wasn't daft. But at least she seemed to be granting me the courtesy of overlooking my intrinsic shallowness when it came to the demise of pets.

This, in its way, was a reassuring state of affairs. When a woman is prepared to overlook the basic shallowness of a man, and the same man attempts to conceal it, then that is most probably the early stages of love.

Actually, though, I'm not convinced that shallow isn't the new deep. Look at a brooding and mysterious body of water like, say, Wastwater. Are the shifting, shimmering shallows any less of a part of the whole than the swirling murkiness beneath? Without a surface, the depths become shallows and over a period of time the whole lake dries up. So if in a committed relationship you look after the shallows, the depths will look after themselves.

Of course, this theory on the nature of relationships,

rather brilliantly concocted whilst listening to Jeannie talk about Whitley and various other dead family pets on the other end of the phone, was of little use when the female half of the partnership refused to come out of her mum and dad's house until she'd sufficiently tortured herself over a drowned labrador.

'You should never have taken your eye off him,' Mum had said when I'd first told her about the curious incident of the dog in the daytime.

'Mum, we were at opposite ends of a narrowboat. How can I watch over a dog that's sixty feet away?'

'Ooh, I know what you're like, Edward Beckinsale. You've got no regard for animals. You were just the same when Snowy passed away.'

'No, I wasn't, I was mortified when Snowy died.'

'Well, you still went to the Wolf Cubs.'

'Admittedly I did, but if I hadn't gone then I'd have had to start my knot badge all over again. And for how long was I supposed to put my young life on hold for the death of a guinea pig?'

'There you go, you see. As far as you're concerned the life of a guinea pig doesn't mean anything.'

'Mum, it wasn't even our guinea pig.'

'No, but you were friendly with Peter Pilbeam from next door and he loved that caviare.'

'I beg your pardon?'

'Caviare. That's the real proper name for a guinea pig.'

'Errm, no, Mum, I think you'll find it's cavy. Caviare is the pickled roe of a sturgeon.'

'Disgusting. But that doesn't change the fact that if you'd been a real friend to Peter you'd have stayed in as a mark of respect.'

'Mother, this is ridiculous. Peter Pilbeam didn't even

stay in as a mark of respect because he'd gone to the fair on Cringle Fields.'

'Well, perhaps he'd gone out to take his mind off things.'

'Well, perhaps I had. Anyway, can we forget about Peter Pilbeam's guinea pig?'

'Oh, forgotten when you're dead now, is it? Well, make sure I'm cremated because I don't want to lie in a grave that no one tends to.'

'All right, enough. Are you seriously suggesting that I will forget my own mother when she's dead because I have failed to spend the last twenty years racked with remorse at the fate of a guinea pig that belonged to our old next door neighbours who moved to Tadcaster in the late nineteen eighties?'

'Well, all I'm saying is that we're all God's creatures and some day we'll all have to move on to that mystical place.'

'What, Tadcaster?'

'Don't try and be smart with me, son. I just can't abide cruelty to animals. Pickled roe of a surgeon indeed. It's barbaric.'

'Okay, Mum, I'll try and be better. Now what's for tea?'

'Ooh, I've got some lovely pieces of veal I could fry.'

To kill time whilst the resident animal rights activist got to work with the crate-reared dish of the day, I returned to my bedroom and lay idly on my back strumming the Grand Old Opry. I was beginning to piece a set together for me and Freddie, safe in the knowledge that if I didn't, then it wouldn't get done.

We had quite a few of our own compositions such as 'Valentine's Day', 'The Old Stamping Ground' and 'Close to God'. We'd played them many times and they'd always gone down reasonably well. At least, they'd never got us bottled off. They weren't as good as Mo's songs, we knew that, but they were good enough until we got round to writing some better ones. Which, of course, we never would. Then there were some old favourites like Simon and Garfunkel's 'Bleecker Street', 'Couldn't Love You More' by John Martyn and, naturally, a selection of songs by the angel Drake, including 'Things Behind the Sun' and 'Northern Sky'. We were also trying out newer tunes that had caught my ear. 'Toxic Girl' by Kings of Convenience was shaping up nicely, and there were two others written by artists who'd died in tragic, and to some degree mysterious, circumstances: Matthew Jay's 'Please Don't Send Me Away' and 'Waltz No. 2' by Eliot Smith.

Both were young men who, it seemed, had taken their own lives when, from the outside, they had everything going for them. When Dad had died I didn't think I had anything much to live for, but it never once crossed my mind to kill myself. I guess you're just a person who falls to the bottom of that particular well or you're not. No matter how pointless my existence felt, there was always something to look ahead to, even if it was only the next pint of Pedigree. I don't suppose you can get drunk when you're dead, can you? It might not seem that the choice between a pint on the one hand and death on the other is an evenly balanced one. Certainly the phrase 'it's a matter of life or a pint' has failed to lodge itself in common usage. All I'm saying is that sometimes living for the small things is enough, and I still like to think that Nick Drake was of the same opinion. For sure, there are many who believe he committed suicide, but I prefer to cling to the notion that he accidentally overdosed on anti-depressants. It just makes my world easier to live in somehow.

Re-learning the songs didn't seem particularly difficult.

It was strange how that dormant part of my brain could be kick-started so easily. The words came back in half mumbled dribs and drabs whilst the fingers rediscovered chord shapes that they hadn't been asked to form for months. Glancing down at them, it was as if they were being controlled by some mysterious outside force. Certainly I felt curiously detached from them, and the sensation of not being entirely in control of your own body is a strange one. I suppose having an involuntary erection is similarly unsettling, and I imagine that acute incontinence would bring its own distinctive traumas and sensations. Thinking about it, in terms of feelings of discomfort, I would put the guitar playing somewhere between the two.

I'd often thought that if I was the guest on *Desert Island Discs*, and I'm beginning to think this unlikely, I would pick a guitar as my luxury item. Perhaps it's an act of great hubris to imagine yourself being interviewed on Radio Four by Sue Lawley about the records you would need if you were a castaway. Maybe it means that somewhere inside you're secretly pretty impressed with yourself, fairly certain that the public would be absolutely riveted by the hitherto unsuspected depths of your remarkable mind. Or maybe it's just that you're an anorak who likes to think of lists of their favourite records. Anyway, at the end of this hypothetical broadcast, during which I've dazzled an adoring Sue with an irresistible amalgam of anecdotal badinage and claustral introspection, after she asks me to select just one of the eight records, and I select *Bryter Later*, and a book, and I pick *The Cornish Trilogy* by Roberston Davies, I choose my Martin as my one allowed object.

This is because there is no end to its possibilities. No matter how many times you pick up that odd contraption of wire and wood there are new avenues to explore. There would have to be. It's such a bizarre piece of apparatus. Who decided that stretching lengths of tensile steel along a thin plank would be a good way to create some of the most amazing music the world has ever known? Sure, there's been the odd decent piece for the symphony orchestra in which the guitar has no part, but beyond classical music into the real world about ninety-nine per cent of all great music has come from the guitar. Think about it: rock, pop, country and western, rock and roll, folk – all spring from the fretboard of a guitar. Admittedly jazz doesn't but perhaps that's why nobody likes it. Not enough guitar.

Historically, of course, there are lots of stringed instruments that pre-date the guitar, such as the lute, the Aeolian harp, the sitar and the two-stringed Japanese banjo that makes a noise like a cat having its innards stretched. In other words, not dissimilar to any other kind of banjo. Each of these has had a notable effect on some area of popular music with the exception of the two-stringed Japanese banjo that makes a noise like a cat having its innards stretched which I understand is not terribly popular even amongst the Japanese. And who can blame them? Why take the trouble to attend a concert of music performed on the two-stringed Japanese banjo that makes a noise like a cat having its innards stretched when you can have REM?

But it is extraordinary that one instrument should have such a hold over the whole spectrum of popular music. Who first realised that an electric guitar going from E to A to B and back again would be a primal force on young people of all generations? And who decided to tune the strings that way? Who worked out that if you damp the top E, put your first finger across the B and D strings on the second fret, your third finger on the A fourth fret, and your fourth on the G string fourth fret, that that would be C sharp minor seventh? Whoever made these discoveries deserves to be awarded a posthumous Nobel Prize for something or other, as their findings will have had more lasting effect on civilisation than the smart-arse who eventually finds top quark.

So even though my days were aimless, I was never bored. Certainly I'd have much preferred to be curled up in some bohemian loft with Jeannie, perhaps I'd have liked to have had some sort of career on the go, without doubt I wanted Dad to still be around so he could take me down the Fox and Barrel and tell me that nothing happened without a reason and that everything would turn out all right. And in truth, only one of these was a cast-iron impossibility.

Life, then, meandered, as all lives are in some part meant to.

Over the rooftops the city clock chimed six.

'Edward, tea's ready.'

'Okay, Mum, I'll be right down.'

I tenderly laid my fellow castaway in her case and headed to the top of the stairs with a rising sense of foreboding. And not just because I didn't like veal. Since coming home we'd become a family again. Dad wasn't there but we'd been used to that. Our Jack wasn't there either, which for a married father of two was not entirely unexpected. But inside the head of Hilda Beckinsale, cohabiting mother and son equalled 'family'. Neighbours regularly asked how I was getting along and she could feign maternal irritation as she told them she couldn't wait till I was 'out from under her feet'. She could shop at

Pickersgill's without feeling that the girl on the till was secretly registering 'meal for one'. How would she take the news that I was moving to the Pines? Badly or very badly?

The kitchen smelt awful, which I knew was going to make things much worse. Having to admit you don't like a meal your mum has cooked for you is something that the male of the species never finds easy. She was actually a pretty good cook and for ninety-nine out of a hundred childhood teas Dad, Jack and I had sat round the table stuffing our faces as she looked on with satisfaction. Strangely, I never remember her eating herself in those days. She always used to fuss around us, fetching plates back and forth from the kitchen, loaded with ever more improbable helpings of cottage pie or corned beef hash, whilst wittering about 'getting a little something for myself a bit later on when my boys are all done'.

I think that there was a general understanding amongst the housewives of Wordsworth Avenue of that era that your qualities as a wife and mother could be directly measured by the amount of food you managed to ram down the throats of your family. Certainly I remember her recounting how Doreen Evans at number 17 had put over five pounds of steak and kidney into a pudding just to satisfy her sons, Bill and Fred. That Jack and I would never manage such feats of consumption was a bit of a disappointment to her, despite that fact that we never left the table without seriously testing the load-bearing capabilities of our knees.

Occasionally, though, she would prepare something that was to all intents and purposes inedible. It wasn't that she risked experimentation with new recipes from far flung places. She always maintained that Dad hated all that 'foreign muck' and had once poured scorn on the idea of holidaying in Spain because she didn't want to spend two weeks living on curry. Dad never contradicted her although, when in the school holidays Jack and I joined him for lunch in his works' cafeteria, he seemed perfectly happy to shovel in industrial quantities of lasagne, chilli-con-carne, moussaka and curry, never once berating it for being 'foreign muck'. Perhaps he intrepidly toured the various cuisines of the world, courtesy of the canteen, safe in the knowledge that what he got at home would be reassuringly familiar, plentiful and, within the relatively tight confines of English cooking, tasty.

Except when it wasn't. What happened on these days was a mystery. The toad in the hole, so succulent of sausage and crisp of batter a fortnight earlier, would be a flaccid, undercooked, grease-laden affair that, with eyes closed, began to worryingly resemble a literal interpretation of the dish. The lean chunks of beef, tender baby carrots and sweet shallots drowning in the rich brown gravy of a hot-pot would undergo a metamorphosis only days later to become a gristle-ridden slop in which lay tendrils of unidentifiable vegetable matter.

There seemed to be no explanation for these aberrations. It seemed unlikely that she had been entertaining a lover in the marital bed, leaving herself insufficient time to prepare the evening meal. If indeed five o'clock counted as evening. Neither could she blame her hectic social life for having left her rushed and flustered. She didn't have one. She chatted to neighbours and went to their houses for what she always called 'morning coffee', despite the fact that she always had tea. She talked on the phone, and received occasional visits from relatives, but she had no interests, no hobbies, no need of worlds outside 37 Wordsworth Avenue. So why the meal that formed the centrepiece of her day could sometimes go so wildly awry was unfathomable. Perhaps further tales of the gargantuan appetites of Fred and Bill Evans had disheartened her to such a degree that her heart went out of the preparation that day. Or perhaps there are days when cooking a dish you've cooked a hundred, a thousand times before just will not go right. I've very little experience in the field of food preparation but I know a bit about playing the guitar and it's certainly true that you can play a song you know backwards much better on some days than others, for no apparent reason.

The other strange thing about my mother's dog's dinner days was that they came without warning. It wasn't as if she was in a foul mood, the kind of pan-crashing sulk that would prepare you for what was to come. She could be sweetly chattering about the blissful nothingness of the day whilst serving up this bilious gruel, seemingly oblivious to its hideousness. The only tell-tale sign that all might not be well in the kitchen was a particular aroma that wafted through the house, a pungent whiff of cabbage leaf and vinegar mixed with the sense of being down-wind of a battery chicken farm. That the meal, when it eventually appeared, often seemed to bear no trace of cabbage, vinegar or chicken only added to the sense of general bemusement. Yet never once did any of us proclaim it anything less than delicious. That was the way of things, our world order, and despite the reappearance of that dreaded smell, I wasn't about to change things now.

The table was set for two. At my mother's end a knife and fork sat at either side of a wicker place mat on which rested the leprechaun ashtray. At the other end a knife and fork sat either side of a wicker place mat on which rested a plate of limp, mutilated flesh, undercooked by way of contrast with the sprouts and potatoes which had, as part of some chemical experiment, been boiled for a considerable period in order to observe their disintegration. It was bad enough that a young cow had to spend its life in a box to create something delicious but to have died for this was an even greater tragedy. I suppose it was the sheer pointlessness of it all. A calf had been killed, and for what?

'This looks good, Mum. You not having any?'

'I'll have a little bit of something later on when my boy's all done.'

Liar.

'I meant to ask you, Mum, do you ever hear anything of Fred and Bill Evans?'

'Oh, didn't I tell you? Oh, that was an awful business that was.'

'What was?'

'Fred Evans. He had a citizen's arrest.'

'Eh?'

'Yes, right there outside the Fox. Keeled right over he did. The ambulance men were thumping his chest like Billy-o trying to get him going again.'

'Ah, a cardiac arrest.'

'And him only twenty-five as well. Mind you he was about nineteen stone. I always said she fed them too much, that Doreen Evans. They always sat down to meals that were far bigger than they needed, those boys.'

'Hmmm, I'm beginning to know how they felt.'

I plucked up the courage to put as small a forkful of immature bovine into my mouth as I thought I could get away with. This proved to be a miscalculation.

'For heaven's sake, Edward, get a decent mouthful. Don't play with your food and eat like a girl, get stuck in. That's a proper man's dinner, none of your poubelle cuisine.'

In this respect she was entirely mistaken. Poubelle cuisine is exactly what it was, but, of course, I wasn't going to tell her that. Would I have to finish it though? I didn't want to hurt her feelings but letting her down gently by leaving at least some of it on the side of the plate seemed wiser than consuming the lot with the pretence of relish before violently vomiting it up moments later. I took a long slug of water to go with what felt like the long slug that was writhing in the back of my throat.

'So, Mum, I've had a bit of an offer of somewhere to live.'

Silence, save for the sharp intake of Lambert & Butler.

'Did you hear me, Mother?'

'Do you want a couple of slices of bread and butter?'

'What, instead?'

'No, to soak up all the juice.'

'No thanks, you're all right. So as I was saying, I've been offered a place to live.'

'Because it's no trouble. I've got a lovely bloomer from Sharpe's. It won't take me a second to cut off a doorstop.'

'Mum, no, I don't want any bread. I've got more than enough with all this.'

'You're not on that Ron Atkinson Diet, are you? It's not good for you, y'know. You need plenty of hydro-carbons inside you.'

'I feel like I'm getting more than enough inside me at this particular moment, Mum, but you're not listening. I'm trying to tell you that I'm thinking of moving out.'

Silence, exhalation of smoke.

'Well, what on earth for, son? You've got a home here. No rent to pay, meals put on the table for you.'

Right now this didn't seem like a particularly persuasive argument.

'I know and it's not that I'm not grateful. You've always been there for me when I need you, and I'll always be there for you, but that doesn't mean I want to sleep in my old bed and let you pretend I'm eleven years old for the rest of my life.'

'Oh, so washing your underpants and thinking about what you might like for your tea means I don't treat you like a grown up, does it? You're my son, and I just like to look after you. What's wrong with that?'

'Nothing, Mum, but there comes a time when you have to move on.'

'Yes, well, that time came and you did move on until it all went wrong and you moved back again. So where are you thinking of going to?'

'Well, you know the Pines?'

'At Cummerton?'

'Yeah.'

'Ooh yes, a lovely place. Your father took us all there for lunch one Mothering Sunday when you and Jack were very small. They used to have a little boating lake in front of the hotel, and after our roast beef we went for a little row. That was a lovely day that was.'

'Blimey, there's nothing wrong with your memory, is there?'

'Why should there be?'

'Oh, nothing. It's just that . . .'

'I'm getting old. Go on, say it. You think I should be losing my marbles, don't you? Well, sorry to disappoint you, lad, but I'm completely compost mentis. Mind you, it's not that great a feat of memory, your father only took us out for a meal three times, as I recall. He was a lovely man in many ways but not too keen on putting his hand in his pocket. Always happy to buy a round at the Fox, he was, but used to hate spending money at restaurants. "What's the point of paying over the odds for food when you can get it for next to nowt at home," he always said.'

Perhaps if confronted with the veal surprise he might have reviewed his position on that one.

'Anyway, what about the Pines?'

'Well, a mate of ours has bought it. It's all a bit scruffy these days and he's got it as some kind of investment. I don't know what he plans to do with it in the long term, but right now he's offered to let us all live there for next to nothing.'

'All who?'

'Mo, Freddie, Matthew, Lane Fox.'

'Jeannie?'

'I don't know about that just now. Maybe.'

'Right, so you want to leave a perfectly good, warm house where everything is done for you to bed down in a damp, draughty old hotel in the middle of nowhere with your sweaty mates, do you?'

'That's about the size of it, yes.'

'Well, go right ahead then. Leave me on my own. My mind's not what it was but I'm sure I'll cope.'

'A minute ago you were telling me you were fully compost mentis.'

'Oh, you can always twist things round to suit your own point of view. Your dad was just the same. Men! They all leave you eventually.'

I felt for her, but I had to make my point.

'Mum, Jack left you to get married to Kirsty and make you some grandchildren. And Dad didn't leave you – he died.'

'Well, he still left me, didn't he?'

'Well, yes, I suppose so in the most literal sense, but I don't think he did it on purpose. I can't imagine that he planned on having a coronary to spite you.'

Silence, slight wheezing of the nicotine-filled chest cavity.

'So when is this all going to happen then?'

'Tomorrow.'

'Tomorrow? Well, thanks for giving me plenty of warning.'

'I know, I'm sorry. Look, Mum, I love you to pieces and I would do anything for you but I need to have my own space. I need to go out into the big wide world and stand on my own two feet again.'

She began to clear the table noisily.

'What, with your little gang for company in a hotel that someone's providing you with for free. Very independent, I'm sure. It's hardly Laurie Lee, is it?'

'Eh?'

'*As I Walked Out One Midsummer Morning*. The book by Laurie Lee.'

'I know. I just didn't know that you did.'

'I can read, you know.'

'I know you can, Mum, I know you can. It's a wonderful book. And no, I'm not exactly going to seek my fortune with all my belongings in a knotted handkerchief tied to a stick. But I do need to go.'

'I know, son. I knew you'd be off eventually but it doesn't stop me getting upset.'

I'm ashamed to admit it but, sensing a means of escape, I resorted to a little emotional blackmail myself at this point.

'You don't have to tell me, Mum, I'm not entirely

insensitive, you know. In fact I'm pretty cut up about all this myself. I want to go, but I hate to leave you here on you own. It's so upsetting I seem to have lost my appetite.'

Silence, then the sound of a match scraping the side of the Bryant and May box to ignite another king-sized.

'Ah well, Edward, don't you worry about me. It'll be nice to have the place to myself again. I'll be glad to have you out from under my feet.'

14

The Pines was a Georgian manor house set in about ten acres of grounds, most of which had fallen into some state of neglect. All the features I remembered from that rare family trip out for Mother's Day half a lifetime ago remained, but only as faint echoes of what had been there before. The small lake of clear waters, goldfish and splashing oars clunking in the brass rowlocks of varnished rowing boats was now an overgrown everglade of writhing lilies and stagnant duckweed. The walled rose garden, so lovingly tended, had become a tangle from which the imprisoned plants tried to grow their way to the freedom that beckoned tantalisingly close over the dry stone walls.

Yet the place had an unmistakable charm. Not faded grandeur exactly but a certain intoxicating decay. Like the ruddy ferns gloriously rotting in a Lakeland October, here was a once genteel country house in the autumn of its existence. Along the main ground floor corridor hung small signs under brass lamps identifying the use of the rooms that lay through the panelled doors like some life-sized game of Cluedo: library, dining room, billiard room and, most tantalisingly of all, cocktail bar. In truth, though labelled so meticulously, some of the rooms had little to identify their former purpose. Two wheezing leather chesterfields sat either side of the fireplace in the library, surrounded by shelving that had no doubt once contained musty hardbacks by the hundred, but no books remained. Unless you counted a selection of ten-year-old phone directories. The billiard room had been stripped of its no doubt slate-bedded table some years previously. The dining room, though, still contained tables, chairs and even cutlery and glassware, lending the cobweb-ridden scene a Havershamesque quality. The cocktail bar, however, was mercifully intact, if bereft of stock. High stools of dark, over-varnished wood with buttoned seats of crimson chenille sat sentinel-like around a small curved bar with front panels of quilted leather. Dusty optics clung to the fixtures on the mirrored wall behind, and on the bar top stood a lonely pineapple ice bucket, browning inside now, but testament to the not so long gone days when retired colonels delved into it liberally to chill their gin and tonics. On the dark green walls chipped frames held hunting scenes, scarcely visible through the grimy glass.

'Bloody hell, Mo, look at this.'

Mo raced into the bar, still carrying his black bin liner of clothes in one hand and his carefully cased Fylde in the other.

'Christ, Eds, this is too good to be true. The place might be falling down, and I imagine we're going to get frozen half to death, but who cares. We've got our own bar!'

Carrying two pricey looking matching suitcases, Matt O'Malley followed us into the room.

'So what do you think of the place then, lads? Not a bad old hovel, is it?'

'It's amazing, Matt, amazing,' I said with a genuine enthusiasm I hoped he would mistake for taking the piss. 'I really think this is going to work for all of us. It's such a romantic notion; your mate from the *Guardian* is going to love it. All these sensitive, tortured artists living under one leaky roof, who could resist that? All of us locked in our separate little garrets toiling away at our craft before coming together for a frugal communal supper in the ruins of a once chic cocktail bar. Terrific.'

'Good God, Beckinsale, don't get carried away. We're only bedding down here for a few months until Danny sends the developers in. We're not launching some hippy dippy commune and promoting an alternative lifestyle.'

'So it's just me, you, Mo, Fred and Lane dossing down here, is it?' I said.

'And Rob Matthews.'

This was a name we hadn't heard before.

'Who's Rob Matthews?'

'Oh, some young legal type who's working at Goulding, Goulding and Latimer. Just moved here and hasn't sorted out anywhere to live, so Danny's stuck him in with us lot. Good bloke apparently. And he's got a National steel.'

This must mean that he was indeed a 'good bloke'. Like anyone with a Raleigh Chopper bike had once been worth knowing for that reason alone, so anybody with a National steel guitar would have to be a complete card-carrying jerk before we'd ostracise him. When newcomers were introduced we usually reacted if not with hostility then a certain ennui, a communal desire to appear impressed by nothing, having collectively achieved very little. Our world weariness, though, could be blown away by something as simple as a National. If you don't know what a National guitar looks like then it's basically an acoustic but fashioned out of bell brass coated with polished steel. There's one floating mid-air on the front of the Dire Straits album *Brothers in Arms*, just in case you want to have a look next time you're browsing.

Upstairs the refined crumbling of the Pines gave way to

a depressingly banal shabbiness. It wasn't that the fabric of the rooms was any worse than downstairs, it was simply that they had been cheaply modernised in the most mean-spirited way. Where once wooden panelling must have glowed in the afternoon sun, acres of woodchip and anaglypta feebly displayed their damp patches to the chilly air. Bedrooms demanding to be furnished with mahogany wardrobes and dressing tables of epic proportions had been shoddily fitted with MFI units whose once pristine melamine now bore the circular stains of a hundred cups of tea and the burns from the illicit fags that had smouldered in the 'non-smoking' rooms. Where once triumphs of sanitary engineering, monuments of porcelain and brass had stood, sad cracked suites in long discontinued shades of ivory and pea green clung desperately to hastily erected stud walls of tragic en-suites. Who could have so heartlessly ripped the guts from such a fine place? Who could have thought that anyone checking in to the hotel and being escorted to their rooms would have been thrilled to discover that the hall lights were fluorescent? Once upon a time I suppose this kind of desecration did pass for improvement. I can still remember Mum and Dad removing a classic Victorian fireplace to install a gas fire. Even as a kid I could see this wasn't right and tried remonstrating with my father.

'But, Dad, that is horrible. I like the real fire.'

'I know, son, but you can't set a real fire to miser rate.'

This was true and in many ways said it all. There was a miserliness to the whole enterprise. A willingness to sacrifice the spirit-raising effect of flaming coal and tinder-sticks for the trite convenience of gas. Then again it was my dad and not me who was having to come in from a day's work only to start messing about with coal scuttles and cinders instead of pushing a button. Fair enough then, I suppose, but where was the defence for boxing in the banisters with gloss-painted hardboard? That involved a lot of effort on his part and what was the point? It was just what you did in those days, I suppose. It was a primitive version of *Changing Rooms* where schemes to ruin perfectly good houses were passed on by word of mouth rather than television. Evidently the plague of the polystyrene ceiling tile had reached beyond Wordsworth Avenue and the city streets to blight the grander residences in the countryside too.

Eventually Mo and I chanced upon a couple of rooms that had been left largely untouched as the redecoration budget mercifully ran out. They were smallish, and were positioned either side of an interconnecting bathroom in which a stained but generous cast iron tub sat resolutely on clawed feet, looking out over the rear of the building to the stables and the delivery yard. They weren't what you'd call rooms with a view, but it was this that had saved them from being ritually dismantled. Naturally, it had been decided, those patrons of discernment requiring accommodation in the front overlooking the boating lake would expect to find strip-light-illuminated vanity units and divans with nylon covered headboards in their suites. Shallow pocketed commoners who could only run to vistas of the goods entrance could just jolly well make do with old oak bedsteads.

The rest of the day was spent unpacking our meagre belongings, trying not to think about the tiny value of our lives if measured in possessions and feeling like over-excited eleven-year-olds on their first day at boarding school. Danny and Jerry rolled up and began filling the empty shelves of the bar with bottles of Bombadier. They were assisted by Rob Matthews, who turned out to be a towering but unassuming bloke, despite his spectacular guitar. Lane made his entrance with Matt flitting around him like a pilot fish, and actually seemed reluctant to shake Rob's hand, saying something about his fingers being insured. Nevertheless it was satisfying to see him temporarily speechless when he found out about Rob's National, not least that it was a 1947 Tri-cone worth close to five grand. He recovered his cool, however, in time to embark on the evening's drinking.

As the sprightly first flames began to lend a convivial flicker to the neglected room, we dragged sagging arm-chairs towards the hearth and began to settle in to life at the Pines. Tops were prised from bottles and pressed into eager hands, as head prefect O'Malley busied himself with logs and coal in the fireplace. Mo gently strummed his Fylde and Matthews produced the treasured National to weave Cooder-like lines of fluid delta blues. Beer followed beer, songs began to flow. Mo treated us to his current repertoire of gems, including yet another new one, a beauty about a mate of his who had died tragically whilst climbing called 'Boys of Glenridding'. Lane ran through a couple of his numbers called 'First Light' and 'Halcyon Days' which, though predictably over-wordy, had a lilting charm that even I had to grudgingly recognise. Sitting in the glow of the fire with his glossy hair brushing the body of his Martin Dreadnought, he looked every bit the romantic hero and it wasn't hard to see why Mulberry would want to sign him up. How I hated him at that moment. There was a residual affection that had always existed between the two of us and for all his faults I did kind of admire the guy. You couldn't help it. In his own way he was charming and talented and stylish and handsome as well as wealthy, which was why you couldn't help trying to push your admiration to one side just to let the resentment show through.

'Evening, all, I'm afraid I haven't made a reservation but do you by any chance have a double room available?' came a voice from the hall.

It was Freddie with his recently acquired shadow, Maria. You would have to say that in her leather pea-coat and Beatle cap she looked little short of stunning but of course for much the same reasons as I allowed my ill feeling towards Lane to grow, I wouldn't have thought to compliment her out loud.

Playing the role of hotelier to full effect Goulding looked the endearingly windswept couple up and down with mock disdain. Using one of the antiquated phone directories as a ledger, he tutted doubtfully and shook his head.

'I'm afraid we appear to be fully booked this evening, Mr and Mrs?'

'Jameson.'

'Right, and it is Mrs Jameson, is it? Only I couldn't countenance letting a room to two persons who have failed to become united in holy matrimony.'

'Oh, yes, she is Mrs Jameson,' said Freddie. 'Isn't that right, Mrs Jameson?'

'Oh, absolutely, Mr Jameson, we are legally man and wife or my name's not Maria McBride.'

'In that case, sir, madam,' continued the makeshift manager, 'I think we may have had a cancellation and might just be able to squeeze you in. How long were you thinking of staying?'

'Oh, I don't know, the rest of our lives or so?'

'I'm not sure if that's going to be possible, Freddie, but

for the time being at least, please be my guests. Bombadier?'

After the shortest tour of the hotel and selection of a satisfactorily drab remnant of a bridal suite, Fred reappeared by the firelight and began to scratch along on fiddle to the prevailing tide of tunes.

'Good to see you, Jameson.'

'Good to see you, Fox.'

'And by the way, I think you've made a very smart move getting it together with Maria. I like her a lot. She's bloody good-looking, has got a few quid coming to her somewhere down the line and doesn't take crap from anybody. Is there any chance you might be booking into the bridal suite for real in the near future, do you think? Should I be thinking about knocking off a suitable epithalamium?'

I couldn't let that pass.

'For Christ's sake, Lane, you're really beginning to piss me off. I'm an English academic and even I have no idea what an epithelium is.'

'Well, allow me to fill you in, Edward. An epithalamium is a nuptial song or poem, and it's a word an academic friend of my father's used over dinner one night. I've been desperately trying to crow-bar it into a conversation for weeks now. The epithelium on the other hand is the outer layer of the skin, and it's a word I only know because it was next in line when I went to look up epithalamium in the dictionary.'

The conversation stalled as Maria walked into the bar, the pea-coat removed to reveal a tight jumper of horizontally striped cashmere that managed to appear simultaneously demure and exotic. The way the garment accentuated her perfect shape made me suddenly miss Jeannie. She should have been here. As so often, she was the lost chess piece without which the game could never really get going.

Maria drew up a fragile-looking footstool and perched at the knee of her gypsy violinist, looking ruefully into the blaze.

'All right, Maria?'

She didn't look up.

'Fine, thanks, Eds. And you?'

'Great. Well, kind of. This place is amazing and it's great to have the old gang back together again.'

'Errm, well, you've never really been together in the true sense, have you? I mean, I know you have this great romantic notion of your long standing artists' colony but none of you ever actually left home, did you?'

'I bloody did,' I snapped.

'Oh yes, I forgot. You took the brave and adventurous step of going to live in a hall of residence funded by the local authority to study books and then came home again.'

'I bloody well went back out and found a job that meant moving away.'

'Of course you did, how unfair of me. Where was that job again? Oh yes, teaching the same subject at the same college, living in the same hall but this time as a warden. You really are one of life's real wanderers, aren't you?'

'Fair enough. I know that the nearest any of us have got to living in what you call an artists' colony is growing up on Wordsworth Avenue and Byron Crescent, but even you have got to admit that this place is a bit special.'

'It's a freezing, damp, tastelessly decorated unloved pile in the middle of nowhere.'

I turned to look at her sclerous profile and detected an

unmistakable faint trace of smile. 'And you're quite right. It is a bit special.'

She hooked her arms around Freddie's legs as they jigged in time to the tunes that he was playing with Mo, Rob and Lane. 'Lanagan's Ball' led seamlessly into 'Morrison's', which in turn gave way to 'Kaliope House'. The beer kept coming and the fire kept crackling. Bliss.

'So are you and Fred thinking of getting hitched then?'

'Give us a chance. We've only officially been an item for a few weeks.'

'Yes, but you have known him for about three-quarters of your life. You know what he's like.'

'That's true, I suppose. Let's just see how it goes, shall we? Anyway what's it to you? Worried that the presence of the dreaded girlfriend will threaten the male bonding?'

'Not really, although you've got to leave a bit of him for me, you know. We are supposed to be partners, if only in the musical sense. No, actually I think it's great that you're here. In fact I was hoping that you wouldn't be the only feminine presence under this roof.'

'Jeannie?'

'No, Denise Baverstock. I've always been entranced by the way she gift wraps a medallion. Of course, Jeannie. Do you think she's likely to come? Do you think there's even a remote possibility that she might come to stay here for a while?'

'I don't know, to be honest. She seemed ambivalent about it when I left but you can never tell with Jeannie. She's my little sister but even I find her hard to read sometimes.'

'I know. Tell me about it. How does she feel about us at the moment?'

'Hard to say really. She hasn't said a lot but I do sort of

get the impression that she thinks your petulant outbursts are under control these days, so that can only be good, right?'

'Dead right but it's just that I thought we were getting closer until that stupid brown mutt went and drowned himself in the canal. Since when she's backed off again.'

'Yes, curious, isn't it, how a man sensitive enough to describe our adored Whitley as a "stupid brown mutt" should find his love unrequited.'

'Yes, well, I wouldn't describe the event to her in quite those terms.'

'But you're quite happy to when it comes to me.'

'Oh, don't be so precious about it, Maria. You're an entirely different kind of beast to Jeannie. You're made of much sterner stuff, as well you know. Anyway, you've got Freddie to be all lovey-dovey and sensitive for you, so to expect the rest of us to be in touch with our gentler side for your benefit is just plain greedy.'

She turned her head away slightly from the illumination of the grate and so it was impossible to easily read her face. I detected a slight tightening of the cheekbones but whether this was sending out signals of good humour or irritation I really couldn't say. Enigmatic facial expressions. Where do women learn that trick? Did they take classes in it at school while we were off doing woodwork?

Perhaps it was her effortless superiority, or perhaps I was overheating from sitting too close to the fire. Perhaps it was the state of increasing inebriation. Perhaps I just missed Jeannie more with each passing hour, but as the evening progressed and the large hours gave way to the small ones, my sense of becalmed contentment began to evaporate.

'Come on, Eds, get the Grand Ole Opry out and give us a song.'

'Naah, you're all right, Mo.'

'Oh, don't be such a boring sod, Beckinsale. Everyone else has done a bit, what's up with you? This is our first night here together, it's supposed to be a big major league bonding session.'

'Look, Fred, just shut it, will you? I'm not in the mood so get off my back.'

'Right, well, that's a brilliant way to engender a strong community spirit, isn't it? What a good job it is that we're not as miserable as you after half a dozen drinks.'

'O'Malley, you're as miserable as me after no drinks at all, so you can back off.'

I'd had enough of this. I felt like I was getting it from all sides and it wasn't my fault. All I'd wanted was to be left alone to think about Jeannie. If she'd been here, she'd have stuck up for me. If she'd been here, they wouldn't have started on me. If she'd been here, we'd have been together. And I didn't feel like singing. Was that such a crime? Under the rules of the new utopia it apparently was. Well, bugger that for a game of soldiers. In my head the evening had lost some of its shine and now I just felt lonely in a room with some of the best friends I'd ever had. The best thing they could do was to leave me alone. All right, I was in a bit of a mood, but it would pass. I could drink myself through it, if given the chance.

'Well, well. Far be it from me to pass comment . . .'

Lane Fox.

'. . . but it seems to me that it's pretty bloody selfish to throw a real sulk on our first night here, Eds. Not to mention bloody ignorant and discourteous to Danny, who's been good enough to put us up here and ply us with drink. Everyone else is getting stuck in and making sure we have a good time, but all you can do is mope around because your girlfriend, who isn't really your girlfriend anyway, isn't here to pander to your every need. You kept telling me to lighten up when we were on the canal, now you lighten up, you miserable sod.'

'Leave him alone, Lane,' said Mo. 'He'll snap out of it in his own time.'

'No, Lane's right,' I said. 'I haven't done much to make the evening go with a bang so perhaps it's time I got started.'

I rose unsteadily from my haunches and took a moment to regain my balance. I put on what I considered to be an enigmatic facial expression, but was probably just the idiot grin of the maudlin drunk, and stumbled towards Rob Matthews.

'Hey, Rob, let's have a look at that National then.'

I took the National from the nervous-looking Matthews and went on a wobbly stroll around the bar, tweaking the machine heads and strumming a few tentative chords.

I didn't play any tunes as such; it was enough to just be handling this most beautiful of guitars. Naturally my doodlings didn't hold anyone's attention for long and they began to drift back into chatting and drinking and basking in the soporific radiance of the fire.

I managed to get the guitar as in tune as I was going to in my current state and stopped behind the chair in which Lane was sitting. I placed the guitar across my chest and gave a sharp cough. Silence fell.

'Right, lady and gentlemen. Thanks for your attention. My name's Edward Beckinsale and I'm going to entertain you for a little while. So here goes . . .'

I began to thread my way through a pretty shaky

version of John Lee Hooker's 'I'm in the Mood', punctuating slurred vocals with inadvisable slide forays up the fretboard. Lane was not impressed.

'Well, this was certainly worth waiting for. Can I just apologise to everyone for having persuaded Edward to attempt this dirge.'

'Oh, pack it in, Lane, he's doing his best. We're not at the Royal Festival Hall, you know. We're just a few mates doing a few songs and having a few drinks,' said Freddie.

'I know, I know, but this is just unlistenable,' spat Lane. 'All right, Eds, you've made your point. We all accept you're in too grumpy a mood to play anything anyone wants to hear, so why don't you give the guitar back to Rob and let the rest of us get on with having a good time?'

I smiled and nodded. Swiftly I moved my right hand away from the strings and held the guitar upright with my left hand around the neck, ready to hand it back to Matthews. As I passed behind Lane, though, I couldn't resist the temptation to propel the steel body directly into the back of his head, accidentally on purpose. I had no intention of really hurting him, but because I was drunk I may have used more force than originally intended.

'Oops, sorry, Lane. Didn't see you there.'

Lane had jolted forward, letting out a yelp of pain and annoyance.

No one spoke for a while. Lane rubbed his head and Maria ran behind the bar to find an antiquated tea towel which she held against the barely noticeable wound.

'Jesus Christ, you lunatic,' yelled Lane as soon as he could speak. 'What the hell are you thinking about? You are a certifiable madman, Beckinsale.'

'Bloody hell, Edward, you did overstep the mark there, mate,' said Freddie. 'I think you've had a few too many, and I know it's only Lane and not someone who actually matters, but it's still no excuse. I think you owe someone an apology, don't you?'

'You're quite right, Freddie, I do. Rob, I am very sorry for any damage to your exquisite guitar.'

Matthews shrugged and said nothing. The reassuring deep burr of Jerry Snow struck up.

'Edward, I really think that you will regret this incident in the morning and that you should go to bed now and sleep it off. I do think that you should make some sort of gesture towards Lane though. You appear to have given him at the very least a bad lump on the back of the head there.'

The room fell silent again, save for the crackling of the fire and the sound of Lane grunting unnecessarily as he rubbed the back of his cranium with the towel.

'Okay, look, all right, I'm sorry. It was just the whole bunch of you ganging up on me that got me riled. No big deal, right?'

Still not a murmur.

'Oh, come on, he's not dead or anything. He's not even unconscious. I've barely grazed the epithelium.'

There was still a deathly hush.

'Come on, for heaven's sake. Somebody say something.'

'Errm, Eds . . .' Mo offered, nervously.

He didn't speak again but nodded over my shoulder in the direction of the door.

I froze for a moment and then turned cautiously to see a petite figure holding a rucksack and a guitar case silhouetted in the doorway.

'Hello, Edward. Having fun?'

15

Dominic Casey was a man who'd built up quite a reputation as a barbed wordsmith in the quality press. His opinionated diatribes on subjects as diverse as nouvelle cuisine, American imperialism and *Pop Idol* had made him something of a mouthpiece for the chattering classes. Whoever they might be. The most chattering I ever encountered from a single group of people was my mum and her friends at one of their WI bingo nights but I doubt that the term applies to them. As far as I can see the 'chattering classes' is a phrase used to describe a group of people who chatter a good deal less than those excluded from the 'chattering classes'. So what's all that about then?

Casey's polemics were often vicious and so it came as no surprise to find that in real life he was a bespectacled wimp under five feet five inches in height who wouldn't say boo to something considerably smaller than a goose. A moorhen perhaps.

O'Malley was showing Casey round the Northern Sky Folk Club with the proprietorial pride of, well, a proprietor.

'Yes, Dom, so basically I try and run a tight ship here whilst making sure the acts all get an equal crack of the whip.'

Of course you do, Matt, I thought, glaring at them. That's why Freddie and I get to go on first when the place is half empty, leaving the good slots for Mo, Lane, Jeannie when she's around, and any guest artists. Mo, of course, deserved better spots than us because his songs were better, and Jeannie could go on whenever she pleased as far as I was concerned. Also I had to admit it made sense, if you were paying a name act to appear, that they went on when most people who'd come to see them had actually arrived. No point slipping Martin Carthy half a grand to play to the bar staff. I suppose my frustration was directed principally at Lane Fox, who was less talented than me but a good deal better looking. Although the surgical dressing attached to the back of his head wasn't enhancing his image.

The days following the half-hearted attack with Rob's vintage Tri-cone had not been the easiest of my entire life, I had to admit. The immediate aftermath had seen Danny and Jerry disappear into the night, courtesy of the instantaneously appearing minicab driver Salim, and O'Malley and the McBride sisters make a colossal fuss of Lane over what was in reality little more than a graze. Well, all right, I admit I hurt him a bit, but he didn't half make the most of it. Freddie refused to condemn me publicly but would only admit that Lane 'had it coming' in private for fear of falling out with Maria. Mo just found the whole thing mildly amusing. At least Fred and Mo were talking to me though, which is more than you could say for Jeannie. Having decided late into the evening at Lanercost that she was going to join us at the Pines after all, and having twisted Penny's arm to run her round in the Vel Satis, the last thing she'd really needed as a welcome was to see her erstwhile lover launching a semi-violent attack on one of her oldest friends. She went back home the next morning. I couldn't say I blamed her for not speaking to me and in fact I only wished that her sister would follow her example. I knew I'd behaved less than impeccably but I didn't need Maria to point it out to me every half hour. Lane naturally refused to utter a single word in my presence but in many ways that was a bit of a blessing. It was his needling that had caused the friction in the first place, so to have him keep quiet suited me fine. There was a noticeable tension around the Pines though and I didn't feel good about that. We'd all come here to pretend to be adults who wanted to escape the petty squabbles of family life and live together in relative peace and perfect bloody harmony. Well, that hadn't lasted long, I'd seen to that.

All in all these didn't seem to be the best circumstances under which to undertake probably the single most important night at Northern Sky since Michelle Shocked turned up unannounced in 1987. Word had spread that there was going to be a review of the night's proceedings appearing in the national press and so the number of people paying to enter the boat-house was well up on the usual for a Thursday.

Matt was making sure that his old pal from the University of Warwick never left his side. Dom Casey was, as O'Malley constantly reassured us, free to talk to anyone connected with the club, who was, in turn, free to express their opinion in any way they liked. Yeah, right. Matt did indeed introduce Casey to all of us, but at no point did he leave him to talk unchaperoned. Dominic seemed keen to find out about the history of the club and this was a subject tailor-made for the Snowman. Jerry sat down and amiably regaled him with anecdotes from as far back as the early seventies, but not without the fatuous interjections of O'Malley, whose only knowledge of these events came from what Jerry had told him. Not that you'd have known that. To hear Matt talk you'd have thought he'd been there in person at every meeting since the club began which, as he'd been born years after it was first up and running, was no mean achievement. A rambling conversation about songwriting, and the resurgence of interest in traditional songs stripped of digital production, should have been left to Mo. But no, O'Malley, who'd written the truly dire 'Days of Yesteryear' and a couple of others that were, if anything, even worse, felt qualified to sit alongside Mo and expound his inexpert views at length. Even a chat with Sally Fisher about how fussy the folk crowd were about their ales was hijacked by Matt as he smacked his lips and riffed on the superiority of Weetwood Old Dog to Beartown Kodiak Gold. Still, O'Malley might have been attempting to use the old pals act to indelibly stamp himself all over the article, but Dom Casey was a hard-bitten hack. He'd be wise to that, wouldn't he?

By seven thirty there were probably about thirty or forty people in the room. The cigarette smoke was beginning to hang in the congealed fog familiar to the backs of singers' throats in clubs everywhere, and the atmosphere was approaching what you might call convivial. Freddie and I were perched on the high stools by the bar chatting to Sally and half-heartedly scribbling possible set-lists on the backs of soggy beer mats when O'Malley sidled up.

'Right, lads, whenever you're ready.'

'That's very kind of you, Matthew, I'll have a pint of the Bateman's, please. What about you, Freddie?'

'Good idea. Yes, cheers, Matt, I'll have the XXXB as well.'

'No, you retards. I'm not buying you a drink. I meant whenever you're ready you can go on.'

Fred and I exchanged glances.

'You are joking, O'Malley. Most people are still eating their tea or pulling on their chunkiest jumper before coming down here. You can't be serious about putting us on now.'

'I'm deadly serious,' Matt said calmly. 'I want tonight to run like clockwork, so you either play now or not at all. Anyway, there's about fifty or sixty in.'

'Oh, come off it, Matt, there's forty in, tops,' I said. 'And most of those are the die-hard care-in-the-community lot. They only come here to keep out of the cold. It might as well be a drop-in centre for all the interest they'll take. We'd get more of a response if we went on there and doled out soup.'

'Conceivably so, Eds. Perhaps they're trying to tell you something. So whenever you're ready.'

With that he turned and breezed across the room to where his simpering little weasel of a journalist was interrogating one of the aforementioned early crowd, a gargantuan woman in tie-dyed t-shirt and patchwork skirt who liked to be known as Saffron. Which was why I always made a point of using her real name, Sandra.

'He's turned into a right bastard and no mistake.'

'You're not wrong there, Eds.'

'Treats us like we're his employees. And junior ones at that.'

'You're not wrong there either.'

'He's the most unreasonable bloke I know.'

'Errm, well, you might be wrong there. There's someone else I know who is prone to knocking people on the back of the head with a steel guitar. He's pretty unreasonable, so I've heard.' Clocking my expression, he went on, 'I can't say that I blame you though. What is it with Lane these days? Many things he may be but stupid isn't one of them, and yet he seems to believe all the crap that Matt tells him. I suppose if you're a rampant ego-maniac you're always ready to believe what the sycophants tell you.'

'I know. They've changed, the pair of them. I suppose I'd still call them mates, just about, but if I met them tonight for the first time I doubt I'd want anything to do with them.'

'I know what you mean. Fair play to Matt for getting all this organised and that, but sometimes I wish the pair of them would bugger off and leave us to it. All right, we might not be having contracts and all that stuff, but we might be having a lot more fun.'

'You may be right, Freddie, you may be right. Come on then, let's get this over with.'

In truth, I'd really been looking forward to playing in public again. If indeed this did constitute playing in public. Fred and I had been rehearsing regularly, some days for up to forty-five minutes before taking a break for Cup-a-soups or Kit-kats, and I'd forgotten just how good he was, not only on the fiddle, but on the guitar as well. Once I sat opposite him again and heard the two guitars and voices blend together in the way they had so perfectly, or so it seemed to us, since we'd first tried it in the sixth form common room, I realised how much I'd missed it. As we slipped into the old songs again every word and chord came back immediately, along with every nod, smile and knee jerk nuance of Freddie's body language. To see him look up from his trademark hunch over his favourite Takamine and grin from beneath his curls like a toddler at Christmas gave me a buzz like nothing else. There's something about that bond between musicians on the same wavelength that's hard to communicate to those outside the playing fraternity. It's that sense of not only

being up there with just each other for support against a
possibly hostile crowd, but the feeling that you have
achieved some kind of deeper understanding bordering
on telepathy with another human being that doesn't
involve sex. Not that sex in bands is exactly unheard
of, but the connection on a musical level was better than
sex. Certainly the way I did it.

We grabbed our guitars and pints and ambled across
the once varnished floorboards of the boat-house to the
small platform of creaking plywood that was laughingly
referred to as a stage. On our way through the sparse
crowd we came across the seemingly inseparable rotund
duo of Goulding and Jerry Snow. They seemed to genuinely enjoy each other's company which pleased me en-
ormously. Although Jerry had long been a fixture at the
club he'd always been something of a loner. Everyone
knew him, everyone liked him and everyone had a chat
with him. It was just that he was a bit older than the rest of
us and, as such, was a bit of a father figure, and there are
times when you're drinking with your mates or kissing
your girlfriend when you'd rather not have your father
sitting across the table staring at you. So it was terrific that
Danny seemed to have become Jerry's new best mate. It
also made O'Malley a bit jealous because he imagined
Goulding to be his new best mate, so that gave me a warm
glow as well.

'Good luck, young balladeers,' thundered Danny, giving each of us a hearty slap on the back. 'Give 'em hell.'

'Do they look like they want giving hell? And even if
they did, which they don't, would they want it at this
time?'

'Yes, it is a bit early,' said Jerry, looking with a degree of
confusion at his gaudily overcomplicated chronometer

wrist-watch, though this may have been because, having been selected from the surplus stock at one of his shops, it had stopped. 'Why don't you wait until the place fills up a bit? I know there's a crew from the Dun Cow coming down, and a good few from the Saracen's Head besides.'

Danny, too, looked surprised that we were on so soon.

'Yes, and there's a whole bunch from the office I've invited who haven't arrived yet. It's only just gone half seven, for goodness' sake. Most of them will still be at work. At least they bloody well should be. It's their dedication to duty that underpins my dereliction of it. Another pint, Jerry?'

'Certainly, m'learned friend. So why not hang on for half an hour or so, lads? Come and have a pint with us.'

'That'd be great in a perfect world, Jerry, but El Presidente O'Malley has issued his instructions and says if we don't go on now then we're not on at all.'

'He really has got into some strange ways, that boy,' said Jerry, ruefully, 'and there's me thinking I taught him to run this club with a lovable ineptitude. If I've told him that no one expects things to happen on time and are disappointed when they do once then . . . well, maybe I forgot to tell him that, thereby proving my own point.'

'And a point well made it is, even if it wasn't when you originally intended to make it,' said Goulding.

To be honest, despite the joy I'd experienced in playing again, the nerves were starting to kick in and, if given the choice at that very moment, I'd probably have opted for sitting and having a few pints with Danny and Jerry rather than putting myself through the stress of performing. Deep down though I knew it was something I had to do. After all, if I failed at music there was nothing left. I'd already failed at everything else. I harboured no illusions

about becoming an internationally reputed singer-songwriter. Being known as far as the Saracen's Head would
do. But I had to feel that I was able to at least do
something that not everyone else in the world could do,
and if that meant holding the attention of three dozen
hobbits in a boat-house with just my acoustic guitar and
talented accomplice, then so be it. Without that I really
was a nobody. Not just to the world in general but inside
my own head as well.

We took our places on the platform which felt like it
might give way at any moment and began to tune our
instruments. Generally speaking, performers at a rock gig
do this in private backstage, or at smaller gigs in the
toilets. This is so they can burst on to the stage and crank
straight into the first number to get things going with a bit
of a flourish. Starting in this professional manner has
come to be seen as something of an affectation in folk
circles where a bit of bumbling about before muttering a
half-heard introduction to the opening song tends to go
down a lot better. The audience at a folk concert does tend
to feel uncomfortable if presented with even the slightest
suggestion of show business. And quite right too. It's that
refusal to be impressed by the trappings of presentation
that has kept the roots of folk alive. You can say what you
like about the diddly-diddly fraternity but they've got very
little time for Kiss. Perhaps if Gene Simmons did an
unplugged tour of folk clubs in full make-up, serpent-
toothed platform boot resting on a beer crate, dripping
fake blood off his celebrated tongue whilst singing 'And
the Band Played Waltzing Matilda', he might earn a
grudging respect, but until that happens the folkies will
treat him with the distrust he deserves.

Tuned to our satisfaction, Freddie smiled his twinkliest

smile and began to murmur in the direction of what would have to pass for the audience.

'Errm, hey, errm, hi . . . errmm, good to see you, errrmm.' He was never this hesitant in real life but was pulling the shy, sensitive routine off a treat. 'I'm Freddie and this is Eds and err . . . we'd like to play some songs for you if . . . errmm . . . that's all right. This is a song written by Matthew Jay called "Please Don't Send Me Away".'

He nodded his curls and whispered the count and we were off, back out on the high wire with no safety net once again. The thrill of performing live with just each other for support. And though thrill might seem an unlikely word to use in the context of that lowly gig, thrill it was. In some ways the gigs where you have to win over a half-populated room, especially one half-populated by people who don't really care whether you play or not, are the hardest gigs of all, and accordingly the most thrilling to pull off. Having said that, I imagine that hearing the crowd roar in anticipation of your appearance as the house lights go down at Wembley is pretty thrilling too, but as that's a particular thrill I will never know, this would just have to do.

We completed the song without any mistakes, always a relief to get the first one out of the way, and whilst it would be exaggerating to say we brought the house down, there was at least a smattering of appreciation rippling across the smoggy room. I opened my mouth to introduce the second tune and even indulged in a bit of gentle ribbing of Freddie's new corduroy trousers, purchased that same day in a shade of yellow ochre that screamed 'Sale' from every seam, but even though my mouth was working and the words seemed to be conveying some kind of meaning to those who could be bothered to listen above the clatter and clank of the early evening tankards, my mind was elsewhere. I was scouring the room for a sight, a sniff of her. I took in Dom Casey by the bar, still shadowed by O'Malley, scribbling the odd word in his dog-eared note-book as he attempted to chat up the admittedly decorous Maria. Whatever she and Freddie were getting up to, and I was beginning to wonder if it didn't involve sex, it was having a fulsome effect on the pair of them. They were positively aglow with the kind of glow that, even though I wasn't presently aglow, I wondered if I possessed.

We picked our way through 'The Old Stamping Ground', 'Bleecker St', 'Valentine's Day' and 'Things Behind the Sun' with perhaps a gentle upwardly curving graph measuring audience appreciation. Not the seismic event we'd dreamt of when allowing ourselves to get carried away by the enthusiasm of Danny Goulding and megalomania of Matt O'Malley, but a rewarding enough experience. Freddie muttered some fumbled words of gratitude to the crowd, which by this time had swelled to around sixty or seventy souls, and we lurched into 'Toxic Girl'.

As we did so our eyes were drawn to the doors which seemed to open with a mighty clatter. Whether they actually did or not I couldn't really say as I have no lasting memory of there being a loud noise, and we didn't find ourselves suddenly looking out on a sea of hairy necks as the audience turned to see who was making such a grand entrance. Maybe then it was just that the appear-ance of that party in that doorway at that moment seemed so dramatic to me, as I sat stranded mid-song on the stage, that it felt like there should have been an accompanying sound.

One of the group of broad, middle-aged men I

immediately recognised, from photographs in *Folk Roots* magazine, as Mulberry Records owner Johnny Leonard. The pair either side of him, a taller man with Alan Whicker glasses, goatee beard and a shock of wavy Titian hair, and a clean cut individual, expansive of gesture, booming of voice, broad of smile, I took to be Bill Foster and Julian Bellerby of Lightwater Concerts. Between the three of them they controlled a good half of the major folk events in the British Isles. However, it wasn't their arrival that so shook me. As they greeted Danny and headed for the bar I could see a second threesome close behind. Rob Matthews was half a step ahead of Lane Fox who was, as expected, elaborately tangled in a multi-coloured-Tom-Baker-as-Dr Who scarf. Hanging from his elbow though, and looking if not exactly aglow then certainly not in an ashen wash of despair, was Jeannie.

Freddie uttered the tentative thank-you's and good-nights as I slung the Grand Old Opry in its case and scuttled across to the bar, the barely courteous applause petering out even as I crossed the room. En route I encountered Mo, Fylde in hand, going in the opposite direction to make ready for his spot.

'Nice work, Eds. I'd forgotten how good you and Fred sound together.'

'Yes, cheers, Mo. And talking of great partnerships . . .' I nodded in the direction of Lane and Jeannie, chattering animatedly with the godfathers of the new acoustic movement. Mo glanced towards them.

'What you mean, Lane and Jeannie? Oh, come off it, Eds. They've only ever been friends. If anything was going to happen between them it would have happened by now. They've had ample opportunity while you've been away, you know. They spent lots of time together walking

Whitley in his pre-drowned days and they've never so much as held hands.'

'Well, not in public.'

'Not anywhere. Bloody hell, mate, don't you think Lane would have bragged about it in words of several syllables if he'd been there?'

'Yes, all right, Mo. Anyway, shouldn't you be starting soon? You don't want to miss your slot as allocated by Commandant O'Malley after all.'

'You're not wrong there, pal. What's he like? I can see we're going to have to get him a stop-watch and clip-board for his birthday. What a loss to the time and motion industry he is. See you later then.'

'For sure, Mo. I'll be listening, even if these big cheeses talk all the way through it.'

Mo smiled that same crinkly smile I'd first encountered at primary school. He was the only person in Miss Boyle's class with crow's feet. Don't ask me why, I think he'd been born with them. Accordingly he hadn't really aged at all over the intervening decades, thanks to nature's cunning plan of making him look about forty-three before he'd sat the eleven plus.

I reached the bar in no time as my progress was, sadly, unhindered by adoring female admirers telling me how great I was. Once there, I stood far enough away from the big-wigs to make it look like I hadn't noticed them, but close enough to make it inevitable that someone would notice me. Unfortunately it was Lane.

'Aah, Beckinsale, how did the set go? Unfortunately I've been tied up with Johnny, Jules and Bill here so I didn't get to hear you. Still, I don't suppose I missed much.'

'How kind of you to ask, Lane. Yes, it went pretty well, you'll no doubt be disappointed to learn. How's the head?'

'No appreciable damage, you'll be disappointed to learn, I expect,' he said curtly. 'I've no plans to take legal advice anyway, despite being the victim of an unprovoked attack in front of several witnesses.'

'Right then. So the wound's healing, is it?'

He seemed to relax a bit. There was even, perhaps, a slight guilty smile. He must have known that I knew he was milking this for all it was worth.

'Yeah, it's healing fine, thanks.'

'So why are you wearing that big white dressing then? Not by any chance wanting maximum sympathy then? Not least from Jeannie?'

The vague smile vanished.

'Beckinsale, don't judge the way others behave on how you might yourself, you little jerk.'

'I'll take that as a yes then.'

I caught Jeannie's eye over the shoulder of Julian Bellerby, which heaved at regular intervals with extravagant laughter at whatever she was saying.

What a flake he is, I thought. She's not that funny. Which was manifestly untrue. She was that funny sometimes and, what's more, Julian Bellerby would turn out to be one of the least flaky blokes you could meet. Or so I thought.

Though our eyes connected for more than a moment, her look was hard to read. The nod of acknowledgement was chilly certainly, but I was sure there was a flicker of sadness, of yearning, of affection too. To read that much into an instant might seem unlikely, but as she hadn't spoken to me in days, just being close to her seemed to constitute some kind of primitive communication. Although not as primitive as I'd have liked; though that sort of thing seemed a good way off.

Somewhere behind my head Mo had effortlessly produced ripples of warm laughter across the rapidly filling room before launching into 'Misty Morning'. The Snowman, good old Snowman, reading my discomfort like an open book about discomfort, placed a stocky forearm around my sagging shoulders and turned me towards the beer pumps.

'Pint of Bateman's?'

'Cheers, Jerry.' I was grateful to him, and not for the first time.

'Nice choice of songs, I thought.' He waved the other arm expansively to indicate the crowd. 'They seemed to enjoy it.'

'Did they? I didn't think they gave a toss, to be honest.'

'Well, you can't expect miracles, Eds. It was early and you were first on. You're hardly likely to take the roof off, are you?' I shook my head. 'Have you met everyone yet?'

'What, the fromages de pompadour, you mean?'

'Well, if by that you mean Johnny and Bill and Julian, then yes. Have you been introduced?'

'Not by Matt. Just look at him slapping them on the back and cackling at their feeble jokes like the little brown-noser he is. Why do you put up with it, Jerry? This club was your personal fiefdom before that toad muscled in.'

'Quite wrong, Edward. I never looked upon this club as my fiefdom. It was never about power and influence. I just sorted it out because nobody else would. To be honest, it's been quite a relief having young Matt take some of the donkey work off me, and if he gets a little carried away with his own self-importance, well, so be it. He's not hurting anyone. It's just his way.'

'Jerry, you're a saint. You see the good in everyone. I think altruism must be your middle name.'

'Actually you're not far off. It's Algernon and, given the choice, I think I'd take Altruism. Either way you've had cause to be thankful for my better nature yourself, haven't you? Ah, thank you, Sally.' The beer had arrived. 'Anyway, you mustn't prejudge Johnny and the guys. I've known them a lot longer than Matthew has and they're good people, I promise you. I'll introduce you later on, after we've heard Maurice. Isn't this his new song about his mountaineering mate?'

' "Boys of Glenridding", yes.'

We sipped the froth off our pints and were soon lost in the music. As was everyone. Well, nearly everyone.

16

'All right, Edmund, I'm Dominic from the *Guardian*.'

It was the high point of Mo's set and Matt's mate had sidled over, speaking far too loudly and getting looks like daggers from nearby punters straining to hear the music. I responded in a forced whisper.

'Edward.'

To no avail. The voice came back, if anything slightly louder.

'No, Dominic.'

'No, I'm Edward,' I whispered.

'And I'm Dominic,' he shouted.

'Sssshhhhh,' someone ssssssshhhhhed.

'I know who you are,' I half-spoke, half-mouthed. 'What do you want?'

'I thought we could just talk about your set and the club in general,' he half-spoke, half-screamed.

'Sure, but don't you want to listen to Mo? He's brilliant. You should hear these songs and tell everyone how good they are. Maybe we could catch up later?'

'Suit yourself, but I'm going to be pretty tied up doing the big interviews later on. I only wanted a couple of minutes but I daresay we can do it later. Unless we don't hook up in which case, no big deal.'

Big interviews? What big interviews? Lane Fox, I supposed. I knew full well that Matthew would have given Dominic a clear idea of the pecking order but, even so, a quick chat with a lanky drip in a soppy scarf hardly seemed like the Pulitzer Prize-winning scoop of an ambitious young reporter's dreams to me. Still, that was up to them. I was lost in the poignancy of 'Summer's End' which sounded better each time I heard it, and as it had sounded breathtaking in the ripe back bedroom at Byron Crescent, that was some achievement.

To the uninitiated the power of the song could be diluted maybe, and I don't like saying this, by the sight of Mo singing it. The world of folk is supposed to be refreshingly image free and yet the vision of Mo's small turnip-like head, bedraggled ringlets, beetroot complexion and piggy eyes did come close to abusing that privilege. It pained me to admit it, but you could see why Johnny Leonard might have gone for Lane Fox. Still, from the few glimpses of *Pop Idol* I'd been unable to avoid, it looked very much as if that tawdry karaoke fest had been won by a hefty Glaswegian lass with several teeth missing so perhaps the tide was turning. Perhaps Mo would, at some point in the future, become something of a Folk Idol. If that wasn't a contradiction in terms.

The reception for Mo was little short of rapturous, and quite rightly so. His songs and the way he delivered them put him in an entirely different league to the rest of us and I felt sure he would have been discovered long ago if he hadn't resembled one of *Pendragon*'s battered Toby jugs quite so much. Not that the same affliction appeared to have hampered Van Morrison's career any.

'Maurice Pepper, you're a seminal genius,' I gushed as he walked towards the bar.

'All right, don't overdo it,' he retorted, with a smile as wide as a face on a head that small would allow. 'It went all right, didn't it?'

'All right? It was brilliant, man. Come on, I'll buy you a pint and we can find a quiet corner where I can tell you how sickeningly talented you are.'

'Sounds good. In fact I wanted your advice on the arrangement of "Boys of Glenridding". Do you think that the bridge should come in earlier because . . .'

But the because never came as O'Malley bludgeoned his way into the conversation, trailing the lovely Dominic in his wake.

'Aah, Mo, come along now and meet Johnny and the Lightwater boys. Quickly before they get talking to someone else.'

'Errm, excuse me,' I interjected, 'but he has just finished his set, in case you hadn't realised. I'm sure you were too busy hobbing and indeed nobbing with your new found captain of industry mates, but he has made a physical and emotional investment in the last twenty minutes and might want a bit of time to cool off.'

'I see,' sneered O'Malley. 'Well, forgive me, Maurice, for interrupting at such an inconvenient moment.'

'Naah, it's all right,' said Mo. 'I was going to have a quiet pint with Eds, but we can get the pleasantries with Johnny and co. out of the way now if you want to.'

'Well, don't let me twist your arm,' retorted Matt. 'If you think it's more important to slope off into a dingy corner and share a grubby table for two with your maudlin mate here than meet the owner of the most respected folk label in Europe, who by the way was dead impressed by your set, then be my guest.'

When put like that I had to admit it didn't sound a close call.

'Come on, Mo, let's go and charm the pants off these guys.'

'I think charming anyone is beyond you at the moment, Edward, but come if you must. I don't suppose Mo, out of some misguided sense of loyalty, will come without you.'

'Why, thank you, Matthew, for that courteous invitation. I will do you the honour of accepting. And anyway, Jerry said he'd introduce us all later on if you didn't get round to it, as I believe he's known them all for a lot longer than you have.'

O'Malley's petty Captain Mainwaring-style one-upmanship drove me to it, but even I was a bit disappointed in myself at stooping to these levels. Mind you, seeing him with a face like he'd just chewed a lemon as he realised that I knew about the Snowman's longstanding connections helped me get over it. As far as Matt was concerned, he was the conduit for everything, and was visibly rattled by anything that threatened to pass him by.

'You really are a snide sod, aren't you, Edward,' said O'Malley. 'If it was down to me you'd be no part of Northern Sky. For some reason though Danny has taken a shine to you and so I'll just have to put up with it, but cause any trouble and I'll find a way of getting you out, Danny or no Danny.'

'Getting all this down, Dominic?'

Matt had evidently forgotten his scribbling friend was still looking over his shoulder, and the momentary look of horror on his face as he realised his faux pas was another delicious moment. We weren't keeping score or anything but, well, two–nil to me.

'So, shall we?'

I gestured in the direction of the large, gnarled refectory table where the major shareholders were having their board meeting and began to head in that direction. O'Malley, swiftly regaining his cool, scuttled in front of us, anxious, of course, to arrive at the table first. To my continued satisfaction Johnny Leonard proved too quick for him.

'Hey, Mo, isn't it, and Edward?'

We didn't say anything at first but nodded with idiot grins on our faces. Not only did he know who we were but he'd robbed O'Malley of the opportunity of putting himself centre stage by making the introductions.

'I thought your set was terrific, son,' he said to Mo with genuine enthusiasm. 'You've got some great songs there, especially "Summer's End". Have you got your publishing sorted out?'

'Errm, not exactly.'

O'Malley, who'd been waiting for his moment, barged in.

'And when he says "not exactly", Johnny, he means no.'

Leonard laughed charitably. He was a bear of a man with unruly black hair and an even unrulier black beard, both liberally sprinkled with grey. His powder blue eyes, though watery and set in crinkled hollows, had a sparkle that somehow led you to think that here was someone you could trust.

'And Edward, I'm afraid I didn't arrive in time to catch all of your set. Why were you on so early?'

'Oh, well, we weren't given much choice in the matter, Johnny. Our best mate, Matt here, said he'd dock our wages if we weren't finished by half past eight.'

The affable Leonard smiled and pumped me warmly by the hand.

'Well, Ed, I must make sure I get in early doors next time to make sure I catch you and your mate, Freddie. In the meantime come and meet everyone. Danny you know,

I think, a complete big fat waste of space but, well, I know his father, so we just have to put up with him.'

Danny roared and shook, sending waves of rippling flesh under his XXL Waterboys t-shirt.

'This is Bill Foster, hard-bitten promoter scum and the only man on the folk circuit to drive an Aston Martin.'

Foster took this in the spirit it was intended and smiled broadly as he shook our hands, but was it my imagination or could that handshake have been firmer? Was there a glint of cold steel in those narrow green eyes, or was I just reading too much into eye contact in general this evening?

'And this strapping public school rugger-loving oaf is Jules Bellerby, Bill's other half at Lightwater Concerts. The only man in folk circles who can afford an Aston Martin but chooses instead to grind around in a knack-ered old Land Rover Defender. I don't know who I distrust the most, his flash partner or this one with his man-of-the-people façade.'

Bellerby slammed his glass down with a mock ferocity that seemed certain to lead to shards of pint pot flying in all directions, wiped the froth from his lips on the back of his hand, wiped the back of his hand on the back of his Levi's, and proceeded to crush every bone in my hand and dislocate several muscles and ligaments along my arm in a violent male bonding ritual more suited to beasts with the upper body strength of, say, gorillas. A firm handshake would be another way of putting it. Mo was similarly assaulted.

'Great to meet you, lads. Loved what you did, Mo. Let's talk later. Might have loved what you did, Edward, but didn't see much of it. Let's talk later anyway.'

Like Leonard, Bellerby was someone you instinctively felt you could depend on. His eyes were less deep set than

Foster's, which made you feel he was a more open character somehow, and he had great teeth which is always a good sign in my book. You can tell a lot about people by their teeth. People who've got cracked and dirty teeth will let you down because they have no sense of responsibility, people with perfect teeth are confident and trustworthy, people with teeth missing are from Glasgow, and women with gaps between their front teeth are sexual predators. This latter theory was, I had to confess, one that I'd held since university, despite having failed to conduct conclusive field research, though not for want of trying.

Sandwiched between Lane and Julian was Jeannie.

'And you know Jeannie, don't you?' enquired Johnny.

I nodded at her nervously, testing the temperature of the water before diving in. She managed half a smile, which was about as good as I could hope for under the circumstances. On these difficult occasions I consoled myself that Jeannie's fits of melancholy were at least easier to deal with than the violent outbursts of her sister that Freddie would have to contend with. But then Freddie was unlikely to ding anyone with a National steel or indeed any other vintage guitar. I didn't know what to do next. Was I supposed to leave her alone and find someone else to talk to or would that look like I didn't care whether we made it up or not? Whilst I was still wondering what to do the sonorous voice of Bellerby rang out.

'So Jeannie tells me you two used to be an item, Edward. How on earth did you let someone like this slip through your fingers?'

Jeannie shuffled uncomfortably. Perhaps it was the effect of sitting too long on a bare, rustic pine bench with no discernible buttocks. Or perhaps, hopefully, she felt less than confident that this was the right thing for Julian to say just now.

'Errm, well, yes, that's kind of true, Julian, only I wasn't quite as sure as you seem to be that us being an item was quite so definitely in the past tense.'

'Oh really? Well, gosh, look, sorry if I've said the wrong thing, old boy.'

'No, you haven't said the wrong thing, Julian. You've probably said the right thing. It's just that I'm a bit surprised that you seem to know more about my relationships than I do. No problem though, it's not your fault.'

This, I knew as I said it, sounded petulant. It also made Bellerby visibly uncomfortable as he'd only been making conversation and had now found himself in an awkward situation. Luckily at that moment Matt got his attention and we were left to talk in private.

'Oh, so I suppose it's my fault then,' said Jeannie, in an angry low voice.

'I didn't say that.'

'No, but that's what you meant.'

'It isn't what I meant. I just meant that quite patently it wasn't Julian's fault.'

'Wriggle all you like but I know what you meant.'

'How come you know what I meant and I don't when it was me that meant it?'

'Oh, honestly, Eds' . . . Aha . . . Eds! Not 'you', not 'Edward' but 'Eds'. That was a good sign, right? We were still on pet name terms. The omens were good.

'Why are you such an idiot that you can't even be honest about what you want to say? You'll never admit you're wrong, will you?'

Not that good then.

'That's not true. I practically went down on my hands and knees to beg forgiveness after that Freddie business. I know when I'm in the wrong and you're right and I will happily admit it. You're quite wrong about that.'

She bit her lip and shook her head, a look of bitter frustration spreading across her face. Brilliant, she still had feelings for me! As Chrissie Hynde once sang: 'it's a thin line between love and hate.' It's indifference you've got to watch out for.

At that moment O'Malley chipped in, looking at his wrist-watch.

'Okay, Jeannie, time for you to get up there and impress our VIPs. Do well and you'll get a good write-up in a quality paper and, who knows, perhaps a record deal off Johnny and some bookings with Jules and Bill.'

'So no pressure then,' said Julian, directing a question-ing stare at Matt. He put a reassuring arm around Jeannie's shoulders under which she ducked a little too readily for my liking. 'Sensitive soul, your friend here, isn't he?'

'Hmmm, yes,' said Jeannie. 'I've got a few of those knocking around.'

I wasn't even going to rise to this. Quite obviously I was going to have to take a few of these on the chin before I'd get near to her again. It was probably no more than I deserved.

'Look, do you feel up to it?' I enquired with a con-scious tilt of the head that I hoped might be interpreted as concern. 'You don't have to do it if you don't want to.'

'Right, and let what you've done ruin this as well. I don't think so. Julian, would you be kind enough to help me to the stage with my guitar.'

What was all this about? Why did she need Bellerby to 'help her to the stage' for heaven's sake? She wasn't an invalid. Yes, she was a woman of small frame and her Lowden was a sizeable guitar, but she'd carried it many times before without needing a prop-forward for a roadie. Julian, to be fair to him, looked faintly embarrassed at her request but also complied immediately.

'Of course I will, Jeannie. Can't have the artiste making her way to the stage unaided.'

Certainly not. God forbid!

Assorted good luck shouts accompanied them as they left the table and headed across the club, like a petite pop princess with her outsized minder. O'Malley was on the stage reading out a few general notices of future events and managed to drone on for ages, giving her enough time to take up that familiar position: hunched over on a small wooden stool, the guitar dwarfing her, ribbons of hair dangling over her face. You couldn't blame Julian for coming over all protective. She had that effect on everyone. There wasn't a man or woman in the place who didn't feel the same. And there was no one who felt it more keenly than me. It wasn't just that she looked like you could physically break her in two with one hand, it was also that she was regarded with genuine affection by everyone in the room, even the ones who hardly knew her.

O'Malley, a man with all the stage presence of a small Tupperware box, reached the end of his interminable mumbled announcements and, checking that she was ready to go, gave her his big introduction.

'So, ladies and gentlemen, I know you all enjoyed Mo Pepper earlier on . . .'

No mention of Freddie and me, naturally.

'But now I'm really pleased to welcome back a very special friend of Northern Sky's, and someone who's had their fair share of problems over the past few months.'

Nice one, Matthew.

'Please welcome home Jeannie McBride.'

17

The warmth of the applause came as a surprise, even to those of us who were expecting it. Jeannie, alone, so alone, alone in the way only she could do alone, in the single spotlight up there, looked as if she'd been struck dumb.

'She's not going to be able to do this,' I murmured to Mo.

'She will, Eds. Have a little faith.'

'I know her, Mo. She wasn't ready for it. Not with this lot in attendance. It was too soon.'

The applause died and a hush fell. A hush that became a silence as the expected song failed to materialise. Instead she just sat there, peering out through the braids of her hair, as if hoping to see a rescuer heading towards her to drag her away to safety. It was a period of perhaps ten seconds but no one present would remember it as anything less than five minutes. We were all rooted, not knowing whether to talk amongst ourselves, clap some more or shrivel up in embarrassment.

'I bloody knew something like this would happen, Mo. I've got to go and help her.'

I made to ease myself out from behind the table but, as I rose, Mo placed a hand on my shoulder.

'Eds, wait. Look.'

In the time it had taken me to stand up Jeannie's eyes had dropped and she was no longer staring at the crowd but at her own fingers as they began to pluck the glinting strings of the Lowden. It was painfully quiet, and from the rear of the room where we were you had to strain to hear it. In fact if there had been anything other than a reverential hush in that room she'd have been inaudible. But there was. And she wasn't. The gentle lilt of Vashti Bunyan's 'Rainbow River' wafted across the boat-house. Willing the tiny breeze of sound to drift towards my ears, I was, along with everyone else in the room, drawn in like a sailor to a Siren. Not that a seaman on the waves would have had a chance of hearing her above the roar of the ocean. But her precise picking and pure, breathy voice, though under-exposed publicly for some time, remained nothing short of intoxicating. She also looked ravishing in an impossibly frail and vulnerable way. Of course, as folkies we weren't supposed to pay undue attention to appearance, but it's hard to say whether the effect would have been as compelling if she'd weighed fifteen stone, and had matted hair and a lazy eye. But the sound she made was so divine, so other-worldly, that it's just possible it might have been.

The song reached its end without the slightest crescendo and there was a beat of silence before the room erupted into fevered cheers and applause led, a little too enthusiastically, I thought, by the stage-side Julian Bellerby. Jeannie slowly lifted her face and produced the same bashful, lop-sided smile she was wearing in that photograph of Maria's graduation on display at Lanercost. It was good to see her smile like that again, although I was simultaneously pained to realise that it wasn't a look I'd been able to bring back myself.

'Thanks, everyone, good to see you,' she mumbled at a decibel level I would estimate at between zero and one, bearing in mind I have no idea what a decibel is. 'I'd like to play another song for you and this is one of my own. Sorry, but here it is. It's called "Heading for the Northern Lights".'

I hadn't heard the song before but it became apparent from the very first verse that we were 'doing a Vashti' here.

'Take me over the water on which the moon shines,
Take me over by night from the shores of Loch Fyne,
Take me away for a year and day,
To where Northern Lights shine over Applecross Bay.'

Even if, like all but a few who were there, you had no idea what she was singing about the effect was still haunting. For those who knew about her fascination with the Vashti Bunyan story, and her dream of one day making a similar journey of her own, the beauty of the song was magnified ten-fold.

She acknowledged the warm appreciation at the end, shaking the guitar to wring the last vestiges of sustain, and spoke once again to the audience.

'Well, look, thank you so much for listening to me again. It's been a big moment for me tonight and I couldn't have done it without feeling that I was amongst friends. Thanks especially to the Snowman without whom I wouldn't have been here and without whom we wouldn't have had a folk club all these years. Jerry, you are a rock for all of us. Also thanks to Matt and Lane and Freddie and Mo and Maria. Oh, and Eds, I suppose, who might be a liability but his heart's in the right place. Even if his head isn't.'

Well, fair comment, I suppose. To be honest, I didn't fully take in what she said. I was just elated that she'd mentioned me at all. With that and the sheer joy of seeing her performing again I felt like I was practically floating.

'Oh, and thanks to my new friends,' she continued, 'Danny and Johnny Leonard, along with Bill Foster and Jules, who've helped a lot.'

Jules? What was all this Jules business? And no surname? A bit over-familiar with someone you've only met for half an hour or so, wasn't it? The sickeningly fit, good looking and rich Bellerby stood close to the stage radiating what I hoped was a paternalistic kind of pride. After all, he was going to be in some ways responsible for her in the future if the bookings from Lightwater materialised, so his keen interest was purely professional, wasn't it?

Jeannie completed her all too brief set with 'Witches' by the Cowboy Junkies, a little pearl of a song, so skeletal it seemed barely to exist. And that was it. Three brief songs and she was gone. A set that had lasted perhaps eight or ten minutes but which must have felt like an hour and a half to her. I burned with a certain pride myself and, even though I wasn't by her side, felt so happy that she'd found her way home.

Eventually she reappeared at the table with Maria, Freddie and Bellerby in close attendance.

'Jeannie, you were fantastic. Bloody hell, I've missed hearing you. It was marvellous.'

'Bless you, Mo.'

'I've just been telling her how good she was,' piped Maria, with obvious pride. 'We've been outside letting her cool off and get ready to face you lot.' She paused, beamed and hugged her little sister. 'She was bloody brilliant though, wasn't she?'

'She was indeed, my dear,' said Jerry. 'Jeannie, you are a rare and precious talent and I want to squeeze you until you snap.'

'Jerry, you're a sweetheart.'

'Hey, little Jeannie,' said Lane Fox, 'you were incandescent. Really, it was quite, quite beautiful. In fact I'm bloody angry that you were that good when you know I've got to follow you. We are supposed to be friends, after all.'

'Well, sorry, Lane, but that's showbiz. Oh no, I was forgetting, we're folk singers, aren't we? Not in showbiz at all.'

Bellerby guffawed with appreciable gusto. Jeannie, unusually, seemed to be revelling in the attention. O'Malley and Leonard also voiced their approval before the ever generous Danny Goulding arrived with a bottle of sparkling white wine.

'Sorry but Sally couldn't find a bottle of proper bubbly. Not much call for it in skin-flint back street folk clubs apparently, so this'll have to do.'

'That'll do very nicely, Danny. It's a lovely thought if a pretty average wine.'

Once again 'Jules' burst into a gale of laughter.

'Anyway,' said Lane, pushing back his chair, 'time I wasn't here. Mustn't keep the punters waiting for the headline act.'

With the silent but watchful Casey in close attendance, O'Malley rose from the table to perform the totally unnecessary task of guiding the 'star' of the evening across the room. That it was a route he'd taken dozens of times before without the need of an acolyte to assist him seemed not to bother either of them. Once they completed their arduous two-man trek to the other side of the boat-house O'Malley climbed on to the stage to make another utterly pointless announcement. Curiously, Rob Matthews was also hovering by the stage, messing about with guitar cases.

'Bloody hell, Freddie, look, Lane's got himself a roadie. Delusions of adequacy or what?'

'Actually no, Eds. Didn't you know? Rob's playing with Lane now, adding a bit of the old steel to the songs.'

I didn't know and I didn't like it. I had nothing against Rob, it was just that we'd all always played on our own with no additional musicians to back us up. Well, all right, Freddie and I were a duo but that was different, we were mates. And I couldn't sing lead. But this was a breaking of an unwritten rule as far as I was concerned.

'That doesn't seem right, does it, Fred? Rob Matthews is a good bloke but it seems somehow that we're letting an outsider into the circle.'

'Oh, I don't know, Eds. It seems like Lane's the outsider these days. Except where the women are concerned. I see him eyeing up Maria all the time. And the annoying thing is that when I catch him doing it he hasn't even got the decency to look apologetic. It's as if he thinks anything and everything is rightly his.'

'Greetings, folkateers.'

Fox's practised, insouciant, seductive tones flowed out of the speakers.

'My name is Lane Fox and this well sculpted youth is Robert Matthews, who's going to embellish these songs. This piece is entitled "First Light".'

Anyone else spouting this crap would have been laughed off stage but, as Lane had perfected the pose of a tortured and sensitive genius, he seemed to get away with it. In fact, due in no small part to his all-round gorgeousness, the audiences seemed to lap it up, men and women alike. The female contingent I could grudgingly understand but blokes worshipping at the altar of Fox left me entirely bemused. He must have had something, I suppose, and I was just determined not to see it. Or perhaps he had something and I wanted it. Either way I wasn't going to hang around watching him. I nudged Mo.

'I'm going outside for a breath of air. Coming?'

'You don't want to hear his new songs then?'

'Not really. They're all more or less the same, aren't they?'

Mo laughed. 'Yeah, they are really but look at Johnny there, he's absolutely hooked. Whether it's the music or the, shall we say, marketing potential of the complete package, I wouldn't like to say. Anyway I'll just stay and make sure he hasn't got anything as good as any of mine. He's off to master his album tomorrow, you know.'

I was taken aback.

'No, I didn't know that. I didn't even know he'd recorded it.'

'Yes, he's been tinkering with it on and off for weeks. Danny was paying for him to go into the studio even before Matt first floated the idea of this whole Northern Sky thing and Johnny's been keeping a close watch on it all along. Proper job it is too by all accounts with session musicians and the full works. It's out in a fortnight to tie in with this article Dominic's doing apparently.'

'Hmm, just a coincidence, I'm sure. And wasn't Matt at pains to reassure us that we'd all be treated the same? Fat chance. I'll see you in a bit then.'

As I made my way through the maze of tables my feelings alternated between envy and pleasure. Yes, I was annoyed and peeved that Lane was going to get an album released so soon, but even so, I couldn't help being pleased that after all those years of talking about being proper recording artists, one of us was actually going to do it. Perhaps Michael Collins, alone in the command module, felt like that when the other two stepped out on to the moon. It was just a pity that Lane Fox had got the part of Neil Armstrong. Still, perhaps Mo would be Buzz Aldrin and then I could get a place on the next mission.

Pint in hand, I walked round the side of the boat-house on to the balcony at the back, directly looking out over the river. It was a clear night of trembling blue stars reflected in the twisting, treacly waters of the Arn. I'd stood here many times before, often smoking and spitting with the lads or, less regularly, holding Jeannie. Mo and I had sat here with our legs dangling over the edge, talking of how life would be when we were famous, as far as being famous and folk was possible. How many dreams had evaporated on this rotting terrace?

'Thought I might find you here.' It was Jeannie. Swamped in a huge parka that made her look about twelve years old.

'Nice coat. Pity they didn't have it in your size.'

'It's Julian's.'

'It would be.'

'Why's that then?'

'Oh, come on, Jean, I might be a bloody idiot in some ways but I can see what's in front of my face. The guy is besotted with you.'

'He isn't. He's just taking a keen interest in what I do and happens to be a very nice person actually.'

'I don't deny any of that for a second but he might take a different kind of interest if given half a chance.'

She turned away and stared into the water.

'So what did you really think of my performance then? Come on, you can give it to me straight because despite everything I still value your opinion for some reason. I must try and cure myself of that one of these days.'

'Oh, Jeannie, you were amazing. Nobody moved or spoke when you were on because you just held them right there. We couldn't take our eyes off you. You really have no idea how good you are, not like this chancer here,' I said, gesturing over my shoulder to the back wall of the boat-house, through which we could hear Lane singing.

'You're wrong there, Eds, and maybe just a teensy-weensy bit jealous. Lane's stuff is great and if it wasn't, Johnny wouldn't be releasing his album in two weeks. And Lightwater are putting him on at the Royal Festival Hall as part of one of these Meltdown festivals.'

'Bloody hell, the Royal Festival Hall? Where Nick Drake played that famous gig supporting Fairport?'

'Yes, it's a Mulberry Records night or something. He's playing with Doc Russell, the Charlie Cargill Band, Don Allen, Big Jock Watson and Christy Lee and the Prospect.'

'But they're all brilliant, so he's going to look a right buffoon in that sort of company.'

'No he isn't, Ed, because he's really very good. It's just that you refuse to see it.'

Maybe, but I didn't want to think about that now.

'Anyway, never mind about him, what about you, us? Are you coming back to the Pines? You can't hold that steel guitar thing against me for ever. Rob's let me off and it was his guitar after all, so I don't see what your problem is.'

She laughed. Just about. 'Look, I will think about giving it a try there but it won't be for a week or so.'

'Why's that then?'

'Because I'm going up to Scotland for a few days. You know, on the Vashti trail.'

'What, you're taking off in an old camper van on the trip you've talked about for half your life? That's brilliant.

I didn't think you'd ever really do it to be honest. That's great, Jeannie, it really is.'

'Well, thanks, but it's not exactly like that.'

Through the wooden slatted wall I could hear Lane Fox finishing his set and Matt O'Malley making a stumbling farewell announcement.

'Right, so how is it not exactly like that?'

'Errm . . .' She hesitated momentarily. 'Well, you see Julian . . .'

'Oh, you do surprise me. I might have known Clark Kent would be involved.'

'Oh, honestly, you really are pathetic, do you know that?'

'I do have a vague idea, yes.'

'Anyway it turns out that his family have a house in Plockton and so we can do the whole West Coast thing using that as a base.'

'Oh well, that's all just bloody hunky-dory then, isn't it? Bully for Jules and his family estate. Mind you, it's going to take you an age to get up there in that knackered old Land Rover he insists on driving.'

'Fortunately we're not going in that. We're taking Bill's Aston.'

'Oh, the Aston now, is it? Can I remind you that Vashti Bunyan went in a horse-drawn caravan with a dog and a cat. Not in a flash sports car with a posh rich boyfriend.'

'He's not my boyfriend.'

'He's not?' I couldn't help but perk up at this news.

'No, and neither are you.'

The conversation that had been growing ever more heated suddenly froze in the chilly night air. There, she'd said it.

'Well, at least we know where we stand.'

211

'Oh, Eds, I'm sorry. I'm just not sure what to think at the moment. Just leave it until I get back and by then my head will have cleared.'

'And I don't suppose the close proximity of Jules will affect that thinking at all, will it? So when are you off on this rustic adventure, getting back to nature in one hundred and fifty thousand pounds worth of automobile then?'

At that moment Bellerby's voice called out her name across the pub garden.

'Well . . . now.'

'What, right now?'

'Yes. Julian reckons it makes more sense to travel overnight.'

'How very romantic. You've only known him five minutes, Jeannie.'

'Yes, and I've known you half my life and where has that got us?'

Bellerby approached, his huge deck shoes trampling the bedding plants.

'Don't make a scene, Eds. Please!'

I nodded, reluctantly.

'Ah, there you are, Jeannie,' said Julian. 'All right, Edward? Beautiful night, isn't it?'

I nodded again.

'So,' he continued, 'all set for the big adventure then?'

She nodded. Not as reluctantly as I'd have liked. He put his arm around the tiny shoulders lost in his own coat and began to lead her towards the car that was worth as much as all the others in the car park put together. They took about a dozen steps before she stopped, broke free of him and ran back towards me. I knew it. He had money, looks, power, influence and a house or possibly small baronial castle in Plockton but it was me she wanted. And under a starlit sky as well!

'Eds?' she said. A V12 Vanquish engine purred into action.

'Yes?'

'Will you get my guitar from in there?'

'Eh?'

'And look after it until I get back?'

Across the meadows the city clock began to chime eleven.

'Of course. I knew that's what you wanted.'

She pecked me on the cheek and was gone.

18

The days that followed seemed like some of the longest and most aimless of my entire life. Which was saying something. The Pines had all the atmosphere of a decrepit seaside boarding house, huffing and wheezing its way through the twilight of the season before slumping back into hibernation. The bar and the library, rooms that had so recently appeared elegantly wasted and rich with the promise of decadence, now seemed tired and soulless, like lounges at retirement homes used by people with no reason to get up in the morning. I was beginning to understand how they felt. Physically I was as fit as a man who hadn't regularly exercised since fourth form cross-country could be, but mentally I was in a daze, unable to escape the creeping languor that lay in every dust-filled corner of every dust-filled room. I've never had much sympathy for people who go around feeling sorry for themselves, but in the absence of anyone else to feel sorry for, I appeared to have become one.

I could have felt sorry for Mo, I suppose. He was still around but I'd spent so much of my life feeling vaguely sorry for him that I couldn't work up the enthusiasm to do it any more. And anyway, compared to the preceding decade this was one of the more fruitful periods of his life. Admittedly he didn't have a job or a home to call his own, but he did have some terrific new songs and a great deal of interest from a man who might put his record out. Plus he'd stumbled across a real find in the local Cancer Research charity shop. One of his routine weekly rummages had unearthed a tweed overcoat with attached cloak in that particularly nauseous vomit-of-small-child-mixed-with-urine-of-adult-with-kidney-infection shade of green so beloved of tweed manufacturers the world over. When he also found a battered deer-stalker in close proximity, I doubt if those who discovered the cave paintings of Lascaux could have matched his excitement. His new ensemble gave him the look of Sherlock Holmes as created by Tolkien and not Conan Doyle, the effect only slightly spoilt by his recently purchased bright orange trainers.

Freddie and Maria were floating around too, but I didn't see that much of them. Patrick McBride had begun to experiment with the concept of retirement and was taking the odd day off here and there to see if the prospect of being at home with Penny was as trying as he thought it might be. At these times his timber yard fell under the control of his eldest daughter and her faithful lackey. That sounds a bit unkind to Freddie, I suppose, but the way he just fell in with whatever Maria said irked me. Or perhaps I was just jealous. He did have a McBride sister after all, and it wasn't as though he'd changed himself to be what Maria wanted. He was just one of those people who drifted through life, keeping his own stress levels low by being nice to everyone. It would have annoyed the hell out of me if he hadn't been so, well, nice. And it wasn't even that horrid nice which is just bland acquiescence with the occasional village idiot grin. This was proper sparkly-eyed-charm-and-anecdotal-wit nice which only those with an allergic reaction to niceness could resist. You know, people like, off the top of my head, Lane Fox.

In some ways I resented Maria because she was forceful, opinionated and domineering and I don't suppose I thought she deserved someone as nice as him. In reality, though, even I could see that they made a pretty good pairing. If he'd been with a woman who was as nice as he was they'd have ambled through life being nice but not much else. She had the steel he lacked, and he lent her a warmth she would be incapable of radiating on her own.

So for most of most days the creaking pile of the Pines throbbed with silence, pulsed with the slow beat of my own indolence. Lane had gone to London to finish off his album and perform at the Royal frigging Festival sodding Hall. He'd taken Rob Matthews with him, given leave from the office by the ever benevolent Danny Goulding, who'd also gone along for the ride himself. That was the benefit of having twenty or so minions who could cover for you when you wanted to swan off for a few days. It was a luxury I didn't have myself. If I went away to have fun who would stand in for me by lying in bed and wondering where my life was going? Where was my willing assistant who would lumber around the corridors looking glum?

Matt O'Malley had, of course, gone with them to play the attentive manager and, in his words, 'get to know more about the business from Bill'. This seemed to me entirely appropriate as Bill Foster, the more I thought about it, was the kind of hard-nosed character who thrives in the music business. Yes, he'd shaken hands with me, in a slightly limp way, and smiled vaguely, but there was something you couldn't trust about him. Although this feeling may have had something to do with the fact that he'd said that as a concert attraction or recording act 'those two other blokes, Fred and Edmund, don't have much going for them'. He had evidently expressed this opinion to O'Malley, who had, naturally, quoted it verbatim back at me to share with Freddie when I felt 'the time was right'. In a rare show of thoughtfulness Matt had entrusted me with choosing the best way to relay this information to Fred as 'he didn't want to hurt his feelings'.

What about my feelings? At least Freddie had a girlfriend who hadn't rushed off to Scotland with one half of Lightwater chuffing Concerts, although the thought did occur to me that Bill Foster and Maria could have been made for each other. But what about me? I was on my own with only the perpetual image of Jeannie and Julian gazing into each other's eyes on the banks of the loch for company. And a good friend it wasn't. It kept me awake nearly as much as Sherlock Baggins snoring in the adjoining bedroom. It sidled up to the deserted bar and plonked itself on the tatty stool next to me. It jumped out from darkened recesses along the musty passageways to catch me unawares. At no point could I count on being safe from this mental stalker. I could be enjoying a pint of Old Peculiar, or listening to Jim Moray singing 'Early One Morning', or Richard Thompson doing 'Meet on the Ledge', or chatting about the weather with Jerry Snow whilst watching Patrick Gallagher torment customers, and it would suddenly spring from its crouching position somewhere in the back of my brain and rear up in the frontal lobe. Again and again it happened, a recurring vision of the pair of them in an intimate embrace on the outskirts of Plockton on the shoreline of Loch Long.

I tried to tell myself it was a stupid thought, not least because Plockton wasn't on the banks of Loch Long but Loch Carron. There was also no absolute certainty that their relationship, such as it was, had been in any way consummated. It'd taken me about ten years to get there, so what chance did Bellerby have in just a few days? Admittedly the stumbling, fumbling advances of a geeky, pock-marked schoolboy with only a drop-handlebar racer to recommend him might pale besides a millionaire in an Aston Martin, but Jeannie wasn't that shallow, was she? And for all my resentment of him, Julian didn't seem to be the kind of guy who would push her into anything she was unsure of. If she'd gone off with Foster I'd have been really worried. It was just the uncertainty. If they were going to make a go of it, I was better knowing and dealing with it, although the thought that that might happen scared me half to death. Which got me thinking what would happen if you got scared half to death twice, such was the blackness of my mood.

Mo, God bless him, could see I was in a mess and tried his best to haul me out of the pit I'd tumbled into. On one occasion he forced me to go busking on the city walls but that proved disastrous. In his tweeds and day-glo sneakers he soon attracted a gaggle of astonished onlookers, many of them American tourists delighted to have stumbled across a genuine English minstrel. A fair percentage of these might have been tempted to hang around and give generously, had it not been for the glowering accomplice scowling from under the hood of his demonic duffle-coat. I didn't mean to scare them away, it just sort of happened.

'For heaven's sake, Eds, I don't mind doing most of the bloody work, and I'll even divvy up down the middle with you, but you could at least smile.'

'I'm sorry, Mo. Perhaps this wasn't such a good idea.'

'Right, and what better ones have you got? Go back to the Pines and feel even sorrier for yourself? If that's possible.'

Unfortunately, it was possible, as I sank even lower when we were moved on by a member of the local constabulary. There we were delighting gullible Americans with a shallow facsimile of Olde English street culture, when we were pounced upon by a lumbering copper with nothing better to do. What made it worse was that it was a snivelling creep who'd been in the year below us at school called Russell Mabbutt. I mean, the indignity of it. Only a few years earlier he'd have been begging us not to flush his head down the lavatory and pinch his crisps, and now he was in a position to tell us what to do. The fact that we had in fact flushed his head down the lavatory and pinched his crisps didn't seem likely to help the situation at all. I couldn't even recall why we'd singled him out for this treatment in the first place. Lane Fox was generally the instigator of things in those days, and would often issue challenges that we were foolish enough to carry out just so that we could still be in his gang. Even so, bullying younger lads was a bit out of character, and the crisps were roast chicken flavour which nobody liked anyway. I suppose that Mabbutt was just in the wrong place at the wrong time, which is pretty unfortunate for someone who'd gone to a lavatory to pee. Here, then, was a chance to settle some old scores. If he hadn't held a grudge for all these years then he'd succeeded admirably in finding one now.

'Beckinsale and Pepper, well, well, well.'

In for a penny, I thought.

'Oh, hello, Russ. Tell me, do they have special courses down at the cop shop training you in bobby-speak?'

'You what, Beckinsale?'

'It's just the way you said "well, well, well". It was just

so, well, rozzer-ish. Can you do us a quick "Hello, hello, hello, what's all this then?" You know, just so as our friends from across the pond really feel like they've been in an Ealing comedy.'

'Leave it, Eds,' advised Mo. This was undoubtedly sound advice but it fell on deaf ears as this was the most fun I'd had since Jeannie left. Mabbutt looked perplexed, in the way young policemen often do if confronted with anything other than mindless violence.

'What are you on about?'

'No, I'm just impressed that you've picked up this Old Bill lingo. Do you still insist on calling dope "cannabis resin"? Are suspects with the regulation straggly shoulder-length hair still described as wearing "denim jeans and blouson jackets"?'

'What?'

'I mean, why do you feel the need to specify "denim" jeans? What other kind of jeans are there? Chiffon?'

'Eds, pack it in.'

'You'd do well to listen to your little chum here, sir.'

Ah, Beckinsale no longer but 'sir'. In my limited ex-perience, when a policeman calls you 'sir' you know you're in a bit of bother. Mo made an attempt to smooth things over.

'Look, Russ . . .'

'PC Mabbutt to you.'

'Sorry. Look, PC Mabbutt, we're only trying to cheer Eds up. His girlfriend's buggered off on holiday with a richer and better-looking man. Plus he's not long since lost his job.'

'Oh well, thank you very much, Mo. Call yourself a mate? Why not reveal all my misfortunes to PC Mabbutt and a bunch of complete strangers.' The enthralled tourists had remained frozen to the spot, lapping up this vibrant vignette of the British urban experience. 'I mean, why not just come right out with it and tell them all I've only got one gonad.'

'Really, Eds? What happened?'

'Nothing happened. I'm just making the point that I'd prefer to preserve what little dignity I've got left by keeping a few things between ourselves.'

'Oh dear, oh dear, oh dear.'

'PC Mabbutt, you really are a slap in the eye for anyone wanting to stereotype the average bobby on the beat, aren't you?'

'I have absolutely no idea what you're talking about, sir, but if you'll just produce for me your street entertainer's licence, I'll allow you to continue for the benefit of these good people.'

'Licence? You're having a laugh, aren't you?' whimpered Mo, hopefully.

'Do I look like I'm having a laugh, sir?'

'No, you look like a right miserable sod now that you mention it. Look, Mabbutt, if this is all about the crisps and the toilet I'll nip off and buy you a bag of Monster Munch and we'll say no more about it.'

'Right, Beckinsale, I've been very patient with you up to now but you always were a smart arse and I've had enough. To clamp down on the number of beggars thinly disguised as itinerant musicians,' he paused to look Mo up and down at this point, 'the council issued a notice that any person or persons wishing to perform within the city walls must apply for an official permit from the council and, having received it, must carry it at all times and produce it on request. So, I'm requesting.'

'Well, Officer Dibble, we are not in a position to

produce it on account of the fact that we don't have one. So what are you going to do about it? Arrest us?'

Our time in custody was not especially traumatic. We were not subjected to intimate strip searches or scandalous police brutality. Our fellow cons did not offer us Class A narcotics, nor did they force us to take part in homosexual acts of a painful nature. Whether you would reasonably expect any of these things to happen in a general waiting room where the only other inmate was a sozzled septua- genarian picked up for urinating in the Cathedral cloisters is open to question, but you've got to be prepared for any eventuality when you're banged up. Not that we were actually banged up in the real sense, which I must say I found a little disappointing. Never having been in a cell, I was quite looking forward to it in a perverse sort of way. At least it would be a break from the routine. The stultifyingly tedious routine of the drab, drifting days thinking of no one but her. And him.

They let us go, after about an hour and a half, with a warning delivered with a gentle finger wag by an avun- cular sergeant with ruddy jowls and peppermint white hair parted low down over one ear and swept across the roof of the head to not quite the other side. He seemed, somehow, to be a relic from a bygone era when minor infringements of law and order were punished with a firm but kindly word from rosy-cheeked blokes just like this. When he told us he was letting us go, but to get a permit for the future, I felt almost inclined to ask him for a clip round the ear just to make sure I'd learned my lesson.

Mo and I took a detour off Crossway to wander through the soot-ridden snickets and pallid flagged yards until we emerged from the west gate and headed across the City Avenue, lined with whispering maples, towards the meadows. Without speaking we crossed the Arn by the footbridge and made for the Old Boat-house.

Once there, the hiss and putter of the gas fire, the incessant burble of the spinsters and widows and the heavy breathing of the over-worked kettle created a womb-like rumble of comforting sound. Here, in a glorified shed, sipping stewed English breakfast tea and biting into stale, partially cremated currant teacakes, I had reached some of the most Zen moments of my life. Actually, I daresay true devotees of that particular strand of Buddhism are not unduly preoccupied with teacakes, but the vague principle must be right surely.

'Do you mind if we don't sit by the window, Mo?'

'Of course not. Why would we want to sit and admire the view across some of England's most lush urban pasture towards the golden stone bearing lasting testament to the skill of Roman wall and fortification building when we can sit in the dingy bit at the back?'

'I know, it's just that I used to sit by the window with her and it just gets to me if we sit there.'

'I know, I know. It must be very hard for you,' he said, nodding sympathetically. 'But as your girlfriend, sorry, ex-girlfriend, is off in Scotland with a man much richer, better-looking and nicer than you and has not died, I am not prepared to have the pong of the bogs spoil the taste of my toasted teacake. I suppose what I'm saying to you, Eds, is pull yourself together or don't, sit by the lavvies or don't, but I am going to sit by the window, whether you want to or not.'

This discussion proved ultimately pointless, however, as in the time it had taken us to have it, an elderly couple in matching beige anoraks had shuffled in and taken the table by the window anyway.

'Well, thanks for your support and understanding, Mo.'

'Piss off, Eds. Thanks to you I've wasted half a day's valuable busking time sitting in a police station being treated like a naughty schoolboy, so don't come to me looking for support and understanding. I'd have a good deal more of it if you hadn't insisted on baiting PC bloody Mabbutt until he had no option but to haul us in.'

'Brilliant. Whose side are you on?'

'I'm on mine from now on. That's the last time I try and help you. I only took you out busking to cheer you up because you've been mooning round the Pines like a jilted teenager for the last few days. I'd have been better busking on my own anyway. At least I look like a lovable English eccentric to these idiot Americans. You just look like a serial killer.'

'Oh, don't talk nonsense. You do like to exaggerate. I do not look like a serial killer.'

'All right then, a part-time nutter who's only done in one or two dossers up to now but who might become a serial killer if he doesn't get help soon.'

'Thank you. That's nearer the mark, I reckon. Now shall we sit?'

Mo shook his head in silent frustration and plonked himself down on a distressed wicker-seated chair, weakened at every joint by a hundred thousand senior citizen backsides. He was right and we both knew it, but at least I'd won the argument over where to sit, although, as the aroma of lavatory was, if anything, slightly stronger than usual, as victories go it had a distinct hollowness to it.

We didn't say anything for a while except to order tea and four teacakes. It was that deep a crisis. Eventually Mo broke the silence.

'Look, mate, you're going to have to let her go. I know it's hard, but you've just got to start accepting it.'

'I can't, Mo. Do you remember that Wordsworth poem "To a Butterfly"?'

'What do you think?'

'Sorry, silly question. But I can't get it out of my head just lately. The first lines go:

Stay near me – do not take thy flight!
A little longer stay in sight.'

'Sounds crap.'

'All right, there's a bit of the doggerel about that bit, I'll admit, but it's a lovely poem. The butterfly, or at least the chasing of it, becomes a metaphor for happy times that have flown away. Do you see? The nature of happiness being that you don't realise it's transitory until it's too late.'

'Well, thanks for the tutorial, Professor Beckinsale, I'll have my essay in by Friday. Look, mate, you can't carry on like this. The Folk and Boat Festival is only a couple of weeks away and we all need to be on top form for that.'

He was right there. The Folk and Boat Festival was an annual event that had originally been little more than a gathering of the local folkies at small venues around the city, close to the water. Over the years though it had become a mid-ranking fully fledged folk festival, not up there with Cambridge or Sidmouth or Cropredy, but an event that attracted really good players all the same. Its attendances had grown massively too. Where once a few hundred locals gathered on canal banks and at local hostelries, now around four or five thousand souls descended on the city to hear three days of quality music on a specially erected stage, and in a cavernous marquee on the meadows close to Windrush Marina. Whole families came with kids of all ages who seemed perfectly content to listen to wall-to-wall folk music with their parents without feeling the need to phone ChildLine.

Personally, and never having shared my father's affinity for Al Jolson, I had always been suspicious of kids who liked the same music as their parents. Where's the rebellion in that? Still, who was I to knock it when it provided a marvellous platform for our songs right on the doorstep, especially as this year Johnny Leonard, O'Malley and Danny had persuaded the promoters to showcase all the Northern Sky acts on the Saturday. That Lightwater Concerts were the promoters may well have had a bearing on things, keen as they were to support any new artists of Johnny Leonard's in order to reap their own rewards from putting their tours together in the future. Needless to say, Freddie and I would be first on at a time when the field would be half full, if we were lucky, but what the hell, it would still be the biggest crowd we'd ever played to by a mile.

I played vaguely with the toasted teacakes on my plate, attempting to give the impression of a man too troubled by burning issues of the heart to bother with confectionery. In *The Return of the Native* is the emotional turmoil of Clym Yeobright demonstrated by his ravenous consumption of toasted teacakes? It is not.

Mo returned from the counter, where he'd paid the modest bill.

'Are you going to eat those, Eds, because I've paid for them and if you're not having them then I will.'

Without a second thought I pushed them into my mouth, the frenzied gobbling in marked contrast to the ruminative cud-chewing of the previous half hour. Well, hot buttered toasted teacakes probably weren't indigenous to that part of Wessex in the 1840s. If they had been I felt sure that old Clym, heart-broken or not, would have scoffed half a dozen. You can't cut furze on an empty stomach.

'Right then,' said Mo, with the disappointed air of a man who's had two extra toasted teacakes snatched away from him. 'Do you fancy a pint? We could nip up to the George and Dragon and you could play with a bag of pork scratchings for an hour or two.'

'I don't think so, mate. I'm not really in the mood. Do you mind if I give it a miss?'

'Mind? I'm bloody thrilled. You're my best mate but even I've had enough of you for today. The thought of sitting and having a couple of IPAs without having to listen to your moaning is quite pleasant, as it goes. Where you going to go then? Back to the Pines?'

'No, I think I'll drop in for a brew with my mum. Maybe my head'll clear a bit in that Lambert & Butler smog.'

We scraped our chairs away from the table with a noise that was inevitable and yet still drew looks of disapproval from the other customers, none of whom looked a day under ninety. Outside Mo gave me a friendly hug and, after crossing the footbridge as the city clock struck five, we went our separate ways.

19

I strolled at an easy pace through the back lanes, arriving at 37 Wordsworth Avenue in no time. Strange how as a child, clinging on to the sleeve of my dad's gabardine raincoat, that same walk had seemed an epic trek, and yet now it was nothing more than a gentle saunter. I was so wrapped up in my own gloom that it was only later that I realised what a fatuous observation on the passage of time this was. That a walk undertaken at the age of four, with an inside leg measurement of a foot, should appear tougher than the same route tackled as a fully grown adult is hardly what you might call an earth shattering revelation.

I pushed the gate, splinters of rotting timber flaking in my hand, and hoped that the corroded hinges wouldn't choose this moment to finally surrender to three decades of elemental battering. Not that Wordsworth Avenue's prevailing weather conditions were like those experienced by the South Stack lighthouse, but the way I was feeling the hinge seemed like a symbol of the sad state of my life. And if Julian Bellerby's life was a set of gates they would almost certainly be big, electric ones at the end of a long tree-lined drive. Or was I reading too much into this?

I went around to the back of the house and peered in through the rivulets of condensation running down the single-glazed pane from which the lines of false leading had started to peel away. Mum was sitting at the table, cigarette-wielding hand flicking ash idly leprechaun-wards, absent-mindedly turning the pages of some magazine purchased without enthusiasm from the check-out at Pickersgill's, eyes flickering over some reality goon show on the Decca television that had been the envy of the neighbours when it was bought twenty years earlier. She looked alone, lonely, and yet not without the handsomeness, the suburban nobility even, that had characterised her many years ago. It pained me to see her on an upright dining chair because that was where she'd always perched while Dad slouched in the long empty armchair by the fire.

I tapped on the window and she looked up without a start to smile through the fug and beckon me in.

'Hello, son. What brings you round here?'

'Just came to see you, Mum. Do I need a reason other than that?'

'You don't need one but you usually have one. Cup of tea?'

'That'd be great. So how have you been?'

'Oh, I'm all right, you know, mustn't grumble. There's a lot worse off than me. The Ethiopians. Marjorie Pimlott. Her husband's left her, you know.'

'No, I didn't know. Mind you, I haven't caught the news for the last few days. That's terrible news. And who is Marjorie Pimlott?'

I don't know why I bothered to ask that question. I had no interest in finding out who Marjorie Pimlott was or what she'd been up to, but now I was going to get a full account. It took perhaps ten minutes, and countless detours, to establish that Mr Pimlott had recently left 33 Wordsworth Avenue after twenty-seven years of marriage. Marjorie and someone called Mavis Brindley had then tracked him down to a house on Coleridge Close where he was shacked up with someone else I'd never heard of called Nora Granville. There was a big slanging match in the front garden apparently, after which the heartbroken Marjorie had fallen back into the arms of her long-time lover Billy Cundall, who stacked the shelves at Pickersgill's mini-mart.

Obviously it's a shame when any couple split up, but the love life of a sad, semi-detached woman whose hedge you may have once thrown a kebab wrapper over on the way back from the Fox hardly seemed cause for concern to me. Yet these were the kinds of events that had come to dominate my mother's world, perhaps they always had, and so it seemed only polite to listen patiently until the saga came to an end.

The extra-marital exploits of the Pimlotts exhausted, Mum took a lingering drag of her cigarette and looked me up and down.

'So how are you, son?'

'I'm supposed to say "Not so bad because there's plenty worse off than me" here, I suppose, but I'm a bit down really, Mum.'

'Why's that, son? As if I didn't know.'

'How do you know?'

'It's always the same with you. Money, jobs, houses, cars, none of that has ever bothered you. Come to think of it, your dad was just the same. As long as we had this place and a few pork chops to stick on the table he was happy. Your brother was different. He always wanted more, had a bit of ambition. You and your dad needed a rocket under you to get you to do anything. Look at the hinges on the front gate.'

'Eh?'

'That gate's almost falling off because your father never

got round to replacing the hinges. He put it off again and again and then he died and it was too late.'

'Well, if it didn't bother him when he was alive, I can't seeing it being a major concern in the after-life. It's hard to think of him in heaven racked by perpetual remorse over not having fixed the garden gate. It's not really important in the scheme of things, is it?'

'Of course it isn't. I don't care about the gate. Mind you, your brother's got electric gates now. I wish your father was alive to see them.'

'He wouldn't have been impressed.'

'He bloody well would, you know. He'd have been out pressing the buttons and watching them open and close in all weathers. He loved a good gadget, your dad. Hours he used to stay behind at the shop when they got any new devices. I had to sit through many a meal whilst he told me how good the new bacon slicer or weighing scales were. "This new mincer," he'd say, "it's going to save us that much time I won't know what to do with myself." "So how come these time-saving bits of equipment are keeping you at the shop for an extra half hour at the end of the day then?" I'd say. He just shook his head and told me I'd never understand modern butchery. But he never wanted to buy anything new-fangled for the house. Do you remember the fuss we had over getting a video recorder? Went on for weeks, it did. And then we got one of them Beta Blocker ones.'

Betamax. Let it go.

'Your brother's got VD, you know.'

'What? How do you know? Does Kirsty know?'

'Of course she does. She was with him when he bought it from Curry's.'

'Right, a DVD. But what's this got to do with anything?'

'All I'm saying is that you and your dad only ever got down in the dumps over girlfriends.'

'I wasn't aware that Dad had any girlfriends. You're not telling me he was drawn into Marjorie Pimlott's web of vice, are you?'

'Don't be daft. She wasn't his type. Mind you, I don't know who was really.'

'Don't be ridiculous, Mum, you were.'

'D'you think so?'

'Of course. He adored you.'

'Didn't show it much though, did he? He never took me anywhere. We never went on trips abroad. We never went on trips at home come to think of it.'

'Yes, but he never let you down, did he?'

'Well, he left me with a wonky gate.'

'Yes, all right, I'll give you the gate, but he was always there for you, wasn't he? Loads of other men spent hours on end down the pub, blowing the housekeeping money on the ale, but he always came straight home with some choice cuts of meat for our dinner.'

'He did pick out a nice bit of brisket.'

'Well then.'

'Oh, I know, Edward, but sometimes a woman needs more to satisfy her needs and longings than meat! You can have the nicest lamb shank in the world but it's still no substitute for passion. Most women would happily swap prime belly pork for a surprise romantic break in Paris.'

I could see that this might well be the case. My father was a fine and dependable man, but I would have to concede that he was not the most spontaneous of creatures. Romance was, I imagined, something he would have felt awkward trying to pull off. He was pretty awkward pulling off a tank top, so convincingly whisking his wife off for Bateaux Mouches cruises past the Ile de la Cité wouldn't have occurred to him. I was only surprised that it had occurred to Mum. She'd always seemed happy in their world. Perhaps she was at the time. Perhaps it was only now that she could see that there was more to life than wall-mounted tea caddies and hostess trolleys. Perhaps now the true worth of the gadgets she'd dragged him round fading department stores to buy was becoming apparent.

If only they'd spent their time doing things she could now recall with relish. Maybe the gate hanging off its drooping hinges was emblematic of a more carefree life she wished they'd led before it was too late. A life she was never going to lead now. I was, of course, working all this out in the silence into which I'd been stunned by hearing my mother talk about needs. Longings, romance and, God forbid, passion. You don't want to discuss passion with your mum, do you? Mums don't do passion, do they? Sex may be a recreational activity for the vast majority of the human race but not for mums surely. Call me old-fashioned but my mother's carnal needs were not something I'd come here to discuss. I'd come to discuss mine.

'Anyway, listen to me jabbering on. How are you doing, Ed, and when are you going to bring Jeannie to see me?'

'Well, I'm not sure really, Mum. That's just it, you see. We're not exactly together at the moment.'

'Well, you've not been "exactly together" for half the years you have been together. Had another tiff, have you? Or have you had too much Old Petunia and clocked someone?'

'No, it's a bit more than that this time. She's found someone else.'

'Oh, son, I'm sorry to hear that. It's not that ponce, Lane Fox, is it?'

'No, it's not him. It's a bloke called Julian Bellerby.'

'Sounds like a ponce.'

A ponce? Where did she pick up these words? I did my best to disregard it and carried on.

'No, he's a really good bloke actually. That's what makes it worse. In many ways I think he's perfect for her. He can give her all the things that I can't. I'm not sure if I can make her laugh the way he does any more. I'd love to hear her laugh again.'

'Now you sound like a ponce.'

'Mother, will you stop using that word, please. Do you know what a ponce really is?'

She looked thoughtful for a moment.

'It's a big girl's blouse sort of bloke, isn't it?'

'Technically it's a bloke who makes his living from the earnings of common prostitutes.'

'What, like a pimp?'

Did she say pimp?

'Mum, for heaven's sake will you stop it? I did not come here to sit at the kitchen table with you and discuss pimping, prostitution and passion.'

'Passion's nothing to be ashamed of, you know. If you feel something, then let it out. Don't be like my generation and keep your feelings bottled up.'

'It doesn't seem like the Pimlotts and Nora Wotsit have been keeping much bottled up.'

'So what's this Julian ponce got that you haven't? Money, I suppose?'

'Yes, plenty of that.'

'But Jeannie was never bothered about cash. Has he got a nice big car? Oh, I do like a man with a flashy sports car. You can tell a lot about a man from the car he drives.'

'How does that work? Dad never had a car.'

'Exactly.'

'Well, as it happens, old Julian is running about in an Aston Martin at the moment.'

'Ooh, lovely! Mind you, Jeannie wouldn't be impressed by that. She's not a materialistic kind of girl. Is he good looking?'

'Well, if you like that kind of thing.'

'What kind of thing?'

'Oh, you know, that tousle-haired, effortlessly craggy, public school charmer type.'

A pause.

'Yes, well, I can see that you might be running a poor second there.'

'Oh well, thanks very much.'

'I'm sorry, Edward. Look, you know I think you're a lovely boy, and sort of handsome in a kind of, errrmm, not obviously handsome kind of way, but you were never the kind to make a girl go weak at the knees, were you?'

'Wasn't I?'

'Not really, son. Neither was your father. But you're funny, and musical, and cheeky, and odd.'

'Odd?'

'In a cute way. Perhaps you're going to have to accept that you've had enough chances to make a go of it with her though, and if it was going to happen it would have happened by now.'

I could see the wisdom in what she was saying but that was no comfort.

'I won't accept that, Mum. I can't. I just feel like if I can't have her my life's over. I know it sounds dramatic,

235

but since she's been gone I can't eat, sleep or do anything properly. I love her and I want her back. It's probably too late though, you're right.'

'Well, have you told her all this?'

'She knows how I feel about her.'

'Are you sure? Have you sat down and looked into her eyes and let her hear you talk from the heart?'

She saw by my expression that the answer was no.

'Well, don't you think it might be worth giving it a go before you write the whole thing off and come moping round here putting me off my fags?'

'You're right, Mum. As soon as she gets back I'll sit her down and give it to her straight.'

'As soon as she gets back from where?'

'Somewhere in the west of Scotland.'

'Well, it's hardly the Great Barren Reef, is it? Don't wait for her to come back. Do something impetuous for once, like your dad never did. Hire a car and go and get her. What's the worst that can happen?'

'Being made to look a fool in front of another man and the woman I love.'

'Well, that's hardly going to be a first, is it?'

'Thanks, Mum, you're saying all the right things.'

A beat.

'Actually, Mum, you are saying all the right things. Do you know what? I'll do it. First thing tomorrow I'll be impetuous and hire a motor and get up there.'

'You can't be impetuous tomorrow, you fool, do it now. Hire a decent car and drive through the night to sweep her off her feet. You'll regret it for the rest of your life if you don't.'

I slapped both hands on the table top, indicating that here was a man who had decided on a course of drastic action. She was right. I had to give it a try.

'Okay, Mum, I'll do it. I'll throw some things in a bag and then I'll rent a car from the station and head off tonight.'

'Good lad. What kind of car will you get?'

'A great big flashy sports thing with a huge long bonnet and noisy exhausts.'

'Ponce. Mind you scrape the gate shut on your way out.'

20

Taking the deserted A82 along Loch Lochy, I pressed the accelerator to the floor and felt the 4,244 ccs of the Maserati Cambiocorsa Coupé effortlessly cruise up to eighty-five before I touched the brakes and took a screeching left on to the A87 heading for Loch Garry.

I didn't really. The 973 ccs of the Vauxhall Corsa Expression kept me at a steady, if rattlesome, fifty-five as I wrestled with the atlas to see how far the junction with the A87 was. When I'd got to the car rental place by the station, as the city clock struck nine, I'd found that Maseratis were unavailable. They did have a Mercedes CL 500 Auto Coupé for a hundred and thirty pounds a day, the merits of which I weighed against the Corsa on special offer at sixty quid for three days. On the one hand the notion of breezing into Plockton in seventy grand's worth of Merc to sweep Jeannie off her feet was a romantic one. On the other hand the Corsa does fifty-three to the gallon. Romance versus frugality. The perennial equation.

Dawn was threatening to break as I trundled by Loch Garry, then Lochs Loyne and Cluanie on what must be the most breathtakingly beautiful road in the British Isles. Perhaps my head was full of the heart but the sight of the sun peering out at the Highland landscape as I rode over the Five Sisters is something I will never forget. Would there be a similar golden radiance on the return journey?

Would I be basking in the comfortably numb silence of a passion rekindled or in the monastic isolation of a lover spurned? These were questions I couldn't yet answer but one thing was for sure, if I was thinking in terms like 'golden radiance', 'passion rekindled' and 'monastic isolation', then I really had got it bad.

Dropping down over Shiel Bridge, the road continued along the side of Loch Duich before I took a tentative right towards Plockton, leaving the A87 to wind its lonely way to the Kyle of Lochalsh and Skye beyond.

Coming into Plockton itself just after first light was another high. A fishing village for which the word quaint could have been invented, the walls of its white cottages glowed with a lustrous warmth as the dark heads of bobbing seals peered inquisitively from the dancing waters of Loch Carron. For the first time my resolve threatened to fail me. If Jeannie had been in any doubt whether to fall for Julian, then surely this setting would be seductive enough to remove any reservations. There were so many things he could give her that I would never be able to match, and although she was never impressed by material wealth, you had to say that a cottage on the water in a spot like this had to count for something. If Julian had brought me here I think I'd have let him have his way with me.

It didn't take long to find them. I didn't have an address but Plockton is a small place and the number of houses with Aston Martins parked outside was relatively small.

The Bellerby family retreat stood on a spit of mossy land jutting out into the loch and had recently been painted a virginal white. Was this a happy omen? Not that Jeannie was a virgin, and not that every other house didn't gleam with fresh whitewash, but it was hard not to feel a certain optimism. On that shiny morning, in that shiny place, anything seemed possible.

I parked the Corsa on the main street, not wanting to attract attention by driving up to the house itself, and in no way because I didn't want to invite comparison with the Aston. Or is it a Martin? I got out and stood for a moment sampling the snap in the air before setting off, relatively purposefully, towards the front door. I say 'relatively' because, even though I hadn't driven all this way to bottle out at the last moment, it's hard to stride as purposefully as you might like when there's a strong possibility that you're going to be told to go away.

The front door was painted a deep green and was set within a storm porch of rough-hewn stones plastered with stucco. Entering the porch I was glad of the cover it afforded because there was no way of seeing who was at the front door from the small bedroom windows dotted along the eaves. This, it seemed, might be to my advantage. I paused for a second and took another deep gulp of what felt like pure oxygen before rapping firmly. I waited for what seemed like several minutes but must only have been a couple of seconds before trying again. This could have been a mistake as anyone inside would immediately know that here was someone whose call had a degree of urgency beyond simple neighbourliness. Still I waited, tormenting myself with the thought of them lying in each other's arms under freshly laundered linen as the first of the day's rays streamed through the leaded window. Or perhaps they weren't in at all but lost on some lovers' ramble hand-in-hand by the shoreline, pausing occasionally only to see the sparkling ripples reflected in each other's eyes. Still the signs of life refused to materialise. Murkier thoughts began to form. How well did she really know him before she consented to hide away in this remote location? Would he have shown his true colours once the cast-iron latches and bolts were fastened? Or was there an altogether more mundane explanation? I glanced at my watch. It was six forty-five a.m.

Eventually a succession of heavy footsteps echoed from somewhere within the house; the stumbling, groggy, unwilling steps of someone dragged from a warm bed a good three hours early. There was a grunt, a cough, a rattle of chain and the turning of an aged key in an antiquated lock before the door swung open to reveal Julian in a pair of boxer shorts and a Waifs t-shirt. He lowered his eyebrows and looked at me quizzically, as if waiting a moment or two to check that he really was seeing what he thought he was seeing. In turn, I looked at him with the slightly embarrassed look of a man who's just driven eight hours to spoil the fun. To his eternal credit he soon recovered his customary good manners.

'Edward, what a pleasant surprise. Come in, you must be frozen.'

I could almost have killed him. Why did he have to be so bloody charming all the time? Why couldn't he have behaved like a normal bloke and sneered something about half expecting me to turn up? My arrival may have been several things but 'pleasant surprise' cannot have been one of them. He didn't even ask me what the hell I thought I was doing there. Breeding, I guess. The thought crossed my mind that I should leave there and then so as not to make trouble for him. He deserved her, and she deserved better than me. I soon got over it though.

'Thanks, yes, it is a bit parky out here.'

'Errm, right, yeah. What time is it?'

'Just gone quarter to seven.'

He looked perplexed but was again too polite, or befuddled with sleep, to ask any awkward questions.

'Errm, right, well you'd better come in then. Unless you've got a pressing engagement elsewhere in the village, that is.'

We both knew the answer to that one.

'Well,' he said, 'come through to the kitchen.'

I followed him along a corridor hung with montages of photographs picturing numerous sickeningly healthy looking Bellerbys baring perfect teeth in broad smiles as they indulged in family games of rounders on wide sandy beaches. This led on to a kind of sun room furnished with tastefully battered leather sofas, beyond which was the kitchen with a refectory table and chairs seemingly created out of polished railway sleepers. A dark green Aga pumped that peculiarly all enveloping warmth into the room. Apart from perhaps Lanercost, it was the nicest house I'd ever been in and how I hated him for that. It wasn't even his first home.

'So can I get you some coffee or something?'

'Tea would be good.'

I preferred coffee but was determined to be awkward. After all, I held the stronger moral hand, didn't I? He was the one who'd run off with my girlfriend, so he was in the wrong, right? That she wasn't actually my girlfriend at the time they absconded was a minor detail. As was the fact that I was technically gate-crashing.

'Tea, right.'

Julian filled an old tin kettle from the tap and put it on the stove.

'So what brings you all the way up here then, Edward? If I'd known you were planning a trip to these parts I could have offered you a lift. The back seat of the Aston is a bit of a squeeze for a big lad like yourself but I'm sure we could have managed.'

Why was he doing this? Even in my suspicious state he managed to sound utterly convincing. Giving me a lift to Plockton must have been the last thing he could have wanted and yet I was in no doubt that he would have done it. Why was he making this so difficult, the reasonable bastard? Why couldn't he behave with a bit of spite like a normal person?

'Yes, well, I'd always heard what a beautiful part of the world this was and thought I'd come and see for myself.'

'Right, and Jeannie being up here with me was just a happy coincidence, was it?'

Aha. The first sign of sarcasm.

'Well, obviously not a coincidence entirely. She did happen to mention your itinerary and so I thought if I was going to come up here I might as well have friends to hang out with.'

Pitiful. I'd surrendered the high ground immediately. Possibly because I didn't have very much to begin with, but even so, I could have held out longer than that. She may not have been exactly beholden to me when she decided to take this trip, but he'd moved in with unseemly haste, hadn't he? I could have made him sweat for at least a few minutes, couldn't I? Apparently not.

'We haven't, if that's what you want to know.'

'Haven't what?'

'Oh, do me a favour and cut the crap, Eds. Sugar? We haven't slept together. I don't blame you for wondering. We've all been there. We've all had to wonder what our exes are up to after they've finished with us. I've been dumped too, you know.'

This seemed extraordinarily unlikely though not

unwelcome news. We did have something in common after all.

'I haven't been dumped.'

'Right. But you and Jeannie aren't together, are you? I did check before I invited her here. I'm not a complete shit, you know.'

All resistance crumbled. What feeble belligerence I'd mustered quickly evaporated in the steam bursting from the kettle. I spoke to him in a shamefaced mumble.

'I know you're not a shit. I find it hard to believe you've been chucked though. Who'd get rid of you with your looks and money and nice bloody houses all over the place.'

'Don't you believe it. For your information my wife left me for a man with more money and more nice bloody houses. And he was my business partner.'

'Foster?'

He nodded.

'The lowlife scum. I knew there was something I didn't like about him. He's not as good looking as you though, is he?'

'Well, you'd better ask my ex about that.'

'But you're still working with him.'

'Because I wasn't going to let him take my business as well as my wife. We'd spent years building that up and I'm pragmatic enough to know that we make a great team. In many ways it's a more important relationship than any marriage and so I just let them get on with it on the condition that she didn't come to me for money.'

'Right. I see. How very grown up of you all. I suppose you think I'm an immature cretin, don't you?'

'Not at all. I understand. Jeannie's very special. I don't

know how to describe that quality she has. She's so frail and everything and yet she just radiates something. A special light. Do you know what I mean or does that sound a bit poncey?'

'Not poncey at all. Not where she's concerned anyway. I know exactly what you mean.'

'And she's more talented than she can even guess. I see a lot of performers, Ed, and what she's got is a very rare thing. For want of a better word I guess you'd call it charisma. You see, when most people talk about charisma they think of confident, up-front, strutting performers who fill the stage with energy. But that's not real charisma. Someone who can sit quietly hunched over a guitar, sing without projecting and yet still hold an audience with one coy look has true charisma. People like that are the really precious ones.'

'I know. She's amazing. But you're not expecting me to believe that you brought her up here just to admire her "special light", are you? Not even you're that nice. So why haven't you slept with her?'

For the first time he looked unsure of himself.

'You're right, of course. I brought her here because I wanted her in every way. I know she's had her problems and there's no better place to be than here to get things into perspective. I do genuinely care about her, even though I've not known her long at all. Some people just get to you like that, don't they?'

I nodded.

'But I won't pretend that I didn't hope that there'd be more.'

'But there isn't.'

'Not yet. Doesn't mean to say there won't be though, does it?'

'You're asking me? My experience with women hardly matches up to yours, I wouldn't think.'

'Maybe not. But we're not talking about women, are we? We're talking about one woman who's asleep upstairs and in that department you're way ahead of me.'

'I suppose so.'

'So d'you think there's any chance?'

'I bloody hope not.'

We both laughed and took slugs of our tea. It seemed strange to be rivals for Jeannie's affections and yet so comfortable in each other's company. Was I being permeated by his infectious sense of fair play or was I finally becoming a fully fledged adult of my own accord?

'To be honest, Julian, I don't really think you're her type.'

'Well, who is? You?'

'I bloody hope so. So has she actually told you she doesn't want to have a physical relationship with you?'

Only moments ago I'd been praying that their relationship hadn't progressed to the damp patches in the bed stage, and yet now I was feeling almost sorry for the guy.

'No, she hasn't said it in so many words but then I haven't pushed it that far. I don't know, it just hasn't seemed the right thing to do. I'm a bit confused to tell you the truth. There's just something I can't put my finger on.'

We looked at each other for a second before giggling like two spotty schoolboys, united in snotty innuendo. It was during this bout of adolescent sniggering, when the heartily brewed and sweetened tea threatened to explode back down my nose, that the kitchen door swung open.

'Edward, what the hell do you think you're doing here?'

'Hi, Jeannie. I was just having a cup of tea actually. How are you?'

'Do not on any account try and bullshit me. Why are you here?'

'I would have thought that was obvious.'

'And you, Julian, what are you doing drinking tea and laughing with him? Why did you let him in?'

'Oh, come on, Jeannie, I could hardly turn him away after he's driven through the night to see us, could I? Come and sit down and I'll make a fresh pot.'

Jeannie paused for a moment in the doorway, her tangled hair catching the sunlight. She'd never had a terribly convincing angry face she could use in situations like this, and the attempt at tight-lipped petulance just made her look even cuter. It wasn't hard to see why Julian had become captivated so quickly.

Resigned to the fact that I wasn't going to do the honourable thing and leave straight away, and unable to face the day without caffeine, she made her way to the table and plonked herself down with a sigh. The sigh of someone who has had perfection snatched cruelly away in a manner they'd come almost to expect.

'So what are you doing here, Eds? Why have you followed me? It's hardly fair on Julian.'

'Oh, don't worry about me,' chirruped Julian from the range. 'It's really no problem at all.'

'Julian, you're too nice for your own good,' said Jeannie.

'I think she's probably right there, mate,' I agreed. 'I've really messed things up, haven't I?'

'Forget it, Edward. You're most welcome. Stay as long as you like, there's plenty of room.'

'Julian, for goodness' sake. It's bad enough he's here for breakfast. Don't invite him for a week's holiday. What sort of bizarre love triangle do you have in mind?'

Bellerby handed me and Jeannie our tea and looked at her in a way that seemed simultaneously protective and yet lustful. He wanted her, but more than that, he wanted her to have what she wanted herself.

'Jeannie, I think it's more a question of what you've got in mind, isn't it? Listen, Edward, why don't you go for a walk along the shore or down to the paper shop or something and let us two have a chat. Don't go far and one of us will come and find you in a while. I think we need to straighten a couple of things out.'

Jeannie didn't speak or look in my direction. She stared out of the window towards the loch, the bottom half of her face buried in an oversized mug. In the absence of further instructions I nodded, put down my own mug, and left the house.

I wandered the main street aimlessly, absent-mindedly glancing into front parlours, checking out snug bars, reading the hoardings for boat trips without taking in any of the details. Why had I come? What could I possibly have to say to her that I hadn't had the opportunity to say to her a hundred times before? This was all my mum's fault. If I hadn't listened to her then I could have been back home going down the Sun or the Fox for a pint with Mo. But what good would that have done? I'd only have been thinking about her. And him. No, whatever was coming to me, it was better to get it over with. At least this way I'd have the long drive south to get my head round it.

I must have passed about half an hour before she came. I was standing looking out over the water, wallowing in the self-pity that seemed appropriate, when I became aware of someone behind me. Sure it would be him, I turned to deal with the bad news. But there she was. Alone.

'No Julian?'

'You've got a car, I presume?'

'Err, yes. Not in the league of your new boyfriend's motor but a car all the same.'

'He is not my new boyfriend but don't you dare say a word against him or his car. He's got more to offer than you'll ever have in some ways.'

In some ways? That had to be a positive sign. From where I was standing he had more to offer in every way.

'Yes, he's a good guy.'

'He's just unbelievably reasonable and nice and gallant. I'm not used to that. He even offered to lend us his Aston Martin for the day. Imagine trusting you to drive a car like that.'

'I daresay he's not that bothered what happens to it. It's not his car technically, and after what Bill Foster did to him he's every right to take it back in any state he likes.'

'Don't make the mistake of assuming that everyone sees the world the way you see it, Edward. He has managed to rise above that fourth form tit-for-tat mentality, which is more than can be said for some people.'

All of this was perfectly true, but why then was she here? I pondered this in silence as we ambled back along the street until I stopped by the Corsa.

'Here we go then. This is it. Maroon's such a vibrant colour for the modern automobile, don't you think? It's got a sunroof though. If you open it and put a beach ball on the back seat it could pass for a referee's whistle.'

'It's a perfectly nice car. You know me well enough by now to know that I wouldn't know an Aston Martin from a . . . a . . . oh, I don't know, another car that's much cheaper than an Aston Martin.'

'Like this one.'

'Like this one.'

'So why do we need a car? Are we going somewhere? Or is it just me that needs transport? If so, do you think I could nip back and use your facilities? There are a couple of pints of tea that I'll need to offload before heading off. Don't worry, I'll steer clear of the master en-suite.'

'How very considerate of you. Look, just unlock the car and let's get in. Before I change my mind.'

If only I'd been possessed of an unshakeable cool I could have reacted to the news that she was getting into the car with me as if it was no big deal. Not being possessed of it, I fumbled with the keys before dropping them on the roadside and then picking them up in the blind panic of a man who couldn't believe his luck. I opened the passenger door, swept the ploughman's sandwich cartons, Bounty wrappers and Red Bull cans into the foot well, and helped her into the stained and smeared seat. Slamming the door before she had a chance to change her mind and make her escape back into the well toned arms of Bellerby, I bounded round to the other side and leapt into the driver's seat practically out of breath. I don't know why I felt so elated. She hadn't said anything yet and there was a distinct possibility that she was building up to the last goodbye. But she was here. We were alone together and for the moment that was enough.

'So where are we going then?' I panted.

'Applecross Bay.'

21

I started the engine and handed her the road atlas, still open at the right page from my arrival in Plockton at first light. We rode in silence back along the edge of the loch as far as Achintee, where we crossed over to the northern shore, heading through Lochcarron and Kishorn, before leaving the main road to wind up to Applecross. It was a stunning drive, unhindered by other vehicles on the road. The last thing you want is sluggish drivers getting in your way when you've got the throbbing horsepower of a Corsa to unleash.

On to Sgurr a'Chaorachain the road rose in tortuous twists around the tectonic folds of the mountain, and if I said I felt like my head was in the clouds it would be to resort to cliché, but the combination of altitude and euphoria made it feel just that way. Jeannie didn't say much except to give directions and marvel at how beautiful the countryside was. I didn't say much either as I was still unsure why we were going where we were going, and didn't want to say the wrong thing.

Heading towards the silver sliver of the sea we dropped down from the pass into Applecross village before swinging right to the beach and the bay. I brought the car to a halt by the roadside and we both gazed across the caramel sand to the breaking surf.

'Let's go then,' whispered Jeannie, already climbing out of the car.

We left our shoes and socks by the large boulders at the back of the beach and began to stroll towards the sea. Cirrus clouds bobbed gently across the bright sky, casting tendrils of shadows on to the smooth beach. It looked breathtaking.

Striding into the shallows, we paddled, then walked, then ran, shrieked, and splashed each other as if we were just any loving couple horsing around. Eventually we wandered back to the rocks and sat side by side.

'So this is the famous Applecross Bay,' I ventured.

'Famous?'

'Immortalised in song, as I recall.

Take me over the water on which the sun shines,
Take me over by night from the shores of Loch Fyne,
Take me away for a year and a day,
To where Northern Lights shine over Applecross Bay.'

'You've got a good memory, although it's actually the water on which the moon shines. Otherwise you wouldn't get the Northern Lights, would you?'

'True, but if you're being pedantic then we're a long way from Loch Fyne.'

'Yes, but you could come over Loch Fyne on your way here. You know, through Inveraray or something.'

'Well, hang on a minute whilst I nip back for the atlas and we can get down to some serious route-planning. You can never know too many A road numbers off by heart, can you? Where do you stand on the A87 versus the A4085 through Beddgelert debate?'

She smiled.

'So have you been here before?'

'Not until two days ago when Julian brought me here. Wonderful, isn't it?'

'It really is. So how did you come to write the song about it if you'd never been here?'

'My mum and dad came here for their first holiday together and there's an album of old photographs of them at home. Just the pair of them looking young and in love, a battered Volkswagen Beetle convertible and the most glorious surroundings you could wish for. Heaven.'

'I can't imagine your mother ever being young and in love.'

'Don't think you're in any sort of position to start having a pop at Mum.'

'Sorry.'

'But as a girl, I'd look for hours at those pictures and say to myself that one day, when the time was right, I'd go to Applecross Bay with my man and it would be special for me too. And it just fitted in with the whole Vashti thing that I cling on to when the darkness comes down again.'

I paused and looked at her profile as she stared out to sea. I couldn't resist the obvious question.

'So when is the right time?'

'Hmmmm?'

'You said you'd come here with your man when the time was right. So does that mean now or two days ago?'

'Oh, I don't know. Maybe neither. Look, Eds, I know you're really jealous of Julian but I'm coming to the conclusion that you've no need to be.'

'Jealous? Me? Of what? Looks, money, charm, success?'

She giggled.

'He is a bit yummy, isn't he?'

'You're asking me? You don't seriously expect me to pass judgement on his yumminess when we're rivals, do you?'

'Is that what you are?'

'Oh, come on, Jeannie, don't mess me about. At least you can drop this innocent coquette act. He's crazy about you. Anyone can see that.'

'Could you see that?'

'Well, not exactly but then I'm a bloke. I'm not supposed to see stuff like that.'

'So how can you be so sure?'

'Because he bloody well told me.'

'Oh, that's brilliant. You follow me up here and burst in on us unannounced and he chooses to confide in you that he'd like to get me into bed.'

'Well, why did you think he'd brought you here, for goodness' sake? You didn't think he'd driven all this way just to show you all this, did you? Come on, Jeannie, not even you could be that naïve. And not even Julian could be that nice. He is a man, you know.'

'God, you're so cynical. Not everyone is after a physical relationship.'

'Perhaps not, but Julian is. I daresay he's very happy to be back up here at one of his family's many hideaways, and I'm sure he thinks the world of you as a person and an artist. That still doesn't mean he doesn't want to sleep with you.'

'So what should I do?'

'That's not fair. I don't want to be your confidant, the wise older brother you never had. I can't tell you who to sleep with because I only want it to be me. If you want unbiased advice, then I'm sorry, I can't help you. If it's completely biased advice you're after, then I'm your man. Tell rich boy to sling his hook and jump into the sack with me.'

'I can hardly tell him to sling his hook when it's his house.'

'So if it wasn't his house you could give it to him straight?'

Silence.

'Jeannie?'

'I suppose.'

I summoned every ounce of maturity I had to greet these words with uncharacteristic calm. Jutting what I thought of as my stoic chin towards the ocean and screwing up my eyes against the sunlight, I gazed into the middle distance, trying to look contemplative. My natural impulse was to strip down to my underpants and prance along the dunes emitting a frenzied high-pitched trill. She'd rejected him. For all his charms and attributes, she'd turned him away. Sometimes life's grand, isn't it?

The wind had picked up and the temperature had dropped perceptibly. I edged six inches closer and stretched my arm around her shoulders. She didn't pull away. I leant round and pulled back a few strands of hair from her face, and wiped away a tear with the back of my index finger.

'He'll understand.'

'Will he?'

'Of course he will. He's not daft, Jeannie. He will have noticed that you haven't exactly thrown yourself at him since you've been here. Men may be a bit slow on picking up subtle signals but I think most of us usually begin to wonder if we're on to a loser when separate bedrooms are involved.'

'But I've been so unfair to him. I came here with the intention of sleeping with him, but somehow, when it came to it, I couldn't go through with it. And then you turn up and everything's turned upside down all over again.'

'Well, it looks to me as if things just got a whole lot simpler. Certainly a lot simpler than if you'd got yourself involved in a full-on relationship with Julian, only to decide it was a mistake. Look, he's half-expecting it anyway. More than half. Don't you think he was desperate for you to send me packing when I turned up at the house at the crack of dawn? But you didn't, and now you've left him at home while you sit on a romantic, windswept beach with your ex-boyfriend. I think he's probably getting the message, Jeannie. Anyway, don't worry about him, these public school types are bred to deal with this sort of stuff. Stiff upper lip and all that.'

'That's such a pathetic generalisation.'

'Maybe. You don't need to worry about how to tell him though, Jean. He already knows.'

We sat huddled there for quite a while without another soul crossing those sands. Just the two of us, the fidgeting clouds in that mighty sky and the perpetual pounding of the waves. It was dramatic and beautiful and romantic and I was trying to sense how she was feeling. Was the time finally right?

'It's getting late. We should go.'

'Do we have to?' I sighed.

'I have to go back and tell him, Ed. I've kept him waiting for long enough. It's not fair.'

As I drove back to Plockton I hoped I was managing to appear calm because inside I was in turmoil. Of course I was amazed, proud, thrilled, that she had chosen me, but was there still the possibility of a cruel plot twist? I wouldn't feel in the clear until she'd told him, and we were on our way home. She, in turn, smiled and rattled on about the lack of traffic and the clouds and the hills and the lochs and the air and the light and the water. There was no doubt that the scenery was special, but was she chattering like that because she was happy, or because she was nervous about facing him?

I stayed in the car while she went to talk to him. I thought this would be for the best. Firstly it would give him the chance to receive the bad news without me being there, allowing him to keep his dignity intact. Secondly I would be a safe distance from him if his dignity deserted him, allowing me to keep the bridge of my nose intact.

So it was with not only deep joy but also some relief that I saw her through the rear view mirror approaching the car without sixteen stone of irate, gym-toned muscle careering after her swirling an ancestral claymore. She got in, looked straight ahead and said nothing. I didn't want to be the first one to speak. I wanted to be cool and mysterious and tortured and romantic too. Naturally she held out longer than I did.

'So?'

'So what?'

'How did he take it?'

'What's that to you?'

'I do have some feelings, you know. I do feel for a thoroughly decent bloke spurned by you. I do know how that feels.'

'Look, just drive, Eds, please. When you say "spurned" that implies that you've been rejected through no fault of your own and we both know that that's not true. Julian, on the other hand, does fall into that category and he's taken it in the way I suspect we both imagined he would. At least, I don't think he's got any plans to attack the back of your head with a National steel guitar and so I doubt very much whether you know how it feels to be a thoroughly decent bloke spurned in the same way that he does.'

'Oh, great, so even though you've chosen me, I'm going to be subjected to unfavourable comparisons with him every time we have a cross word, am I?'

She looked at me and creased the left-hand side of her mouth upwards into that half-cocked smirk.

'Well, as I'm in a position to dictate terms and you're not, that's about the size of it, yes. So do you want to live with that or do you want to drive south on your own?'

I turned the key and felt the reassuring throb of the Corsa's engine purr into action. The words 'throb' and 'purr' aren't often found in the same sentence as 'Corsa' and 'engine', but I felt so good that not even the throb and purr of an Aston Martin could have sounded better. The comfortably numb silence of a passion rekindled did indeed infuse the journey back over Five Sisters, although, as it was late in the evening, there was no accompanying golden radiance. I certainly had got it bad, and I'd got her back, but there was no way I could describe the glow cast by the headlights of a Corsa in those terms. Not even on full beam.

22

It was close to lunchtime the next day by the time we hauled ourselves from my bed at the Pines. Sleeping with the woman of your dreams in a single bed is a close and intimate affair but it's probably best to do it when you're still a callow slip of a youth. Jeannie was both callow and a slip, but that hadn't stopped us having a bit of a rough night. The constant jockeying for position had left us both bleary eyed and, in my case, aware of a certain stiffness that was considerably less welcome than the stiffness that had manifested itself several hours earlier.

'If I'm going to move in here, Eds, we're going to have to do something about the sleeping arrangements. I can't spend every night wrestling with you like that,' said Jeannie, rubbing her neck.

'You weren't complaining when we got between the sheets last night.'

'Yes, all right, you know what I mean.'

'It was a bit snug after a while,' I admitted.

'And to be honest, I'm not sure I'm ready to share a bed with you permanently just yet. I'd rather have my own space to go to when I need it.'

Bugger!

'Do you think there's room for me here at the Pines?'

Oh, well, at least 'own space' didn't mean going back to Lanercost then.

'Room for you? Jeannie, there's room for whole coach

259

parties of Saga louts who will never arrive. I'll have a word with Danny and sort it out. We are back on though, aren't we? I can make an official announcement? You're not retreating after one restless night under moth-eaten candlewick, are you?'

'Of course not, stupid. I just want a room to call my own and in time, who knows, perhaps we'll upgrade to the honeymoon suite. Just don't rush it.'

As I was trying to work out how quickly this might be achieved without 'rushing it', I became aware of a male presence in the adjoining bathroom. Resonant belches and coughs of expectoration were followed by the sound of stale air reverberating around the toilet bowl. Mo. At that precise moment I quite fancied 'my own space' somewhere else in the hotel myself.

I opened the unlocked bathroom door and a vision of loveliness presented itself. Mo was wearing a rainbow striped cardigan with tortoise-shell toggles, patchwork flares and a pair of desert boots decorated with purple stars. With the tap running he was plunging his hands into the water before running them through his hair in a futile attempt to control the overgrown bush on his head.

'All right, Eds? Mission accomplished then?'

'Errm, yes, I suppose you could put it like that. How did you know?'

'Eds, many things I may be but deaf isn't one of them. I can't imagine you're a skilful lover, and I'm taking a wild guess that you haven't got much staying power, but I know for sure you're not the strong, silent type.' He smiled and raised his voice slightly. 'Good afternoon, Miss McBride, welcome home.'

'Hello, Mo, I'll come and give you a hug when I'm decent.'

'Don't worry on my account,' he retorted.

'Oi, Mo, that's the kind of cheap, sexist claptrap that we new-age sensitive folkies hate. Get your own girlfriend to ogle while she's getting dressed. So what's been happening then?'

'Well, you've seen the *Guardian* piece, I presume.'

'No, I haven't. When did that come out?'

'The day before yesterday. I suppose you were wrapped up heading north on your rescue mission.'

'And?'

'Errm, well, it's probably fair to say it's not exactly what all of us were hoping for, though I'm pretty sure that O'Malley and Lane wouldn't see it that way. It's probably best if you read it for yourself. I've got it here somewhere.'

A couple of minutes trawling through the detritus on the threadbare crimson carpet produced a crumpled edition of *G2*, open at an article titled: 'Bright in my Northern Sky – Dom Casey visits a northern folk club and finds the future of British singer-songwriting alive and well.'

'Well, that's not bad for a start.'

'Read on.'

Settling my backside between prominent springs on the mattress I began to read the piece, safe in the knowledge that whatever O'Malley's mate had written, it would at least be a thrill to see my name in a national newspaper for the first time. Inevitably perhaps, disappointment beckoned.

The description of the boat-house rather overdid the 'sagging, dampened timbers on a charmless marsh' thing, but you could have forgiven him that. A writer has to use a bit of licence to set the scene, after all. His impressions of the clientele, though, went way beyond what was acceptable. Cliché-ridden sentences full of beards, woolly jumpers and pewter tankards swept by before he fixed on two individuals in particular. 'Propping up the bar in the manner of two ageing hippopotami at a waterhole, two gargantuan men, one in an overstretched Waterboys t-shirt and one in a voluminous silk blouse, animatedly discuss the beers on offer. They're the kind of oversized, real ale obsessed specimens you expect to find at establishments like this up and down the land.'

'The little bastard,' I shouted.

'I know,' said Mo, looking over my shoulder, 'not fair on Danny and Jerry at all, is it?'

'Dead right. It's not fair whoever they might be but seeing as one of them is bankrolling the whole operation and the other has run the club for donkey's years it's a bloody disgrace. He makes them look like cartoon characters.'

Reading on I was intrigued, though not entirely surprised, to learn that Matthew O'Malley was 'a local journalist and musical visionary who has, almost single-handedly, revitalised the local traditional music scene'. I was, however, mildly gob-smacked to read that the evening's music had 'started in low-key fashion with a local duo of no fixed ability'. And that was it. No mention of our songs, our sound, our reception or even our names. The little worm had looked us in the eye and used our names in conversation, but when it came to writing the piece up he couldn't even be bothered to write Fred and Ed. Further into the text Mo was praised for the quality of his songwriting, but not before he'd been described as 'an escaped gargoyle from the local cathedral'. 'The fragile beauty and haunted voice of Jeannie McBride' were words I could have chosen myself but the space devoted to her was criminally small. This was because the low-life Casey had to leave himself plenty of room for his eulogy to Lane Fox. Here, apparently, was 'a remarkably charismatic performer'. Oh, really? Not only that but evidently the search for a new Oscar Wilde could be called off because 'Lane Fox is witty, sharp and articulate'. In addition, his songs, at best workmanlike and often trite, were 'the work of a true poet with a real melodic gift. In fact,' wrote dear Dominic, 'as I walked out of that damp, decaying boat-house and heard the chime of the city clock I began to wonder if I hadn't encountered a worthy successor to the great Drake himself.'

I sat there in stunned disbelief as Jeannie re-read the article, emitting sighs of disappointment and snorts of outrage and derision.

'So there it is,' said Mo. 'Lane Fox is a seminal genius, Matt O'Malley is the man who makes everything happen and the rest of us are pawns in the game.'

'At least you got a mention by name.'

Mo tightened visibly.

'Do you know what, Eds, I really wish I hadn't. All right, he said some nice things about my songs, but who wants to be associated with a piece of crap like this? Jerry Snow was hospitality itself to that little toad, and he pays him back like this. Without Jerry there'd have been nothing to write about. The whole think stinks. It just stinks. Oh, and that's not the only thing.'

'Go on.'

'We've all been given complimentary copies of Lane Fox's new album. It isn't actually due out for a couple for weeks but miraculously they've managed to press up a few hundred to flog at the festival. Funny how things can be made to happen very quickly in certain circumstances for certain people, isn't it?'

'And what's it like?'

'Yes, it's all right if you like that sort of run-of-the-mill sixth form poetry and minor chord stuff. I do have one niggling issue with it though.'

'What's that?'

'Here, see for yourself.'

Mo handed me a CD on the cover of which were the words 'Lane Fox – First Light', above a photograph of the suitably tousled, tortured artist in a velvet coat and striped scarf, looking preoccupied as he strolled across the meadows beyond the city walls at dawn. I turned the package over to look down the track listing. And there it was. Even after the shocks to the system I'd received over the previous few minutes, this one still stopped me in my tracks. Track eight on Lane Fox's new album was 'Summer's End', and in brackets after the title came the composition credits. There in black and white it said: (Fox/Pepper).

'Oh, Jesus, Mo. When did you find out about this?'

'When they gave me my free copy of the album.'

'And you had no idea they were using the song?'

'None at all. Matt said I should be pleased that the song was going to be heard by thousands of the people. He said that it should help to convince Johnny Leonard to put my record out.'

'Johnny Leonard would have put your record out anyway. He knows good stuff when he hears it.'

'Possibly. Oh, that reminds me. He wants to talk to you, Jeannie.'

'To me? Why?'

'Well, Eds must be right. He must know good stuff when he hears it because he wants to put something by you out. He's coming here this afternoon to talk to us all.

Didn't Julian tell you? I know Bill Foster phoned him the day after you went to Scotland.'

'No, he never said a thing.' She looked surprised.

'Strange. Still, maybe Matt's right. Maybe getting one of my songs heard will get things started for me.'

'Yes, Mo, but that's such a great song and yours should have been the first version anyone heard. And anyway, since when have you been co-writing with Lane? How come it's credited to both of you?'

'A printing error apparently.'

'Bullshit. Anyway, presumably they can correct that before the rest of the albums are pressed up.'

'No, they say they can't because, although they've not made all the discs yet, they have done the full print run on the sleeves so it's too late to change it.'

'Well, fancy that.'

'I know. Still, it's done now and there's nothing I can do about it. I've just got to live with it and get on with my own stuff.' He shrugged. 'Anyway, can't stand here chatting all day. Things to do, you know.'

'Come off it, Mo, since when did you have things to do?'

'Oh, yes, that's something else I've got to tell you.'

'Yes?'

'Now listen, Edward, I don't want you to take this the wrong way, what with us being best mates and all, but I'm afraid you just can't have me to yourself any longer. I know you really love being in the next room to me and hearing me in the bathroom of a lunchtime, but I'm afraid, and there's no easy way to say this, that I'm leaving you.'

'Oh, Maurice, you heartless cad, how could you do this to me? Seriously though, where are you going? Far?'

'Not that far. About a hundred feet, I reckon. Danny's

said I can have the stables across the yard for the same rent. They used to be staff quarters apparently and there's loads of room over there so I thought, why not? They're in a bit of a state but then so am I.'

'Well, I hope you'll be very happy in your new stall.'

'I'm sure it'll live up to the standards of interior design to which I've become accustomed. I was thinking that maybe you'd want my room, Jeannie.'

'Perfect,' I chimed, a little too quickly, 'you said you wanted your own space, which you'll get, but this way we'll be close together. All we share is the bathroom.'

Jeannie raised an eyebrow.

'If your performance in there is anything like his, then I think I'd rather share a bed and have my own bathroom. You don't make as many revolting noises as he does, do you?'

'Certainly not. Do you?'

'Eds, look at me. Do I look like I have that much air in my body? If I expelled half of what Mo just did I would cease to exist.'

'So what do you think then?'

'We could give it a go, I suppose.'

Outside the crunching of expensive car on sparse gravel signalled the arrival of Johnny Leonard. Looking through the window on to the courtyard, I saw a huge black jeep come to a halt by the kitchens. Out stepped Leonard and Danny, laughing uproariously at some anecdote, followed by the unsmiling Bill Foster and O'Malley carrying what looked like a new briefcase. Last of all came Lane, in the same coat he was wearing on the sleeve of his album. He couldn't have tossed his hair more artfully if there'd been a red carpet and assembled paparazzi.

'Well, it looks like the show's about to begin,' said Mo. 'Shall we go downstairs and get it over with?'

23

The bar of the Pines had lost its mustiness, thanks to our regular gatherings, and had begun to smell reassuringly of stale beer and cigarettes. Sometimes, when you want to leave the world behind, that smell is all it takes for you to start to unwind. It's as good as a drink in itself. Sometimes.

Freddie and Maria were perched on the high stools at the bar, behind which Rob Matthews was busy stacking bottles of Spitfire on to the shelves, along with Pol Roger champagne, which was all Lane Fox would drink now, according to Rob.

'You what? Since when?' I asked him.

'Oh, I don't know but he certainly insisted on it in London before going on at the South Bank. Me and Quentin were happy to have a glass of whatever was knocking around but Lane always had to have a bottle of Pol Roger handy.'

'I see. Anything else he insisted on? M and M's with the blue ones taken out perhaps? And who's Quentin, by the way?'

It turned out that Quentin was Lane's new piano player, something that really made me realise the widening gulf between us.

'Excellent,' I said sarcastically. 'So the solo singer-songwriting genius has got you and a pianist backing him up now, has he? Anybody else? Sly and Robbie on bass and drums perhaps? Earth, Wind and Fire's brass section? The choir of King's College, Cambridge?'

I grabbed a champagne bottle and popped the cork across the room, hitting the wall by the main door. Sadly it flew over Lane's head, as he and his cohorts entered the room as if attending a press conference.

'Mr Fox, over here, sir. Can I tempt you with a glass of your favourite tipple?' I shouted. 'Mmmm, it's yummy, isn't it, I always insist on Jolly Roger, don't you?'

Lane looked at me, not without amusement, I thought. Or was it just pity?

'Right, that's pretty much the reaction I'd expect from you, Eds. What's wrong with having a favourite drink that's not Scruttock's Old Dirigible or something? People can be fussy about the beer they drink but not about their wine or, God forbid, champagne, is that it? I'd call that inverted snobbery.'

'Call it what you like, mate. So do you want a glass of this over-priced crap or not? You'd best be quick, mind, I'm getting a bit of a taste for it myself.'

Lane strode over and whisked the bottle away from me.

'Yes, well, I think that I'd better have a crystal flute of the over-priced crap, as you so charmingly put it, before you swig the whole lot. Don't want you getting drunk in charge of a banjo or anything. At least not until I've had the chance to borrow a crash helmet.'

Jeannie, bless her, decided to bail me out.

'All right, Lane. I think that'll do. You've had your pound of flesh. And stop hogging that bubbly. You're not the only one who appreciates the finer things in life, you know.'

'You're quite right, Jeannie,' said Lane, 'and talking of finer things, like cottages by the loch and Aston Martins, how are things between you and Julian? I can't tell you how pleased I am for you both. He's perfect for you.'

Jeannie dropped her head slightly, and spoke a little more timidly than I'd have liked.

'Actually, Lane, I'm back with Eds.'

'You are joking, aren't you?' said Lane, incredulously. 'Please tell me you're not serious.'

'I'm completely serious, but I'd prefer not to talk about it now, if you don't mind. That goes for you too, Maria. Just drop it, please, Lane.'

'Whatever you want, Jeannie,' he said, 'but Julian had everything. Especially when compared to this loser here. No offence, Eds.'

'None taken, you supercilious tosser,' I said. 'Why should I possibly take offence at being called a loser? Although I think you'll find it's Julian, Laird of Plockton, who's lost this time, for once in his posh life.'

'Oh, here we go,' said Lane, visibly riled. 'This is a victory for the great working-class hero, is it? Pathetic. Anyway, Jeannie said she didn't want this discussed in front of everyone right now, and I, for one, am prepared to respect her wishes. Maybe, if you care about her the way you say you do, you should think about doing the same.'

He was right.

'Fair enough, Lane, we'll talk about it later. So do you fancy having a chat now about why you've stolen Mo's song?'

At this point, fearing the scene was about to degenerate into chaos, O'Malley and his briefcase strode to the middle of the room.

'All right, calm down, everyone. Eds, I understand you trying to defend your friend, but I've already explained to

Mo that the credit for "Summer's End" is a simple printing error.'

'Yes, Matt, of course it is. And Lane having nicked the song in the first place was presumably just a recording error. The engineer's fault, was it?'

'Eds, Lane has not nicked the song, he has covered it. Also you shouldn't forget that Mo's going to be due a good few royalties. He will get paid, you know.'

'What, all the money or half of it due to a banking error?'

'All right, Eds,' mumbled Mo, in the resigned tone of someone who knows when a battle has been lost, 'let's forget it and move on. I just want to say thanks to Johnny and Bill for coming and providing us with lunch. I would of course have been happy to put on a good spread of cheese with the mould cut off, past-sell-by-date pâté and stale bread but this looks a bit better.'

Johnny Leonard smiled through his beard.

'Thanks, Mo, and it's good to have a chance to chat with all of you because things have been happening that you need to know about. The reaction to Lane down south has been sensational and we've got very high hopes not only for the album but also for a tour that Bill here is putting together. Lane will, of course, be the headline act but we really want to represent the other Northern Sky artists and so we'd like to invite Mo here and you, Jeannie, to be the support acts. There won't be much money in it at this stage but we'll underwrite all your expenses and take care of all your travel, accommodation and bookings. We'll also release an EP by both of you to sell at all the dates to see how it goes. What do you say?'

Mo looked at Jeannie and received the faint nod that confirmed he could speak for both of them.

'Johnny, that's great and it's the break we've been looking for all our adult lives. You didn't say anything about Fred and Eds though. We're all in this together and we'd like to know what's in it for them too.'

'Absolutely, Mo, I was just coming to that. The problem we have is that the venues we're looking at generally have a curfew and we can't realistically get more than three acts on the bill. But we know you're all mates and would want to be in this thing together. So Bill here came up with the idea of Fred and Eds coming along, all expenses paid, to sell the merchandise in the foyer each night.'

Silence.

'So what do you think, boys?'

I looked at Freddie for a sign that it was okay for me to speak for both of us. He nodded. Maria raised her eyes to the heavens.

'Well, whoopee. Excuse me if I don't crack open another jeroboam of Pol Roger, Johnny. Lane Fox's song thievery and O'Malley's hack pal might well be launching some careers with a fanfare, but some of us are getting more than a bit pissed off at where we are in the pecking order. If Jerry Snow was here, which of course he never is when stuff like this gets discussed, funnily enough, then he'd remind you, Matt, that all artists at Northern Sky are supposed to be treated equally. Now, I'm chuffed to bits that you are offering something to Mo and Jeannie, Johnny, don't get me wrong, but if you think that Fred and I are going to trawl around the country humping boxes of CDs and t-shirts in and out of a Transit van while the rest of you lounge backstage swilling champers, you can piss right off.'

Johnny tried to maintain his normally fixed smile but he looked as crestfallen as it was possible for him to be. Bill Foster entered the fray.

'Look, Ed, I can understand how you feel . . .'

This was more than I could stand.

'Oh, can you now?' I snapped. 'I very much doubt you know how we feel because I doubt that you've got any feelings at all.'

'Steady on, Eds,' whispered Jeannie. Foster fixed me with his hawkish eyes.

'What do you mean by that, Edward? Please go on.'

'Well, I think before you start telling us all you know how we feel you should spare a thought for how Julian felt when you ran off with his wife.'

'Oh, I see. I'm with you now. For your information, Edward, I did not run off with Julian's wife. Julian's wife left him after he refused to stop his philandering. Do you really think that Jeannie was the first vulnerable willow of a girl to be given the Scottish retreat treatment? I'm sorry to have to break it to you like this, Jeannie, but you were the latest in a long line. Julian's wife Viv, or rather my wife Viv, gave him plenty of chances to be faithful, and he let her down every time. They'd been separated for over three years before she and I got together. You might also be interested to know that when I talked to Julian about the tour this morning, he didn't want you to have anything to do with it. I managed to talk him round on the merchandising idea.'

'Well, pardon me if I don't weep with gratitude,' I said. I realised immediately that this wasn't the most gallant response under the circumstances but I was still reeling from what we'd just heard. The good cop was the bad cop, and the bad cop wasn't so bad after all. Jeannie crumpled into a wing-back chair, one of the wings of which was all but detached.

Freddie, calmer now, though avoiding eye contact with anyone, spoke for both of us.

'Well, perhaps Eds and I had better talk about it. We'll let you know.'

'Okay, Freddie, thanks for that,' said Johnny. 'I realise it's not what you had in mind but at least you'll be out on the road with everyone and we'll have a laugh, I promise you that. And this is only the beginning. There'll be other tours and next time, who knows, we may well get you and Eds on the bill.'

Freddie shrugged as Maria put her arm around his shoulder. Danny Goulding opened another two bottles of champagne, one with each hand, and attempted to cheer things up a bit.

'Anyway, come on, we've got loads of booze here, let's get stuck into it. After all, we've got the festival in a few days and so we need to get plenty of drinking practice in for that. Oh, the rolling English countryside and fine traditional song enjoyed whilst snot-flying drunk. It's good to be alive and no mistake.'

'Yes, wise words indeed, Danny,' said O'Malley, who had never been snot-flying drunk in his entire life, 'and if I might just have your attention for one last moment. I have here the performance times for the festival, so I thought I'd just let you know what you're all doing. As you know, all Mulberry artists are performing on the Saturday, so Lane will be co-headlining on the main stage at Windrush with the Family Mahone. Mo, you're on the main stage too at four thirty in the afternoon. Jeannie, we thought you might prefer to play in the marquee rather than face the main arena crowd, so we've put you on in there at six. Oh, and Edward and Freddie, you'll be playing the festival fringe club at the Saracen's Head at midnight. Right, any questions?'

'Yes, Matt. Why don't you go and . . .'

Ever the diplomat, Mo stepped in.

'All right, Eds, just let it go. What good will it do? Come on, let's grab a couple of bottles of Pol Pot and I'll show you round the stables.'

24

The setting that Saturday morning at Windrush was nothing short of idyllic. The main stage looked out across a lush, sun-baked meadow stretching up to the marina, where the gleaming narrowboats sat proudly on the shiny water. Candy-striped bunting dangled from the marquee, unable to summon the energy to flutter in the still, warm air. Stall-holders chatted amiably whilst rearranging their stock, viewed only by curious squirrels and the first trickle of browsers. A few groups of punters were already staking their plots with travelling rugs and hampers, sitting under wide-brimmed hats on collapsible chairs reading the *Guardian* as 'The Lark in the Morning' dripped from the speakers. The city clock, hovering in the haze above the canopy that covered the stage, chimed a lazy eleven.

Since we were kids, the Folk and Boat had been one of the highlights of our year. Like all good folk events it was completely unpretentious and so warm in the welcome it extended to people of all ages and tastes. Dozens of brilliant musicians, without any rock and roll ego, would arrive from other small festivals, having criss-crossed the summer landscape like wandering minstrels of yore, which I think of as being somewhere between 'olden times' and 'the good old days'.

As local kids we'd wandered the site, being treated to circus skills workshops and mass dancing competitions, whilst marvelling at the sheer variety of folkies scouring the festival market for Sandy Denny rarities, brightly coloured footwear or budget concertinas. They came in every shape and size and dressed however they saw fit, treating fashion with the disdain it deserves. Never once had we felt threatened or excluded and the thrill of it all showed no sign of evaporating in adulthood. Which was why Freddie and I had found it pretty hard to stomach that our contribution would be restricted to a late night session in a smoky back room in front of a scrum of hardened drinkers who'd been on the pop for a good twelve hours at least.

Following the meeting with Johnny, everyone had been spending their time getting ready for the big day. O'Malley had, as expected, manoeuvred himself on to the festival committee and had set up office in the bar of the Pines. There he barked into one of his two mobile phones, issuing unnecessary instructions to bemused volunteers who knew what they were doing anyway as they'd been doing it for years. Opposite him sat Maria, trying to look busy by rummaging through documents that spewed out of Matt's briefcase.

Lane Fox had taken over the old dining room in the company of Rob, the odd bottle of Pol Roger and the multi keyboards, cables, gadgets and devices that surrounded Quentin Hardwicke. It looked as though he had brought the contents of NASA's mission control room with him, and indeed some of the ethereal textures he created did sound like they were being beamed in from another planet. And there was me thinking we were part of some acoustic movement. So was Lane the traitor or was I just a Luddite? I'll say one thing for him though, he was an absolute stickler for getting it right. He worked for days arranging, and finding just the right sounds in

Quentin's memory banks. I would never grow to love his songs, but even I had to admit, privately, that it sounded pretty amazing.

I didn't see that much of Mo. He was holed up in his stable, only coming out to gobble the stuff from the communal fridge that the rest of us might have sniffed, winced at, and chucked in the bin.

I spent time listening to Jeannie sing, trying to get her to eat when she seemed to forget. It wasn't easy. I'd walk down to the village shop for fresh bread, cheese and pickles and make her what I liked to think of as the perfect sandwich. After telling me she was 'starving', she would have a few token nibbles and then leave it to harden on the chipped white plate bearing the once proud Pines crest, now faint after years of pounding in the industrial dish-washer. Sometimes I'd take her leftovers across to the stables, where I could count on seeing my creation scoffed in seconds.

In truth, I spent time doing anything but practising my own material. Freddie, utterly dispirited by the way we'd been treated, was spending as much time as he could at McBride's timber yard. He'd also taken on extra work refitting Danny Goulding's boat *Pendragon*. He would leave early in the morning, and come back only after Matt and Maria had completed office duties for the day. It was obvious he was annoyed that Maria was so wrapped up with O'Malley but it never exploded into an argument. That wasn't Fred's style, but you could tell from the absence of his easy smile, and a dullness in his eyes, that he was brooding somewhere in there. So there seemed little point rehearsing as a duo on my own, and in any case, by the time we took to what passed for a stage at the Saracen's Head the crowd would be too rowdy to hear and too pissed to care.

So it was with mixed feelings that I strolled on to the site that lunchtime. The weather was great, Jeannie and I were hand-in-hand, Mo was infectiously excited and we were going to be on free beer all day. And yet there was a brewing resentment that, thanks to someone, Bellerby, O'Malley, Foster possibly, Fred and I had been sidelined. The increasingly lofty behaviour of the already lofty Lane didn't help either. Whereas the rest of us had shared a taxi to the car park and strolled to the production office carrying our own instruments, Lane's equipment was being delivered backstage by two roadies in a hired van. Who was footing the bill for all this stuff? The celebrated Mr Fox, we were told, would be arriving with maximum ceremony mid-afternoon in Johnny's menacing four-wheel-drive tank.

The production office was located in a small mouldering caravan in which sat the large smouldering figure of Jerry Snow, whose trademark good humour was being sorely tested.

'Bloody hell, you lot, am I glad to see some friendly faces. I've been here on my own since nine o'clock this morning trying to sort this mess out. Everybody needs different passes for different stages and meal tickets for different sittings and has the help I was promised by young Matthew materialised? No, it has not.'

'Poor Jerry. Do you want us to help out?'

'Dear Jeannie, I wouldn't dream of it. You're an artist and you've got to concentrate on your performance. There are lots of less talented people hanging around who can deal with all this admin rubbish. Eds, are you free for a couple of hours?'

'Very funny, Snowman. I have to retire to my backstage Winnebago to centre myself over a crystal in order to play songs no one will listen to in the early hours of the morning. Can't you get O'Malley down here?'

'I haven't been able to get hold of him on any of his mobile phones. He's probably locked in a high-level meeting discussing arrangements for Lane's scarf. Thankfully Danny Goulding picked up a call and said he'd be along any minute.'

'Good,' said Mo, 'and d'you think anyone will be bringing along a bigger caravan because I don't think there's much chance of you and Danny fitting in this one. Not unless you take turns.'

'That's a bit below the belt, Mo, not that I've seen what's down there for some time, of course. It's a fair point though, so I was hoping you might help me get this awning up then we can sit outside because having to put up with the smell of me and Danny sitting in a plastic box in this heat all day is something I don't fancy much myself.'

During the erection of the awning Goulding arrived with a pint in each hand, but it was obvious immediately that here again was someone whose good nature was wearing thin.

'All right, Danny?'

'Bloody marvellous, Eds, thank you. What better way could there possibly be to start the day than by driving round the local supermarkets looking for champagne?'

'Pol Roger, I presume?'

'Correct. Honestly, I had this morning all planned. Out of bed around nine-ish, full English with extra black pudding, an hour with the papers and then on site in time for the bar opening. But no, at eight o'clock O'Malley's on the blower issuing orders like I'm on work experience. I was close to reminding him who was stumping up the capital for his little empire but didn't want to get into a slanging match. To be honest I'd rather not talk to the jumped up little toe-rag any more than I have to today.'

Well, this was helping to lighten my mood anyway.

'Then to top it all, when I get back with Lord Fox's poison, O'Malley tells me to get down and help out at the production office. I nearly hit him until he told me that I'd be on duty with Jerry and what better way to restore one's spirits than to sit in a sauna-like caravan with the big man here and consume our own body weight in Cameron's Strong Arm.'

With this he plonked one of the pints down in front of Jerry, who paused momentarily to lick his lips before taking off the top half in a single draught.

'Mr Goulding, you are a gentleman. Now then, let's sort out all your passes, then you can wander where you like. They're all here somewhere.'

He plunged his hands into one of several carrier bags stuffed with brown paper envelopes and eventually tugged one out marked 'Northern Sky Artists'. He opened it and the contents spilled out across the table.

'Right, here we are. Mo, there's an access all areas main stage pass for you, and the same for you, Jeannie, with a separate wristband for the marquee production area. Eds and Fred, oh, you only seem to have day passes for the festival. Was that what you were expecting?'

Freddie glowered into the middle distance before recovering himself to speak.

'Jerry, we're learning to expect very little, very quickly. We're not actually performing on either of the two main stages but it would have been nice to be able to hang out with Mo and Jean.'

'Well, of course it would,' said the Snowman. Hopefully, he picked up the envelope and shook it to check it
was empty. It was. He was clearly irritated. 'Honestly, this
is bloody ridiculous. I'm sorry, lads, but there's very little I
can do. Lightwater have hired a private security firm so
you won't get anywhere without a pass and I can't give
you one because they've all got to be signed by Bill Foster.
If I can get hold of him then I'll try and sort something out.
In the meantime I'd just go to the beer tent and make the
best of it, if I were you.'

Goulding was having none of this.

'Jesus H. Christ, what sort of a set-up is this? This is
no way to run a sweet shop. These guys are mates and
they want to spend the day together. O'Malley and Fox
might have deserted them but that's no reason they
should be forced to desert each other. I'll sort this out
now.'

Tearing open another envelope, Danny tipped more
access all areas passes out on to the table.

'Here you go, fellas. Now have a good day.'

'Cheers, Danny. Nice one.'

As we clipped the passes on, Jerry sounded a half-
hearted note of caution.

'Do you think we should be doing this, Danny? These
are the Family Mahone's passes.'

'Yes, and they're one of the headline acts, Jerry. Do you
really think O'Malley and Foster are going to turn them
away from the backstage area?'

'You're right. Here, you may as well have some of their
meal and beer tickets as well.'

We stuffed the tokens into our pockets, thankful that
there were still people like Jerry and Danny who we could
call friends, but depressed that they were in danger of

becoming subordinates of O'Malley and the Lightwater mafia.

The next couple of hours were spent in a blissful, bleary haze in the backstage bar, where the seemingly limitless supply of free pints reserved for the headliners was progressively whittled down by the festival chancers. Jeannie was relatively abstemious, but Fred and I saw no alternative to getting rolling drunk at someone else's expense as early in the day as possible. My only regret in hindsight is that Mo saw fit to match us drink for drink, despite being on stage in front of a good two thousand people, hours before we were scheduled to appear. And whereas we were only going to play to three dozen borderline alcoholics, Mo's crowd would be comparatively sober and ready to listen.

Eventually, a rotund bloke in owl-like spectacles, wearing a home-made badge that said 'Stage Manager', tapped Mo on the shoulder.

'Okay, you're on.'

'What, now?' said Mo, looking surprised. 'But I've just got a fresh pint.'

Reluctantly, and unsteadily, he got to his feet.

'Come on then. Watch and learn as the great Mo Pepper stuns the festival.'

With that he staggered off in the vague direction of the stage.

'Well, brilliant,' said Jeannie. 'Well done, you two. He's off his head. And he's forgotten this.' She held up his guitar case. 'Is it likely that the great Mo Pepper is going to stun the festival without his guitar?'

'It's possible,' I said, 'and anyway, why is it our fault? He's a fully grown man . . .'

'Well . . .' murmured Freddie.

'Well, all right, perhaps not fully grown, but he's big enough to decide how much he wants to drink. Anyway, Jeannie, you're the one who's not drinking much. You should have been keeping an eye on him.'

'Right, I should have known that I'd be at least partly to blame, but what's more important right now is that we get him onstage with his guitar. Let's go.'

We followed her to the foot of the side-stage metal staircase, at the top of which Mo was wobbling precariously, and at the bottom of which was a knucklehead in a luminous tabard inscribed with the legend 'Security'. He looked at us and our passes suspiciously.

'What you all doing?'

'He's the act and we're his roadies.'

'What, all of you?'

'Oh, yes.'

'But he's only got one guitar.'

'Yes, but it's a heavy one.'

Grudgingly we were allowed through and found ourselves standing on the side of the stage where the previous act were completing their performance. Dun Carloway were a brilliantly adept sextet of fiddle and mandolin players from the Isle of Lewis who were really getting the crowd going with their lightning fast jigs and reels. We grinned at each other and bobbed up and down as close to the beat as we could get, in our condition, although I was a bit disappointed that they were pulling off one of the oldest folk musician's tricks in the book. This dictates that when playing relatively simple tunes at high speed you should take up a semi-hunched uncomfortable position so that it looks like what you're doing is really difficult, whilst at the same time smiling broadly to let everyone know that, for you personally, it isn't. Still, they finished with a flourish and left an appreciative audience wanting more. The compère then strode up to the microphone and said they would need a few minutes to re-set the stage, after which Mo Pepper would be on.

As the technical crew began to remove forests of microphone stands, leaving only two pointing at a small wooden chair, we began to realise just how far gone Mo was. He'd been prancing like a demented pixie to Dun Carloway, but now the music had died it became apparent that he could barely stand up. Still, that was okay because he was going to be sitting down. Wasn't it?

'Are you okay, Mo?'

'Never better, mate,' he slurred. 'Has anyone seen my guitar?'

Jeannie, being by some distance the most capable amongst us, opened the case and took out Mo's Fylde. She strummed it gently.

'It's not in tune.'

'What, love?'

'Mo's guitar. It's not in tune. Has he got a tuner?'

'I don't know. I'll ask him. Hey, Mo, have you got a tuner?'

'Tuner schmooner! I'll tune it by ear, Eddie baby.'

Considering his degree of inebriation and the volume radiating from the onstage sound system, this seemed unlikely. Fred took hold of the situation.

'Give it here. I'll tune it.'

As he put his ear to the body of the guitar and began to tweak the machine heads the compère took a nod from Mo that he was ready, which he wasn't, and approached the microphone.

'Ladies and gentlemen, we hope you're having a fabulous day. Tonight we've got the mouth-watering prospect of not one but two headline acts in Lane Fox and the Family Mahone. The weather forecast says there might be rain much later but it should hold out until past our curfew, so all's well with the world. Now, though, will you put your hands together and welcome a very fine singer-songwriter, a local lad recently reviewed very favourably in the *Guardian*, it's Mo Pepper.'

At this very moment Freddie gave one last minute tighten on the final machine head, causing the top E string to snap with an audible ping.

'Shit.'

'What is it, Freddie?'

'I've broken a string on your guitar, Mo.'

'Never mind. I've still got five left. Give it here.'

'You can't, Mo. It'll sound dreadful.'

'No it won't, Eds. It'll be fine. Now give it here. I'm on.'

And with that he stumbled from the sanctuary of the wings towards the solitary chair placed centre stage. For what seemed like an eternity he bumbled and fumbled about with the microphones and his guitar before struggling to shape the words with which to introduce his first song, 'Long Shore Drift'. As he embarked on a hesitant first verse it was immediately apparent that, though it was a great song, he was murdering it. Or was that just because I knew it so well? Perhaps those hearing it for the first time didn't quite appreciate just how much of a hash he was making of it. They did, however, realise that here was a man too drunk to perform coherently. There was no heckling, no hurled bottles raining on to the stage. This was a folk festival and there was a collective pride amongst the crowd that they were up the food chain from disgruntled rock audiences. But there was no mistaking a general air of disenchantment.

'I can't watch this,' sighed Jeannie. 'I'm going to find him another guitar.'

'Good idea,' I said, as Mo shot another terrified look across the stage towards us. 'I'd come with you because I don't much want to watch this myself, but if he looks up and sees we've deserted him I'm worried that he'll lose his bottle completely.'

Jeannie scuttled down the steps in search of an instrument with its full complement of strings, whilst Fred and I stood shoulder to shoulder in a show of solidarity and in an effort to stay upright.

By the time Jeannie returned with one of Lane's guitars and an agitated Matt O'Malley in tow, Mo had recovered the situation. A bit. Perhaps it was the panic setting in, the realisation that being drunk in charge of a de-tuned five-string is not a great crowd-pleaser. Whatever it was he somehow found enough of it to get him through a passable 'Boys of Glenridding' and a spirited, though approximate, version of 'Coast to Coast' before calling it a day with 'Misty Morning'. He left the stage to what, if you were generous, you could call polite applause. Which under the circumstances was more than he could have expected.

As he tripped disconsolately down the stairs from the stage, slump shouldered, he had the misfortune to run into O'Malley and Fox.

'Well, what a compelling show that was, Maurice,' said Lane. 'I couldn't take my eyes off you. Couldn't wait to see which song you were going to screw up next. It was almost performance art now I come to think about it. Have you thought of applying for an Arts Council grant?'

'Leave him alone, Lane.'

'What do you mean, leave him alone, Eds? He's very

nearly screwed up the whole afternoon session. These people haven't paid good money to see crap like that. What the hell did you think you were playing at, Mo?'

'You can leave him alone as well, Matt,' I said. 'He wasn't playing at anything. He was just out of his mind on the ale. What's wrong with that? It's a festival, for Christ's sake. People are supposed to be off their nuts. That's what it's all about.'

'Agreed, Eds,' retorted Matt, 'but couldn't he have got off his nut later on? He'd have finished everything he had to do by three o'clock in the bloody afternoon. No one was asking him to stay off the beer till midnight.'

He had a point but I wasn't about to concede it.

'Oh, where's your sense of fun, O'Malley. So he was pissed. Big deal.'

'Yes, well, that's just the sort of attitude I expect from you, Beckinsale. I trust you haven't been pouring drink down Jeannie to jeopardise her set. I know you're not best pleased at having to play at the Saracen's Head but getting your mates leathered before they go on is a low trick, even for you.'

'You snide bastard, O'Malley. They're all adults who can drink as much or as little as they like. They're quite capable of making their own mistakes. I'm not going to be some control freak like you and tell Mo to stop drinking when he's enjoying himself. And for you to suggest that I'd try and sabotage their sets . . . well, if Jeannie wasn't here, I'd hit you for even suggesting it.'

'I'm sure you would and that's why you're not getting any passes for the marquee. I'll take Jeannie over there myself to make sure she doesn't arrive after a succession of fights, arguments and several more pints.'

'You bloody won't, you patronising sod. She's my

girlfriend and she needs me with her for moral support. Don't you, Jeannie?'

She paused and looked at me like an RSPCA inspector looking at a malnourished greyhound found tethered behind a static caravan.

'Just stay here, sweetheart. Have another drink and look after Mo. I'll be back in forty-five minutes.'

She was right, of course, and I knew it, but that didn't make the look of smug satisfaction spreading across O'Malley's face any easier to take. She kissed me lightly on the cheek before making her way from the backstage area with him.

'Don't worry about it, Eds,' said Freddie. 'She'll be back before you know it.'

'Certainly she will,' offered Lane. 'She's a bright enough girl to know when she needs you kept at arm's length. Unfortunately she's not bright enough to realise that that's all the time.'

'Shut it, Lane. I need you like a hole in the head, don't I? Shouldn't you be programming your acoustic folk computers or inspecting your staff or making sure your scarf's been taken out of the portable Corby trouser press or something?'

'Oh, grow up, Beckinsale. You never could take your ale. Even when I used to take you along to gigs, though God knows why, you'd always get paralytic and have to be carried out. Did it never occur to you that I stopped phoning you because you were an embarrassment to be seen out with?'

'And did it never occur to you, Lane, that I might have got sick and tired of hanging around with you, you boring bugger.'

'Oh, right, of course. So all those messages you left with Marielle were just an elaborate bluff then, were they?'

'Might have been. And anyway, don't give me all this boho calling your mum by her first name crap. She's your mum so call her Mum like normal people do.'

'That's your problem, isn't it, Ed? You're so hooked on what you consider normal you feel threatened by anybody who wants to achieve anything out of the ordinary. Well, that's up to you, but don't expect the rest of us to follow suit. Freddie, if you ever get bored of aspiring to mediocrity, I could do with someone who could play a bit of nifty fiddle.'

'Oh, piss off, Lane,' barked Freddie. 'Haven't you got sycophants who are paid to listen to you spout this kind of stuff? Come on, Eds, don't let him get you worked up. We need to check on Mo.'

As Fox retreated to his Pol Roger-stacked Portakabin, Fred and I took Mo to the beer tent and plied him with more ale he didn't really need. Gradually he started to cheer up a bit, musing that it was nothing to get too upset about.

'After all, no one died, did they?'

'True, Mo. But you didn't even do "Summer's End".'

'Didn't I?'

'No. And you know what that means. The first version all these people will hear is going to be by Lane Fox. Then they'll buy his album and see it credited to the two of you but assume that it's more his work than yours. You're losing your best song, Mo.'

Mo slumped again.

'Shall we have another drink?'

Jeannie's set was, by all accounts, even more low key than usual. Rob had been to watch her and told us that she hadn't uttered a single word to the audience but had held them anyway. That was the effect she had on people. You couldn't help but be seduced.

In spite of ourselves, we felt we had to watch Lane Fox. He took to the stage at eight on the dot, waiting for the city clock's chimes to die away before ushering Rob and Quentin into 'Halcyon Days'. Bathed in orange lights, in his velvet coat, with hair wafting across his face, it was easy to see why he was causing something of a stir wherever he went. Also, the textures and soundscapes produced by Quentin Hardwicke provided perfect settings for the songs. Floating in the night air both 'First Light' and 'Summer's End', introduced without any mention of Mo, sounded sublime. Rob Matthews had also taken to playing a Stratocaster through all manner of effects units to add further layers of shimmering sound to the mix. The versions of John Martyn's 'Solid Air' and Nick Drake's 'Bryter Later' they performed I will never forget. It hurt me to admit it, but Lane was operating on a level far beyond the rest of us. I still doubted his talent as a songwriter, but as an overall package, you had to hand it to him. He had it all.

We gathered backstage after his set, as the clatter and thump of the Family Mahone rang out across the fields, and confessed to each other that we thought he had really been rather wonderful. Out of the corner of my eye I could also see him threading his way through a crowd of well-wishers and heading in our direction.

'Well, why don't you tell him that?' said Jeannie. 'It would mean a lot to hear you say so. We are his oldest friends, after all. Despite the impression he likes to give, he cares a lot about what you all think of him. He's easily misconstrued, you know, is Lane. All that superiority stuff is one big act. He's desperately insecure really and uses all that as a front. If you told him how much you'd enjoyed it he would really appreciate it.'

'What, after the way he spoke to Mo? No way. I might have enjoyed his set but I wouldn't tell him that to his face in a million years.'

'Pathetic and childish.'

'Well, he started it.'

'So, good friends,' said Lane, arriving theatrically, 'what did we make of it then? All comments welcome. Even from you, Eds.'

'Lane, it was fantastic,' gushed Jeannie. 'The sound, the lighting, you. It was perfect. It was almost as if the city walls and clock had been designed as some kind of stage set, it fitted together so perfectly. And what a fantastic noise Rob and Quentin make. It was marvellous.'

'Thanks, Jeannie. Your opinion means as much to me as anyone's.'

Even though you don't think she's that bright, I thought. For Jeannie's sake I left it unsaid.

There was a pregnant pause whilst Lane looked at the rest of us and the rest of us looked anywhere but at Lane.

'Maurice?'

'It was good, Lane,' said Mo, keeping his sentences simple to be sure of completing them. 'It was very good. I think you did a much better "Summer's End" than I could have done today.'

Lane seemed genuinely touched. So was I. Mo had more reason to hold a grudge against Lane than anyone, and yet he was still man enough to lend praise where it was due.

'Thanks for that, Mo. Pretty big of you under the circumstances. I do care what you all think, you know. Freddie, Eds, did you find it to your taste?'

The bell for last orders rang out from the beer tent. Saved!

'Come on, it's last orders,' I said. 'We don't want to miss that, do we?'

Mo and Fred giggled as Jeannie shook her head, but with a tight smile just showing on her lips.

'I think that's as good as you're going to get, Lane. Come on, why don't we go for a quick drink, just the five of us? It'll be like old times before all this nonsense began.'

O'Malley, materialising over Lane's shoulder, butted in.

'Did I hear someone say five? I think you'll find there are six of us and if we're going for a drink it had better be a quick one because Eds and Freddie have got to be at the Saracen's Head within the hour.'

'Oh, loosen up, will you, Matthew. You used to be fun once,' jeered Mo.

'I beg to differ, Maurice,' I said. 'He was never fun.'

'Oh, stop it, you lot,' said Jeannie. 'Matt, let's just put all the pettiness to one side and go for a drink. Just the old gang. No one will care if Eds and Fred get to the Saracen's Head on time, or indeed at all.'

'Well, thanks very much for that, love.'

'Oh, I'm sorry, Edward, but you know what I mean. Matt, you've had a successful festival today. Lane's played a blinder. The crowd will all go home happy. Bill and Danny will take care of things here for a while. Let's just be a bunch of mates again and go and have a drink together.'

Mates? Did Lane and O'Malley still fall into that category? Did I want them to? O'Malley's manner, even now, did nothing to recommend him as a good bloke to hang out with.

'Well, I suppose half an hour wouldn't hurt. That's if you're happy to go along with this, Lane. I do have a couple of bottles of Pol here just in case of emergencies.'

'Never let it be said that Lane Fox is a headliner who won't mix with lesser mortals. For all their faults and foibles, they are supposed to be friends. A drink it is.'

'All right then,' said Matt. 'There is just one thing though.'

'What now?'

'How are we going to have a quiet drink when the world and his wife and dog want to talk to Lane?'

Lane nodded, convinced beyond any doubt that this would certainly be the case. Insecure, my arse. Freddie, however, had the solution.

'Well, I do have the keys to *Pendragon* on me. I've been refitting the cabin and I'm sure Danny wouldn't mind if we went aboard to have a night-cap or six. Happy with that, Matt?'

'Perfectly, although we must make sure you get to the Saracen's at some point.'

'Oh, stuff the bloody Saracen's, O'Malley. Let's just have a drink.'

'All right then, Eds, if we must. But no mucking about on the boat. Dangerous places after dark are canals.'

'For heaven's sake, Matt, will you stop behaving like a teacher on a school trip. We're supposed to be having fun.'

25

It was the six of us. Six of us well the worse for wear after a full day's drinking. Jeannie was, of course, only mildly gone. O'Malley had been on the wine but was still desperate to give the impression that he was in control. Not only of himself, but of the whole situation. Mo, Freddie and I were lashed, and Lane, though so full of Pol Roger you could practically hear him sloshing when he moved, seemed ever so slightly distant. Even though he'd agreed to come for a drink with us, he was at one remove as that evening began.

Pendragon was moored at one of the more remote spots in the marina. Freddie said this was because of the intrusive noise of the power tools. We hobbled and weaved down the towpath in single file behind Freddie until he stopped at a pile of cut timbers stacked neatly by the boat.

'Here we are then, all aboard the night boat.'

You could see that Freddie had been hard at work in the cabin. Off-cuts of wood lay everywhere, along with bags of nails and stray chisels. The dresser, holding the little cherished Toby jug collection, had been removed, taking its strange cargo of obese, frock-coated trolls with it. Unfortunately, Freddie had also stripped out most of the available seating, which made the prospect of a long night's boozing an uncomfortable-looking proposition. Fox, as befitted his view of the natural order of things, immediately jumped on the one remaining day bed and arranged the cushions around him like Mark Antony on Cleopatra's barge. Fair play to him though, he offered to share it. Though not with me.

'Hey, Jeannie, feel free to lounge with me on this pile of cushions that don't stink too badly of engine oil. After all, we're the ones who've done the work today, so I think it's only right that we get to relax and unwind, don't you?'

'Thanks, Lane, it's a kind offer, although I think you're being a little unfair,' said Jeannie gently. 'Matt's been working pretty hard and don't forget that Mo's had a pretty stressful day, one way or another.'

'Ah yes, I'd almost forgotten the triumphant Pepper performance. A couple more drinks and I'll have erased it from my mind completely.'

'That's typical of you, that is, Lane,' I said. 'Mo's had a bad day but he still has the good grace to pat you on the back and pump up your ego. Even more, he even told you you'd done a good version of "Summer's End", the song you've stolen from him. And now you're just slagging him off. And stop trying to get my girlfriend to go to bed with you.'

'Beckinsale, you twerp.' Twerp? Steady. 'Don't you think that if anything was going to happen between Jean and me it would have happened by now? It's not as if we haven't had our opportunities. This might be difficult for you to understand but we've sort of come to an adult decision, that we might actually be better suited to a platonic relationship.'

'Don't patronise me. I fully understand the principles of a platonic relationship. In fact me and Jeannie are having one but with a good stiff shag every now and again.'

At this Mo spluttered into his beer, causing a shower to

spray across the cabin. Freddie too made a gargling noise before a trickle of Strong Arm emerged from his nostrils. Surprisingly the other three didn't find it as funny.

'Beckinsale, you are a sad, sad little saddo.'

'Wow, impressive word selection, Lane. It's that command of the language that makes your lyrics so memorable, isn't it?'

'And that's what all of this is about, isn't it? You just don't like the fact that my career is finally taking off. You really have difficulty accepting that people do like what I do. I can't think why. You've just seen several thousand of them lap it up back there but you still have this idea that I'm not as good as you. Or that we're all the same and should stay together, not getting anywhere, forever. Well, I am getting somewhere, so just deal with it. Mo has. Jeannie doesn't have any sort of problem with it. She even seems quite happy for me, which is how mates are supposed to feel. Y'know, I regret the day I ever took pity on you and asked you along to a few gigs when we were younger. Having you for a so-called friend has been like signing up for the Reader's Digest. It's all right at first but when you decide you don't want it any more, you just can't shake it off.'

'Fox, you are the most arrogant arsehole I ever had the misfortune to once call a friend. The reason I resent your success is because you're only where you are because you look the part. I'm a better guitarist than you, Fred's a better singer and Mo's certainly a better songwriter. That's why you've had to pinch one of his good ones to pad out your sad little record. If it wasn't for your girly hair and your Mr Darcy velvet coats you'd be nothing.'

'Well, what a good idea this was,' muttered Jeannie with a sigh.

'For sure,' agreed O'Malley. 'I can think of nowhere I'd rather be.'

'Can't you boys just stop bickering?' Jeannie continued. 'We're just supposed to be having a drink and enjoying each other's company, if that's not too much to ask. Lane, you could try being a bit more gracious. We're all de-lighted at what's happening to you, but we don't want to have to talk about it all the time. And Eds, just because he is getting somewhere doesn't mean he's betrayed the rest of us. Now can we talk about something else because we don't want to just sit here in a moody silence for the next couple of hours. If we're going to do that we might as well just pack up and go home now.'

'You're right, Jeannie,' said Fred, with sudden anima-tion. 'We don't want to just sit here.'

With that he leapt up from the toolbox on which he'd been sitting and began to pick his way through the obstacle course of carpenter's paraphernalia to the stern. O'Malley followed his movements with interest.

'Where are you going, Freddie?'

'Well, Jeannie's right. We don't want to just sit here. So let's get ourselves mobile. We're on a boat, I've got the keys, it's a beautiful evening, so let's go for a little trip.'

Mo and I looked at each other, grinned and stood up to salute.

'Aye aye, Cap'n Jameson.'

Matt was apoplectic.

'Freddie, you are not taking this boat out tonight. It's pitch black out there.'

'Firstly, cabin boy O'Malley, it is not pitch black, there is a considerable glow from the moon up there. Secondly, I don't know what primitive boats you've sailed on in the

297

past, but on the good ship *Pendragon* we're blessed with the technological wonder of a headlamp.'

'But taking a barge . . .'

'Narrowboat, Matt, narrowboat.'

'Oh, whatever. Taking a narrowboat out on the canals after dusk is against the local by-laws and could result in us being reported to British Waterways.'

'My God, you're right, Matt,' said Freddie, 'I'd forgotten all about British Waterways. As soon as we move they'll have their riverborne SWAT teams bearing down on us at speeds of up to three miles an hour in their special barges.'

'Narrowboats, Fred.'

'Thank you for that, first mate Beckinsale. And for your information, Matt, there are no by-laws governing taking a boat out at night on this navigation. It might not be a good idea if you don't know what you're doing but I do, so there's nothing to stop us doing it. It's not like we've got young children on board.'

'I wouldn't be too sure of that,' said Jeannie.

Freddie turned and stepped up to the tiller deck to make ready for our moonlit pleasure cruise. O'Malley turned to Lane and Jeannie.

'Come on, you two, let's get off this tub.'

'Oh, calm down, Matthew,' said Lane coolly. 'Even with these clowns at the helm, there's nothing to worry about. It's not like a sailing dinghy, is it? You can't capsize a narrowboat.'

O'Malley fixed Jeannie with imploring eyes.

'Jeannie, you're my last hope. Put an end to this madness.'

'Chill out, Matt. Freddie knows all there is to know about boats like this. It'll be fine. Anyway, I feel relaxed for the first time today. You know how difficult I find it jostling with the crowds. We're so far away from the world here. Let's stay for a while.'

'Nicely put, angel,' said Lane, 'and you wouldn't want to deny Jeannie a bit of peace and tranquillity, would you, Matt. I mean, feel free to disembark in the interests of your own personal safety if you're worried, but it looks like the rest of us are staying aboard.'

'I am not leaving you here alone with these imbeciles. I don't think Johnny and Danny would see that as looking after the talent responsibly, do you?'

'Very nicely put, Matt. Thank you. I've never been referred to as talent before,' said Freddie.

'He doesn't mean you, boatman,' sneered Lane. 'He means me, and possibly Jeannie. Still, at least when I'm huge you can say you were my personal barge driver or whatever you want to call yourself.'

Freddie looked at him without speaking for a moment, the twinkle in his eyes momentarily icy.

'Great, well, thanks for that, Lane. We all know where we stand now if we didn't before. Right, much as I'd love to stay and continue this chat I'm going to get ready for the off, so anyone not coming had better sling their hook now.'

Realising he was a lone voice of dissent, Matt conceded defeat.

'All right, Freddie, you win. But be careful.'

'I'm always careful,' said Freddie, with a noticeable slur. 'Just up to the Five Locks and back, I promise.' Clanking his bottle on the door post and his head on the cross beam, he made his way up to the steering position, Mo and I following him to cast off.

The engine coughed into life as we untied the ropes and

stepped back on board. Freddie eased the Morse throttle forward and we slipped out on to the main waterway. Matt, Jeannie and Lane remained below, the pop of another champagne cork causing a peal of laughter. Mo and I hung out by the tiller position with Freddie, leaning on the roof of the cabin and swigging from beer bottles as the stealthy progress of *Pendragon* sent unsuspecting waterfowl, sleeping on the deserted towpath, skittering for cover. Somewhere across the meadows the city clock let out a solitary chime.

We didn't speak for quite a while. Perhaps, after all that drinking, it was just too much effort. Glancing into the cabin, I saw Lane topple from the day bed and stumble to the big cupboard housing the small toilet. Jeannie and Matt, calmer now, were chatting quietly whilst sipping Pol Roger from paper cups.

Eventually the skipper spoke.

'You see, this is fantastic, isn't it? All that tension has just disappeared. There's something about night cruising that's good for the soul. Everything's so still and calm.'

'You're right, Fred. This is brilliant,' said Mo.

'Absolutely,' I agreed, 'I feel really mellow now. He is a tosser though, isn't he?'

'Matt or Lane?'

'Take your pick, Mo. I mean, Matt's a right pillock because he thinks he's this big music business executive now and really he's just running errands for the likes of Johnny and Bill Foster. Lane's worse though if anything. I mean, I used to really look up to him, still do in some ways, but that doesn't give him the right to look down on us, does it?'

'He thinks he's got a divine right to do whatever he wants,' said Freddie. 'To be honest, Eds, I don't know why you're surprised by any of this. He was never really a proper mate, was he? He was just someone we hung around with because he was cooler than us, and we thought a bit of it might rub off. He's never actually been what you might call a team player, has he?'

'I know what you mean,' I said. 'Who does he think he is to lord it up on the main stage when we have to play in some dingy back bar where no one is interested?'

'Well, look, boys, I know what you're saying,' said Mo, 'but that's hardly his fault, is it? He didn't decide who was going on where, to be fair.'

'Oh, for God's sake, Mo, fair's got nothing to do with it. It's not his fault but he could just be a little bit more humble about it. Everything he does just rubs our noses in it and I hate him for that. I mean, look at us now. We're all up here taking in the experience together, he's reclining down below like some bloody Middle Eastern potentate.'

'Actually he's in that Tupperware toilet thing and has been for ages. What is he doing in there?'

'Oh, come on, Eds,' spat Freddie, 'don't be so naïve. What do music business people do in toilets, apart from the obvious?'

'I don't know.'

'Eds, even I know he's on cocaine,' said Mo.

'What? Really? Lane's on the coke? How do you know? He's never offered me any. Not that I'd know what to do with it.'

'No, he won't have done. He's never offered anybody any of it. Well, actually that's not quite true. He told Maria she was welcome to try some if she wanted it, and she told me he'd also asked Jeannie.'

'What? She didn't.'

'Of course she didn't, Eds.'

'The bastard. I mean, I'm no prude about the odd bit of blow, but offering Jeannie coke! She's had enough health problems without getting stuck into that muck. Suppresses the appetite as well, doesn't it? That's all she needs.'

'Well, look, I think you might be getting a bit carried away here,' said Mo. 'Even if she'd tried it, which she didn't, it still doesn't mean she'd have been a full blown addict, does it?'

'Of course it doesn't,' said Fred, 'but it just shows you how Lane operates. All for one and one for himself.'

O'Malley's head appeared in the doorway.

'Everything all right up here, Freddie?'

'So far, Matt, so far. You didn't trust me though, did you? You've got to learn to have a bit more faith. I'm as skilled a tillerman as you'll find round here, so sit back and relax. You're as safe as . . . errrmm . . . someone who's very safe in a very safe place on here. How're things below?'

'Oh, well, Jeannie's just sort of dozing, and Lane's been in the bog for ages. I think he must have an upset stomach or something. Probably the pressure of the big day.'

We exchanged knowing glances as the bolt slid back and Lane emerged unsteadily from the toilet, wiping his nose with his fingers.

'I hope you've washed those, Fox, you don't know where they've been.'

'He bloody well does, Eds, and that's the problem.'

'I see the level of what passes amongst the crew for humour has remained in the kindergarten,' said Lane to no one in particular as he advanced in the direction of the day bed in a series of ungainly lurches.

'Dick-head,' muttered Fred, all but inaudibly over the pulse and throb of the engine.

For perhaps another half an hour *Pendragon* made her stately progress along the canal towards the locks. Mo sat on Fred's upturned toolbox, roaring out 'Seven Drunken Nights', whilst cracking open bottles of Spitfire. Even O'Malley, realising that resistance was futile, started to drink more heavily and shout along with the choruses. Jeannie, floating in a stream of Pol Roger, reduced the cabin almost to tears with gossamer versions of Vashti Bunyan's 'Where I Like to Stand' and 'Glow Worms', the nursery rhyme simplicity of the songs suiting her voice perfectly. Spellbound, we sat by the open port-holes as the notes hung like tiny bubbles in the night before being lost over the bulrushes. Lane, save for yet another trip to the en-suite, lay on his back, eyes closed, occasionally dribbling champagne from the bottle down his open throat. It was in this serene state that we reached the first of the Five Locks.

'All hands on deck,' boomed Fred. Immediately the usual suspects hauled themselves to their feet and reported for duty. Matt, evidently, needed to talk to Jeannie about what he'd just heard and the possibility of doing an album of Vashti for Mulberry. Lane seemed incapable of any movement whatsoever.

'Okay, fellas,' Fred barked, recklessly hurling windlasses at us, 'I'll stay at the helm and you two can man the lock gates. Mo, you're on port duty, Eds, look after the starboard.'

'Fine, Freddie. Which is which again?'

'Oh, it doesn't matter. Just take one side each. Obviously.'

As a steady drizzle began to fall, he pulled the throttle back to allow us to leap on to the canal bank on either side. He then ushered *Pendragon* alongside the dripping walls of the chamber, festooned with dejected ferns rendered limp by a thousand soakings. We closed and secured the bottom gates before climbing the stone steps to the top set. There we began to turn the rack and pinion paddle gear that lifted the sluices which, for men as intoxicated as we were, was by no means an easy job. As the water roared and careered in the darkness the moon set upon the torrents of foam boiling around the hull. Slowly, *Pendragon* began her ascent. Mo wiped the sweat from his forehead with his sleeve as the violent eddies began to subside.

'Bloody hell, Eds, that was hard work at this time of night. Still, only four more to go, eh?'

'Don't remind me. And how predictable that it's you and me doing the donkey work. No sign of his lordship, I presume.'

Freddie hammered on the cabin roof with an anger I didn't know he possessed. Certainly he hadn't been like that in our distant bout over the honour of Nick Drake. 'Lane bloody Fox,' he shouted, 'get your butt out here now and help us with this boat. We are not your servants.'

As we entered the next lock, Lane's tangled, beautiful head appeared from the front of the cabin and looked back along the roof towards Freddie.

'Did somebody call?' he might have said. I say 'might' because it was now apparent that Lane had reached a place where words had almost ceased to exist. Our own senses were dulled by what we'd drunk that day and so our hearing wasn't all it could have been but, even so, he was sounding pretty messed up.

'Diddssomebody call?'

'Yes, Lane, I bloody called,' Freddie yelled back.

'What d'you want? I's nice and cosy down there.'

'Exactly. Whilst the rest of us are up here working our balls off.'

The rear gates attended to once more, Mo and I wearily negotiated the staircase to the next set of sluices. Taking up our positions, we gazed down at the spectacle of Lane, teetering on the forward deck, hurling his drunken sentences at the visibly agitated Freddie in the stern.

'Okay, lads,' shouted Fred, 'away you go. Lane Fox, you are a good for nothing, worthless piece of shit who expects everything to be done for him. How come you're too high and mighty to give a hand with the locks, eh?'

As the metal sluices began to lift from the old timber gates *Pendragon* was caught in the cauldron of surging currents again. Lane, arms stretched outward towards the heavens, opened his mouth and practically screamed at Freddie.

'I don't need to be involved with your little lives any more because I'm off to bigger and better things. Be nice to me and I might send you a postcard when I get there.'

As the words left his mouth, Mo and I completed the last turns of the cranks to unleash the full force of the water. At precisely that moment, whether by accident or intent we will never know, perhaps he will never know, Freddie leaned on the throttle and pushed it fully forward. This, combined with the brutal power of the water raging under the hull and emerging at the stern, caused *Pendragon* to hit the lock gates with a mighty thump. Any minor bump or sway would have been enough to cause Lane Fox, that night, in that haze, to lose his balance. As it was, the second the impact was felt, he was tipped into the lock. For how long, I couldn't say, but for a beat of the heart or a few seconds, we did nothing. I can't know for sure if we were frozen in shock or just waiting. I stared at Freddie, whose face was clear to me in the moonlight. His expression was hard to read but there was no twinkle in his eyes, I'm pretty sure of that.

It was Mo, who had already scuttled down the steps to reach the boat, who brought us to our senses by banging feverishly on the roof.

'Jeannie, Matt, get out here,' he screamed. 'Get out here now. Lane's in the lock.'

Having alerted them, he then sprinted back to the top of the lock gates to try and stem the flow.

The craft shook as Matt bounded from the cabin with his face a ghastly white. Jeannie, petrified and sallow, followed. They looked over the side. Mo and I were, I swear, struggling as manfully as we could to lower the sluices in order to stop the water. Freddie was plunging a boat hook into the depths along the starboard side and calling for Lane. I looked around at the screeching faces and yet I recall hearing nothing. I was aware of the panic but also braced for the inevitable. I would have done almost anything to save him. But sometimes 'almost' is not enough.

The sluices closed, and calm gradually returned to the surface of the water, the only ripples being caused by *Pendragon*'s engines, puttering away, oblivious to the nightmare. Peering over the tiller, Fred and I turned away as we caught sight of the body. I will never forget that waxy, ruined face staring dully up at the moon. Matt and Mo stood motionless on the towpath, oblivious to the now heavier rain. Jeannie, sobs sweeping over her, trembled at the door of the cabin. I put my arm around her. She shrugged it away. For good.

26

'Edward, it's all right to cry.'

I'd held it off all day, but the moment the coffin slid behind the curtain brought the biggest lump yet to my throat. It felt like I could have choked. But still I refused to cry. The arm around me grew tighter as I turned my face into the folds of her coat. Under the other arm, Jack sobbed uncontrollably with huge heaves that shook his whole body.

'Edward, don't hold it all in.'

But I was going to hold it in. All of it. I'd held it in for weeks, even though it had struggled to escape many times. On the way to the crematorium it had threatened to break right through my chest, but I'd crossed my arms over my ribs to keep it imprisoned. He was my dad, and whatever it was that I was holding in, I wanted to keep it there. For him. I was frightened that if I did as Mum told me and let it out, it would run like a wild animal let out of a cage. And then it would be gone. Forever. So I kept it in.

I didn't cry for Lane either, but I was surprised by how similar some of the feelings were. Somehow, I didn't want what I had of him inside to disappear either. We'd fought, we'd argued, we'd grown apart, but somewhere down the days, we'd connected. And he'd been right. I didn't want him to be successful. What was it about his ambition that I found so difficult to deal with? Perhaps our early years as friends, drinking, laughing and loving the music, meant he understood me better than I thought he did. It was a shock, but I missed him terribly. In some ways I'd started to think of him as the brother I never had. No offence to Jack, he was the brother that I did have, but I'd never looked up to him like I looked up to Lane. And why could I only admit that now? Why couldn't I talk to him about it while he was still around? And maybe there was even more to it than that. Maybe Lane Fox being my brother wasn't enough. Maybe, in some way, I wanted to be him.

There was a police investigation, of course, but what could they prove? We weren't at all clear what had happened ourselves. And in any case, his post mortem found veins pumped full of alcohol, barbiturates and cocaine. The coroner had no qualms about pronouncing it death by misadventure. It worked wonders for sales of the album.

We were all questioned at length but even though, inevitably, our versions of events differed because of the booze consumed that day, no one could point the finger at anyone else. Not even O'Malley. Lane, out of his mind on drink and drugs, had been alone, in the rain, on the slippery forward deck of a moving boat when it hit the gates of the lock. Simple. We never colluded to get our stories straight. We just told it how we remembered it. We may have forgotten to mention the throttle though. And that possibly fatal pause.

There was a big funeral at the cathedral attended by hundreds of people, including not only family and former friends, but music business figures and members of the press. He'd have liked that. His father, Arthur, gave a moving speech packed full of genuine emotion and long words. He'd have liked that too. Marielle read Words-worth's 'Great Men Have Been Among Us'. I thought that was a little over the top myself but, again, he'd have liked it and I suppose that was all that mattered. As his coffin was carried out Nick Drake's 'Northern Sky' echoed around the lofty vaulted ceiling. We all liked that.

There was an obituary in the *Guardian* written by Matthew O'Malley. He'd have adored that. And Matt got to write for the nationals at last.

Jeannie moved back home straight away, as I knew she would.

Without her I was lost. So I went home too.

About nine months later, out of the blue, I received a letter from Bernice asking me if I wanted my old job back. Well, actually she was letting me know on behalf of the faculty that 'following departmental restructuring candidates are being sought for newly re-designated positions'. That was the official line but Bernice's handwritten note gave the translation of the bureaucratic gobbledegook. Evidently Bede Raynsford had been dismissed. She didn't go into too much detail but suffice to say there was a lay-by incident in his Jaguar involving a bottle of Glenmorangie and a female passenger of seventeen summers well known to the local constabulary. His chair had gone to Mark Lambert, a man half Raynsford's age with at least twice his intellect, hence the reorganisation. According to Bernice it was just a formality that I'd get back in if I re-applied, and pretty much certain that a senior lecturer's gig would follow within half a dozen semesters or so as a matter of course. It was the best offer I was going to get. And what was there to stay for?

Arnold Pickersgill, having lost his wife and sold the mini-mart on the corner of Wordsworth and Keats Avenues, had blown some of the proceeds on a bright red BMW Z4 sports car and had got into the habit of whisking my mother off for days out. They'd even stayed overnight at a country house hotel in the Lake District, though Mum was at pains to point out they had separate rooms because she 'wasn't ready for any of that malarkey just yet'. Just yet! I begged her to leave it there as, even though I was a grown man, as far as her sex life was concerned I preferred to remain a small boy. The chat at the kitchen table about passion and a woman's needs before I went to Plockton to retrieve Jeannie had been excruciating enough. Still, I was glad she was being made to feel special again. There had been no moonlit dinners by the Seine as yet but, well, you never know.

Mo was away a lot on tour. He wasn't massive or anything but he earned a living on the small concert hall and arts centre circuit here and in Europe. He was moderately big in Holland. He also earned a decent royalty from Lane's record, on the re-pressing of which he was correctly credited with being the sole writer of 'Summer's End'. He's got his own album out now on Mulberry called *From the Pines* which got four stars when it was reviewed in *Q* magazine. There's a version of Lane Fox's 'Halcyon Days' on it which, in my opinion, is much better than the original.

The Pines has been done up to within an inch of its life and is now home to Goulding and his brood. Danny spends a lot of time there supervising his estate, having handed on a lot of his legal commitments to Rob Matthews. The stables have been done up to within an inch of their lives too. Not by Mo, who still lives there occasionally, but by the contractors working on the main house. Inside the stables I imagine the carnage to be every bit as unpleasant as Mo's old bedroom at Byron Crescent. I don't know for sure though because I haven't been back.

Northern Sky still happens at the Rising Sun, and Jerry Snow and Matt O'Malley continue to run it. Attendances have fallen off a bit but it still gets decent crowds. It's packed when Mo Pepper plays. I know that for sure because I sometimes creep in at the back and hear that unmistakable voice. If I close my eyes I can almost go back to before it all happened. Strangely, it's not so packed when Danny Goulding plays. I know, ridiculous, isn't it? Danny just decided to learn the guitar and, being Danny, it only took him about six months. He's now the proud owner of a 1966 spruce top Martin Grand Ole Opry limited edition. It cost him four grand. Screwing a lawyer, that was sweet. I imagine he can afford it. The law firm money rolls in and with Matt he manages some fairly successful acts. There's Dun Carloway, a guitar band you might have heard of called the Rainmen, and a trio of country tinged girl singers from Vancouver who go by the name of Scirocco. Oh, and they still look after Mo.

Freddie still sings occasionally at the club, but he spends more and more time at the timber yard where he's absorbed with mastering the art of boat-building. He never took the tiller again though. He's still with Maria and so I get occasional snippets of information about how Jeannie is. She never did get to 'do a Vashti'. Not the way she wanted to anyway. She rarely ventures beyond the grey rendered walls of Lanercost but I believe she's getting a bit better. She's by no means what you'd call well, but she's going to be all right in the long run from what I can make out. Fred tells me she still sings. She doesn't sleep well and quite often anyone else awake in that house will hear her gentle strumming and spectral voice behind the bedroom door, wafting down the hallway. She doesn't sing the old songs though, always new ones. Or at least bits of them. Fragments that will never be properly heard. She never sings in public any more. Her strength isn't up to it but, even if it was, I'm pretty sure she wouldn't want to. I still love her, of course, but that's the least of her problems.

And the city clock still chimes. Life goes on. For some. There were six of us and now there were five. Lane was gone never to return and Jeannie wouldn't ever really come back. Even if she did, it wouldn't be to me. Mo was away all the time. Matt would always suspect, and every time I saw Freddie I would see the awful truth in his eyes. It was all over. We had reached our summer's end.